PRAISE FOR *ALL THE OTHER ME*

"I'm a sucker for a good sister story and Jody Holford's *All the Other Me* absolutely delivered. The relationship between Isabelle and Elaina is complicated and poignant and real… *All the Other Me* is a book that will stay with you."

—ALICIA THOMPSON,

USA Today bestselling author of *Love in the Time of Serial Killers*

"A moving and beautifully written novel… This layered, thought-provoking story about embracing who we are in order to discover who we want to be is the kind of story readers will be dying to discuss. Holford has crafted a book club gem!"

—MELISSA WIESNER,

bestselling author of *The Second Chance Year*

"*All the Other Me* is an emotional page-turner. Beautifully written and lyrical, raw, and witty at just the right moments, it will stay with you long after the last page."

—JESS SINCLAIR,

award-winning author of *What We Could Have Been*

all *the* other me

BOOKS BY JODY HOLFORD

STANDALONE NOVELS

All the Other Me

Caught Looking

Damaged

With These Shadows

THE WANNABE SLEUTH SERIES

Home Is Where the Body Is

Homecoming & Homicide

Spring Break Slaying

THE ISN'T IT SWEET SERIES

A Convenient Christmas

Lessons in Love

THE FOR THE LOVE OF THE GAME SERIES

Covering All the Bases

Catching Her Heart

THE BRITTON BAY MYSTERIES

Deadly News

Deadly Vows

Deadly Ride

Deadly Drama

THE LOVE UNEXPECTED SERIES

Let It Be Me

Never Expected You

Story of Us

THE SOME KIND OF SERIES

Some Kind of Christmas

Some Kind of Love

Some Kind of Forever

Some Kind of Always

THE KENDRICK PLACE SERIES

More than Friends

The Bad Boy Next Door

Hate to Love Him

THE MENDING HEARTS SERIES

(with Kara Leigh Miller)

Dangerous Love

Jaded Love

THE ANGEL'S LAKE SERIES

Forever Christmas

Forever Plus One

Falling for Home

Falling for Kate

Falling for Christmas

Falling for Love

Falling for Holly

Falling for the Holidays

all *the* other me

JODY HOLFORD

Inspired by a concept by Sandra Leigh Vaughan
Published in 2024 by Blackstone Publishing
Cover and book design by Larissa Ezell

Printed in the United States of America

First edition: 2024
ISBN 979-8-212-63819-7
Fiction / Women

Version 1

Blackstone Publishing
31 Mistletoe Rd.
Ashland, OR 97520

www.BlackstonePublishing.com

To my girls.
You can be any version of yourself you choose to be.

"People think that good and bad are opposites but they're wrong, they're just mirror images of one another in broken glass."

—Alice Feeney

ISABELLE

ONE

The line between arrogance and pride was razor-thin.

Arrogance meant Isabelle Duprees wasn't surprised to be accepting one of New York's most prestigious business awards at a party held in her honor. Pride was knowing she'd earned it. And then some.

She took the stairs with the same careful efficiency she applied to all areas of her life. Gripping a handful of silk, she crossed to the podium without incident. Tripping was something done in private. The spotlight blocked the expressions of her peers and associates. She'd always appreciated the way that worked—being illuminated without having to read faces.

There were people in the audience who believed she didn't deserve to stand in this spot—in front of a group of people whose combined wardrobes cost more than she'd earned in her first year out of MIT. Those same people would kiss her cheek and shake her hand when she mingled later. They'd tell her they weren't surprised before talking behind her back about luck and timing.

Pride and arrogance. The room was thick with it.

Inhaling deeply, she made sure not to exhale directly into

the mic. The room was nearly silent except for the gentle whir of hidden fans and the breathing of New York's most elite.

She hadn't prepared anything, but, for this sort of thing, she worked better off the cuff—balancing on that thin wire.

"It's easy to say we don't do this for the accolades," she said. "Especially since we all know we do it for the money."

The resulting laughter settled the nerves dancing in her stomach. No matter how many times she did this, it never got easier to be the focal point. It was just a by-product of her ambitions.

"The truth is, I admire and respect everyone here." She didn't have to like them all for that to be true. Those mutual feelings never got in the way of a deal. Which was why she was the one accepting the award.

"To be honored in this way is oddly humbling because I know how many worthy candidates there are in this very room. When I have my head down and I'm lost in my work, awards and accolades are never the end goal. But they're a damn nice side effect. So, thank you. Truly."

A few seconds of quiet followed her words, of people wondering if she'd say more, before the audience clapped. Isabelle stepped back, grateful the award was on a table at the back of the room, like a miniature guest of honor, and she didn't have to hang onto it while the more relaxed part of the evening commenced.

Her Cinderella slingback heels hadn't reached the final step down before Kaia Huxley was at her side. The young, dark-haired woman played so many roles in Isabelle's life, she defied labeling. At the moment, though, as she hooked her arm through Isabelle's, steadying her in a way few people could, Isabelle was glad one of those roles was friend.

"You rocked it," Kaia said, lips barely moving as the two of them floated through the crowd, stopping for people who rose out of their seats to congratulate her more personally.

"The night just started."

"But the hard part is over. Now it's the good stuff."

They wound their way to the back of the ballroom where guests could come to her, where Kaia could quietly whisper forgotten names in her ear, pass her a glass of champagne whenever hers ran dry, and run interference when people dove too deep into business chatter. Tonight was for celebrating. One of *Vanity Fair*'s Most Interesting People, *Time* magazine's Rising Wall Street Star, number seven on *Forbes*'s Top Ten Richest Women list, and now, the Best in Business award. She'd *earned* a fucking celebration.

Music filled the room as tables were moved, a dance floor was created, and hair was let down both literally and figuratively. The first party of this magnitude she'd attended had left her speechless. She'd stood in the corner of a room just like this one, staring out at a sea of diamonds and glitter like a little girl who'd dropped into the pages of a favorite fairy tale. Awe at being in the room with business giants, celebrities, and sports stars had consumed her, left her unable to do more than stare as she absorbed every second.

Her dress had come off the rack, something she hadn't let happen again in the ten years since. People's gazes had passed over her with the same interest they had in the furniture. She was an invisible shadow, only there because she'd made a smart suggestion to her then-boss the morning of the gala and, wanting out of it anyway, he'd offered his invite as a thank-you.

Now, everyone was here for her. Her dress had been designed and made solely for Isabelle Duprees to wear to this event. It would be auctioned off for charity the following week. The deep navy color made the blue of her eyes pop even without the expertly applied makeup. The silk fit her skin like it'd been painted on but let her move with confidence. She accentuated the backless design by putting her dark mahogany tresses up in a sharp twist—Kaia's smart suggestion. Isabelle smiled, finding her assistant in the crowd doing what she did best, engaging and disarming the best of the best who'd let champagne loosen their tongues.

"You look like the cat who not only swallowed the canary but made it think it was his idea," a familiar voice said close to her ear.

Despite the heat emanating off the bodies dancing and mingling, a shiver ran up Isabelle's spine.

"How do you know it wasn't?" she asked, not needing to look at Jonathan Fairbanks to know exactly how good he looked. His dark-blond hair would seem sun-kissed in this lighting despite the fact that New York hadn't seen steady sunshine in months. It'd have just enough product to hold it in place but not so much that anyone would even realize he used it. His wide shoulders and strong arms would fill the custom tux with sinful perfection.

"With you? I can't be sure. You look incredible, Ms. Duprees."

Her mouth ticked up in one corner. "As do you, Mr. Fairbanks."

"You haven't looked at me yet," he said, the side of his body brushing the side of hers.

I have you memorized. "No need."

"We could dance," he suggested, his fingers grazing hers, sending sparks along her skin.

"No need."

His rough laugh brought out her full smile. "Jesus, you're good at compartmentalizing."

A necessary skill for her own survival. She looked at him

now, ignoring the way her pulse jumped. "The upside is when something has my attention, it's absolute."

His gaze burned into hers, heightening her awareness not only of him but their surroundings.

"Don't I know it."

She could give him something, just for his ability to look at her that way. "You're the only one who does."

Fire flashed in those almost black eyes. "A deal is a deal." He stepped back, still holding her with the heat of his stare. "Congratulations."

Her smile softened and her pulse slowed. "Thank you."

Because it'd look strange if he didn't, he shook her hand and they both pretended there was nothing more than business between them.

Until later.

As Jonathan walked away and moved through the crowd, Isabelle went back to observing the partygoers. Every year, these events grew bigger and smaller at the same time. She knew fewer people but the ones she did, she knew like books she'd studied.

She'd read Sun Tzu's *Art of War* so many times, her first copy had fallen apart. When she needed reminders, she still turned to the battered one, where she'd highlighted more of the pages than she hadn't. *It is more important to out-think your enemy than out-fight him.* These events were treasure troves—weapons in the form of words and secrets.

It had only taken a couple of these parties to shatter the illusions of the fairy-tale magic. While from a distance the glitter was dazzling, the reality was more Grimm than Disney. These people danced and laughed, shared anecdotes, champagne, and expensive brandy in this setting. But put a boardroom table or a deal between them and the gloves came off. Isabelle loved the duality of it.

Kaia appeared at her side, handing her a bottle of water. "You need to mingle. Donovan Westbrook is hoping to chat about a merger. Vivian Cho wants advice on branding. Stanley Sinclair is currently taking credit for your, quote, unquote, "overnight" rise to the top. Ben McNair is regretting taking his brother's advice over yours. Your schedule is clear until lunchtime tomorrow when you have a phone interview with *People*."

Isabelle slid a sideways glance to Kaia. "Is that all?"

"Not entirely. Estelle Moore is cheating on her cheating husband with his former partner but they're still moving forward with the Bayer Hotel acquisition. And your sister called. Again."

Isabelle's shoulders immediately tightened. "Set up a phone call with Bayer for first thing tomorrow. If the Moores are one-upping each other with their infidelity, their focus will be scattered. We can pick up the acquisition."

"Tomorrow is Sunday."

Isabelle's brows rose. "Your point?"

Kaia tapped something into her phone which rarely, if ever, left her hand. She glanced up through lowered lashes, knowing Isabelle well enough to be cautious but not well enough to know exactly why. "And your sister?"

The bottle in her hand creaked with the pressure of Isabelle's grip. "I need to mingle."

This was her world, she thought as she slid through the crowd. She was no longer that girl who stood in the corner taking it all in, wondering where she fit. There'd been no overnight rise to anything. It was hours stacked upon days, months piled into years, one cautious and calculated step at a time. She'd earned this. It was hers. The award, the night, the party, this life. All of it.

Shattering the glass ceiling meant there were shards left

behind, leaving a trail, some piercing her own flesh. Her sister was one of those shards. Instead of tending to the wound, Isabelle preferred to pretend it didn't exist.

She knew enough about success to know it meant moving forward. Nothing good ever came from looking back.

TWO

There were unwritten rules to every facet of . . . well, every single thing. Which was why Kaia didn't call the car for Isabelle until nearly midnight. It was also why she climbed into the backseat, alone, without saying goodbyes. *Leave them wondering.* After the requisite polite small talk with her driver, Steven, she rested her head back against the cushion, closed her eyes for just a sliver of a minute. Breathed in, held it. Out. Once more.

Opening her eyes, she stared out the window, knowing others couldn't see in. Didn't matter. New Yorkers weren't overly concerned with who was being driven in the fancy car beside them. They were too busy living their own lives, making their own way, leaving their own mark. It was part of the appeal of the city. One tiny part in a city with a whole hell of a lot of appeal.

In her brain, Isabelle went through a list of things she wanted to file away for further reference. The biggest takeaway from the night was the Bayer acquisition. She could swoop in on that, close the deal before either of the Moores returned to their own sides of the bed. A smile tugged at her lips. It had been a good night.

About to get better too, she mused, thinking of her plan to

get Jonathan out of his tux. Despite the exclusivity—his term in the deal—there were no labels between them, which was one of her terms. Only moments. No couple outings, no details shared, no posing for *Page Six* together. Like most things, she'd learned the hard way that attending an event with a date—even a friend—was cause for speculation. It didn't have to be print-worthy speculation, but she couldn't stand people wondering about her personal life when she was clearly so devoted to her professional one. She refused to be discussed for anything other than her drive, determination, and enviable business acumen.

If she were a man, it wouldn't matter. Having someone on her arm at The Met Gala wouldn't negate her power or influence. It was easier to keep the pieces of her life in tidy little boxes that only she controlled. That didn't stop the chatter. She knew all the derogatory monikers she'd earned for her unwillingness to share anything personal with the world.

No amount of money shut down people's opinions, so Isabelle learned to drown out the white noise. But it took effort. Concrete buildings zipped past outside the window, the soft light of the moon allowing little glimpses of the street's heartbeat. People milled, a few leaving clubs, others walking, some in groups, some alone, someone dragged a trash bag around the corner of a restaurant, a couple was pressed together in an alcove. There were more stories in one New York City block than some libraries.

As the driver pulled to a stop in front of her place, she gathered herself, grateful Kaia had insisted on the thin wrap to protect her from the evening chill. Spring was being a moody bitch.

The driver held the door, offered a hand, which she accepted. "You look lovely, Ms. Duprees. Congratulations on another well-deserved award."

She smiled, genuine happiness offering more warmth than the wrap. "Thank you, Steven."

Nodding, he walked to the driver's side door, where he'd wait for her to get inside. She stepped up onto the cobblestone sidewalk, smiling as she walked toward the high-rise she called home. The first time she'd seen it with its strong columns, clean lines, and the many stained-glass windows, which provided a fanciful contrast to the cement structure, she'd fallen in love. The only kind she allowed.

Multiple outdoor lights, some attached to the building, some under the wide portico, made it easy to find her key in her purse. She had a hand on the door when a sound to her right startled her enough to look in that direction.

Isabelle wished there were a reverse spotlight or no light at all so she could cover the instant shock, her sharp intake of breath, the widening of her gaze. In seconds—milliseconds—she schooled her features, stiffened her spine, squared her shoulders.

But it was too late.

Elaina Duprees's smile made it clear that she'd already noted, and tucked away for future use, her younger sister's show of weakness. Some people were made or destroyed in split seconds.

Eyes not unlike her own, though perhaps a clearer blue, sparkled with satisfaction. Her sister's rich brown hair had been cut so it hung longer in the front, curls framing her face, softening the angles of it. An oversized T-shirt slipped off one shoulder, Audrey Hepburn's face splashed across the front. Cropped jeans and vibrant flats made her look like she'd tossed the outfit together without a care, but Isabelle knew better. The strap of a duffle bag across her chest, right through Audrey's hair. Older by two years, Elaina clapped her hands together in a slow, sarcastic round of applause as Steven stepped forward, away from the vehicle.

"Everything okay, Ms. Duprees?" he asked.

Elaina turned her head, made a show of looking Steven down, then up, before holding his gaze. There was enough light to see his cheeks flush. Stronger men had tried and failed to resist her immediate charm. The only person who seemed immune was Isabelle. And even she wasn't entirely exempt. She wasn't sure what that said about her, and she hadn't had to wonder in a very long time.

Irritation tightened the spot between her shoulders like pulling a string back on a bow.

"Everything's fine, Steven. Thank you." She stepped into his line of sight, blocking him from looking at her sister or, more aptly, blocking Elaina from looking at him. Tidy little boxes.

And one of them had just upended all over the sidewalk.

THREE

"Let's take this inside," Isabelle ground out.

She hated surprises. As a person who liked to keep her emotions locked tight, for more reasons than she could count, the unexpected made her feel weak.

With quick, efficient movements, she opened the door, let Elaina go ahead. Relief and gratitude filled her when she saw that the opulent lobby, lit by a single crystal chandelier the size of a smart car, was empty. Her heels clicked along the marble floors toward the elevator as she brushed past her sister, whose rubber-bottomed soles squeaked when she followed. An audible reminder that the past was impossible to escape.

When the doors slid shut, Isabelle ground her back teeth together, noticing, with a small pang of satisfaction, that the doors' shimmering gold reflection gave her sister a funhouse-like smile.

"You don't seem happy to see me," Elaina observed. "I came all this way to congratulate you on your big night and you haven't even said hello."

Champagne, anger, and—maddeningly—the slightest kernel of happiness rolled around in her stomach. She shot her sister a glare. "Why are you here?"

Without the reflection, Elaina's smile was just a little mean. "To see my baby sister."

The ride to the penthouse felt longer than usual. As the doors slid open, Elaina stepped out, whistling through her teeth in a way that made the muscles around Isabelle's heart loosen. Their father had done that.

Goddamn Elaina.

"And the rich get richer," Elaina said, slipping her shoes off, leaving them in the middle of the floor before walking farther into the open-concept, high-ceiling room that Isabelle adored.

The curved wall of windows made it seem even bigger than it actually was, and the city lights sparkled against the black sky, bouncing off the glass in a breathtaking display.

In the daytime, the view of Central Park was stunning, but Isabelle preferred the night. Slipping off her heels, she slid open the closet, tucked them on a shelf, and hung her purse and wrap on the same hook, using the moment to gather herself. The bodice of her dress felt too tight, too restrictive. When she turned back, she watched her sister move around her space, unknowable feelings tumbling around inside of her like a foreign object in a dryer.

In front of the windows, a long and wide L-shaped couch took up a generous amount of floor space. A live-edge coffee table sat in front of it, on top of a rug Isabelle had purchased at auction. Like the rest of the things in her home, she'd bought it for comfort, not cachet—it felt like the softest cotton on her bare feet.

The L of the sofa faced a freestanding brick wall, which housed a narrow gas fireplace under a flat-screen television. To the far right, two oversized white chairs with another live-edge table between them formed a sitting area. She loved relaxing there with a cup of tea, a great book, and the view of Manhattan spread out like a magazine. Behind the chairs was a floating wrought iron staircase to a loft area where Isabelle had a home gym set up. A stained-glass balcony hid the equipment while creating another artistic focal point.

Beyond that was a hallway leading to the bedrooms, bathrooms, and her home office. To the left of the elevator was a long, modern dining table she rarely used. The kitchen was tucked back into an alcove around the corner, along with a door that led to a stairway giving her access to a private rooftop patio.

Art prints, painstakingly chosen for the way they made her stomach flutter when she looked at them too long, hung on the white walls. The splashes of color, the abstract emotion that emanated off them, made her feel alive.

Other little snippets of color danced over the furniture in the form of a throw blanket, ceramic vases on tabletops, and unique sculptures on shelves. She'd chosen every single thing in this apartment, cherished each item like a curator in charge of special exhibits at The Met.

Elaina dropped her duffel to the floor before collapsing onto the couch. "Nice place."

Isabelle had to laugh even as she stood perfectly still, arms folded, nails pressing into her skin. "It works." She stared at her sister knowing that after concentrated effort, her face now gave nothing away.

"It's good to see you."

Nothing was ever that simple. "How did you know I'd be home?"

Elaina leaned farther back into the cushions, tucked her feet under herself, getting comfortable. Of the two of them, Elaina was able to settle wherever she landed. Isabelle was the one who always felt like she had to carve out a space for herself. Except in her own home. Usually.

"Unlike you, Kaia doesn't pretend I don't exist. Sit down, Iz. Take the stick out of your ass."

Closing her eyes, Isabelle clutched the last tethers holding her temper in place. "*Don't* call me that."

When she opened her eyes, she saw that Elaina was smiling. "I'm sorry. *Ms. Duprees.*"

"It's not a good time for company right now. Where are you staying?"

A lightning-quick flash of hurt lit up her sister's gaze, which Isabelle worked to disregard.

"I'm thinking you have a guest room. And I'm not company. I'm *family.*"

"Who only shows up when she wants something," Isabelle said, her feet aching, her back stiff. *Most of the time, never shows up at all.*

Elaina sat up, lowered her feet to the ground. Her movements were measured and slow like she didn't want to be the one in the spotlight now.

"I was in New York. I wanted to see you. A moment of misplaced nostalgia combined with hearing about your award. From your assistant. Never from you." The silence roared between them until Elaina stood up. "I'll see myself out."

Guilt clawed at Isabelle. She couldn't deal with this right now. Couldn't and didn't want to. But she spoke regardless. "Down the hall, second door on the left. There's a guest suite. We'll talk in the morning."

Elaina didn't smile as she picked her bag up off the floor, stared at her sister like she could see all the way through her. "Congratulations on the award."

Isabelle blinked, not trusting the sincerity in her sister's tone. "Thank you."

After another beat—a useless game of chicken since Elaina

knew Isabelle would never look away first—she walked around the couch and down the hall.

Isabelle's shoulders sagged, her body wanting to slip into a puddle on the floor. Seeing her sister, as rarely as it happened, always did this to her—turned her into the weak version of who she used to be. Someone she would *never* be again.

Before she could entertain any ideas, the elevator doors slid open and Isabelle turned to see Jonathan stalking toward her, still in his tux, a bottle of Dom in one hand. He used the other to grip her hip, pull her flush against him before he took her mouth in a kiss more intoxicating than the alcohol she'd had.

She let herself fall into it, just for a moment, absorbing the taste and feel of him, the heat of his body pressed against her own. His hand streaked down, up, locked around her waist like a vice.

When he pulled back, it was hard to say which of them was breathing harder.

"I've wanted to do that all fucking night. I'm so tired of pretending at these events, Isabelle," he said, his voice a little rough and a lot sexy.

Feelings scattered around inside of her like they didn't know what to do with themselves. "It's part of the deal. I can't do this right now. Tonight. I'm sorry." And she really was. Incredibly sorry that she couldn't use him as an escape at that moment.

He lived downstairs, on the fourth floor. They'd met just over a year ago and the attraction, the connection, had been instant. Still, Isabelle fought it for weeks. She rarely allowed complications into her life. Time was precious and she couldn't waste it worrying about relationships and feelings. She couldn't focus on something that would leave her with more scars.

But it was one of those times the universe didn't care what she wanted. The pull was too strong. They'd started talking about the hotels he owned, one thing literally led to another, conversationwise, and she realized she *liked* him.

"Why's that?" His tone cooled. He set the champagne on a narrow table behind the couch, shoved both hands in his pockets.

She breathed through her nose. "Something came up."

The heat in his gaze disappeared. "I'm tired of playing games. Do you mean some*one*?"

"I don't. Well, I do but not like you're thinking." God. This was why she avoided this sort of thing. It was never supposed to be about feelings. Maybe, given the look on his face, it was time to cut her losses. One more thing she could thank Elaina for taking away from her.

Jonathan pulled one hand from his pocket, stroked his thumb over her cheek. Isabelle leaned into his touch, hating how much she craved it. He stepped closer, lowered his head, and kissed her with a gentleness that could undo a weaker woman. One who wanted to be undone.

"Every time I think we're making progress, you put up a wall," he said against the corner of her mouth.

She put a hand on his chest, sighed. Maybe—

"Well, well. Looks like the Ice Princess melts at a very specific temperature," Elaina's voice said from behind them.

Jonathan startled, his head popping up. "Jesus Christ. You have company."

Isabelle went stiff, wishing she wasn't still in her dress. She turned to look at her sister, who stood in the arch of the hallway, wearing only the T-shirt that hit midthigh.

"What do you need?"

"How about an introduction?" Elaina said, staring at Jonathan.

In response, he stepped into Isabelle, as if he could somehow protect her from this woman. She appreciated the sentiment.

The gesture. Appreciated it *too* much, which stiffened her back, reminded her she didn't need saving.

"Who is this, Isabelle?"

Elaina smiled. "I'm her sister. Who are you?"

Isabelle looked up at Jonathan in time to see the surprise in his gaze. The hurt he didn't bother to mask. "You have a *sister*?"

"Aw, Iz, you didn't tell him about me?"

Anger whipped through Isabelle like a flash storm. "Go to bed or go to a hotel. *Now*."

With a quiet laugh, Elaina turned and left them alone.

Jonathan shoved his fingers into his hair, stalked forward and back, before stopping in front of Isabelle and dropping his hands.

"I've tried not to push you, not to ask for too much, to stick to your ridiculously rigid relationship terms, but this is too much. You have a fucking sister?"

Isabelle inhaled deeply, exhaled slowly, her fingers twitching. "She's not part of my life."

He shook his head. "You *know* me. You know my family—I talk about them. You know why I had a falling out with my brother, how we mended things, what I want to do with the hotels. Goddamn it, you *know* me. All this time, I thought you were letting me in. Slowly . . . but I thought it was happening."

She'd felt it happening as well. She'd even told herself to back away, lower the castle gates and protect herself, but his pull was magnetic. Soothing in ways she didn't want to need. And some days, she was just so fucking tired of being alone with her own thoughts, so she'd let him in. Further than anyone.

"It was. It *is*. I'm sorry. I can't do this right now." Something like panic clawed at her chest.

Jonathan nodded, like he finally understood something. "Maybe we shouldn't do this at all."

When he turned to walk away, Isabelle's hand shot out, gripped his arm without warning. She hadn't meant to stop him but the thought of letting him go made her throat want to close.

"Don't leave like this." She swallowed. "Please."

He turned back to face her, looked at her hand on his arm. She dropped it, held his gaze. "I care about you. You don't know what to do with that and I have no idea how you feel about me. I'm not an acquisition, Isabelle. I want more. Unless you do, unless you want everything, I'm done. I won't be the one thing in your life you do halfway." He sighed, reached out but dropped his hand. "If you stop being scared or want to stop hiding or whatever it is you're doing, you know where to find me. Congratulations on your award. You're a hell of a businesswoman."

She watched him leave, wrapping her arms around herself to ward off the chill running over her skin.

When the doors to the elevator closed, Isabelle wondered how such a great night could fall apart so easily.

"It's fine," she whispered to herself. "You don't need him. You don't need anyone."

It was better this way. She would have done it soon, anyway. If Elaina hadn't shown up, it might not have been that night but she would have ended it eventually. It would have been on her own terms, which rankled a little, but the result would have been the same.

You're on your own, Isabelle.

That was nothing new. The only thing "new" was that it had never bothered her before.

FOUR

Isabelle walked to the kitchen, forcing herself to calm down, regroup, breathe through the tidal wave wreaking havoc in her chest. She hated the feeling and intentionally lived her life in a way designed to avoid it. Grabbing a Waterford flute from the glass cabinet, she went back to the champagne. Opening it, she didn't even blink when it spilled over, dribbling onto the gleaming floors.

Pouring a half glass, she downed it like a shot, refilled the glass and set the bottle down, and walked to the windows, the flute clutched in her grip.

She stared out at the pockets of darkness that hovered around the lights. Elaina's last ambush was eight years earlier. Isabelle, only twenty-five and already knocking people out of her way on the climb up, had been on her way out of the office for a meeting and nearly ran right into her sister. She didn't regret agreeing to coffee since it had led her to Kaia. But she damn well resented every other moment about it. Elaina was, much like their mother had been, a taker. A fucking world-class champion taker. She was so good at it, she made a person think it was their idea. The thought sent a jolt through Isabelle. *The apples fell right next to the goddamn trees. One of them anyway.*

Elaina had needed money. And Isabelle had plenty of it. It was easy to give, so she did. On her terms. No more contact. Of course, Elaina had never intended to hold up her end of the bargain, but Kaia ran interference and Isabelle never opened that box. It was useless to wonder how she'd gotten to the point she was at now. It wouldn't change anything. Her sister was in her guest room, Jonathan was done with her, and she was still Isabelle Duprees. For tonight, she'd drown out the noise with really good champagne and an empty bed.

"Got enough to share?" Elaina said, padding into the room.

Isabelle didn't bite back the sigh. "Glasses in the kitchen."

She slipped her phone out of the discreetly hidden pocket on the side of her dress, checked her texts. The top one was from Kaia.

People interview at noon. Phone call scheduled with Henry Bayer for nine. I'll pick up the dress to be cleaned in the afternoon. Dinner at Waldorf with Klein Agency is at seven on Monday.

Fresh fruit in your fridge. Eat some. Your sister may ambush you. You can get mad at me Monday. I've blocked out 9-9:15 for it.

Isabelle shook her head, typed back.

Only 15 minutes?

The response was almost instantaneous.

> You're a busy woman.
> Sleep. If you can.

"Your lips twitched. Careful. I might think you know how to smile." Elaina stood next to her, a matching Waterford in her hand.

"It's been known to happen." Isabelle tucked her phone away.

"Sure as hell not in public. You look tired, Izzy."

She winced. She was too old for nicknames. "Isabelle. It's after midnight. It's been a long day."

Elaina sipped her drink. "Not that kind of tired."

Draining her glass, Isabelle turned to look at her sister, doing her best to keep her expression unreadable. "Is everything okay?" She wouldn't ask the real question, but it was implied: *Is Mom okay*?

Elaina's mouth tightened like it used to when they were kids and Isabelle wouldn't listen to what she was saying. "Everything's fine. I wanted to see you. The timing was good."

"For you."

"If I waited until it was good for you, I wouldn't be standing here," Elaina said. "And I never would."

Isabelle had worked hard to build a guilt-proof suit of armor but like anything, there were holes. Sometimes hard to see, but they were there, and her sister had a map to every one of them.

"Do you think I don't know my own finances? My own life? That my assistant sends you enough money you don't have to want for anything? I don't tell people about you, but I've made sure you're okay. We had a deal. No contact."

"Because then you'd remember where you came from,

remember who you are, maybe remember that you're far from perfect. And it was *your* fucking deal. I never agreed to it."

Isabelle stalked away from her sister, irritated at having the same thing said to her twice in one night. She filled her glass, took a long swig.

"I'm turning thirty-five, Iz. Forty is right around the corner." There was a heaviness in her tone that made Isabelle's heart squeeze.

Their dad had made it one week past forty but what happened to him had been an accident. A tragic, life-altering accident.

"That's not how it works and since when am I the person you come to for comfort?"

Elaina's laughter rubbed over her skin like sharp fingernails. "Is there anyone on this earth that *would* come to you for comfort?"

Smashing the glass down on the table, Isabelle glared across the room. "Then why are you here?"

Having no trouble matching the temper Isabelle worked so hard to keep under wraps, Elaina marched over to her sister and gave her shoulders a little shove, knocking her back a step.

"I've answered your question. You can keep asking it, but the answer won't change. I'm an idiot. I thought maybe you'd want to see me. I forgot you're a fucking robot with no feelings. The more money you make, the less human you become. My bad. I forgot the rules. You don't need me. You don't need anyone." Her hands flew into the air. "You can sit around in your literal fucking ivy tower counting your money and googling yourself to see if you're still number one at everything. The rest of us are out there feeling *real* things. Things money can't bury. Like fear about turning forty, like terror when the doctor tells you they found a lump, like going through test after test to 'make sure' and then the sheer, absolute relief when, weeks and more tests later, they say, 'Oops, it was nothing.' Like regret that you let so much time go by when you know everything that matters to you can be snapped away in an instant. I wish I was you, Izzy-belle. I wish I didn't feel a goddamn thing. It was a mistake to come here, I see that now. I knew it all along. I know I've fucked up. Bad. Enough to warrant the anger you'd feel if you let yourself feel anything. You're not who you used to be. And you know what? I miss that person. She died right along with Dad. The first version of you died at eight years old and I don't know who the hell you are now. But I'm not who I used to be either and if you'd thaw that icicle you call a heart, you might find you like me. Maybe even still love me."

Spittle had flown into Isabelle's shocked face and her hands went limp at her sides as she stared at her sister, whose chest was heaving up and down, her breath ragged and raw. She tried to process everything Elaina had just said.

They found a lump.

"Are you okay?"

Her sister pushed her hair back away from her face with a harsh huff of breath. It fell back into place easily. "Yes. I'm fine. Other than suffering from severe idiocy, I'm fine. No need to worry." She arched her brows. "Did Kaia program a worry option into you?"

Isabelle narrowed her gaze, the tightness in her stomach loosening. She kept her features blank, her fingers still. Remembered who she was.

"For the record," she said quietly. "I don't stay up nights counting my money and googling myself. In fact, I've never done either of those things."

Elaina's chin dropped, hiding the flash of a smile. She put her hands on her hips, stared at the floor, shaking her head. Her curls bounced back and forth.

When she looked up again, Isabelle noted the exhaustion etched into the creases of her eyes. "Bullshit."

Isabelle picked up her glass, finished it off. "Are you calling me a liar?"

"You've *never* googled yourself?" Her tone was incredulous.

"Why would I? Google is a place to look for answers. I know everything I need to about myself."

Elaina made a dismissive noise, picked up the champagne, topped off her glass, then Isabelle's. "I get it. You don't like what people say about you."

The stem of the glass was damp. "I don't care what people say about me. I don't look. It's a waste of time. There's nothing out there that could tell me anything about myself that I don't already know."

Tipping her head to the side, her sister regarded her carefully. "You've *really* never typed your own name into Google?" Her tone was the same goading one from childhood. The one that convinced her to take an extra donut only to find out Elaina had added salt to it. How could it still piss her off? How could a *tone* send her back to a time she'd spent her life putting behind her?

"Jesus Christ, Elaina. What difference does it make? You're relentless. Let it go."

"The difference is you think you're above it all. Too good for anyone or anything. Guess what? You're *not*."

Even knowing there was so much more under the layers of anger, Isabelle fixated on this moment. She pressed her front teeth together, breathed through them. "I may not know you now, Elaina, but at the moment, I can tell you with absolute certainty, I do not like you."

A sharp bark of laughter rang out from her sister. "Back at you. Where the fuck does that leave us?"

Isabelle plucked up the bottle, swung it a little without

meaning to. "I'm going to bed. If you're here in the morning, if anything you've said is true, we can talk then."

As she walked toward her bedroom, a full glass of champagne in one hand, the bottle in the other, she did her best to hold her head high. It was never hard when Elaina wasn't around.

"I'm not the liar, here, Izzy-belle," Elaina shouted.

It took everything in her to tamp down on the childish retort of "Are too." Instead, she gritted her teeth hard enough to hurt and kept walking. Letting herself into her bedroom, she leaned back against one of the French doors and thought, if her sister *wasn't* lying, maybe she had changed just a little.

FIVE

Her sanctuary inside of her sanctuary was her bedroom. The house she'd grown up in could easily fit inside of it. Two narrow floor-to-ceiling windows met in one corner, where she'd arranged another sitting area. Her California king–sized bed sat high, piled with pillows and throw blankets. It faced a television mounted, once again, over a gas fireplace. There was another fireplace in the bathroom—around the corner made by a built-in wall of bookshelves—at the foot of her beloved freestanding stone-resin tub.

Moving to the side of her bed, she set the bottle, her glass, and her phone on the table. She slipped her arms behind her to lower the hidden zipper of her dress, letting it fall to the ground before picking it up, hanging it over her arm. Sliding one of the white pocket doors open—they contrasted nicely with the dark gray tones on the walls and soft wood shades of her furniture—she stepped inside, hung the dress on a hook.

Heading straight for the comfort gear, she opened one of a dozen dresser drawers, pulled out her favorite pair of Celine joggers. Her champagne state didn't leave her capable of pushing away the memories flashing through her brain. Nothing good came from seeing Elaina. Yanking on the pants, Isabelle opened another drawer, pulled on an old T-shirt. She'd get ready for bed and deal with her sister in the morning.

On the way to the bathroom, she snagged the champagne glass, wishing she had a shot of something instead. Elaina had a knack for burrowing under her sister's skin and poking around without even trying. Like all experts, she'd been rehearsing how to best pull at the threads of Isabelle's life since childhood.

In the high-ceilinged bathroom with its opulent light fixtures, heated floors, the bathtub, and a ridiculously huge shower, she went to one of the bowl sinks. She'd had the gold fixtures replaced with brushed nickel, preferring the look. Pulling one pin out of her hair at a time, she set each of them in a small case inside a drawer, then placed each of her skin-care products on the gleaming countertop. Pushing her hair back with a cloth headband, she proceeded through each of the steps of her skin-care routine, forcing herself not to scrub her skin with too much vigor. It was supposed to calm her, settle the restlessness she often felt before bed. As she completed the routine, she sighed, taking the time to put everything away. Yanking the headband out, she tucked it away in its place. Her long hair flowed down as she gripped the edges of the bowl sink.

"You always let her mess with your head. You're stronger than this," she told her reflection. With her makeup off, in the stark lighting, she couldn't hide the dark shadows beneath her eyes. Whatever Elaina wanted, Isabelle would deal with it and then send her sister packing.

She brushed her teeth, shut off the light, and went to turn down the bed. The champagne didn't taste nearly as good with a hint of mint. She topped off the glass anyway, ignoring her own reminder that she wanted to speak with Henry Bayer in less than eight hours. Tapping a button on her bedside, the blinds lowered, shutting out the city, leaving her alone. *At least in this room.* Usually, she didn't mind.

Alone was good. She'd been alone on the bus ride from Tennessee to Boston. Alone when she graduated from MIT, when she'd made the move to New York City. Really, she'd been alone since her dad died when she was eight years old. That might have been the only true thing her sister had said that evening. That version of Isabelle was long gone. *Thank God*, she thought as she settled into her soft sheets. *That* version of her was weak.

Picking up the remote, she turned on the television just for the noise. The books on her bedside table weren't calling to her but she wasn't about to let her sister's stupidity get in her head.

Like a highlight reel, all the times Elaina had told her things that turned out to be false whipped through Isabelle's brain. She took another gulp of champagne. It was going to drive her nuts, having her sister sleeping down the hall. This was her *sanctuary.* Everyone had different versions of themselves. In her work, she was a force. At home, she was herself. *With Jonathan, you're a softer version of you.* Not anymore.

She threw back the covers and hopped out of the bed, glancing at her phone. Elaina wanted to talk about googling yourself? *That's* what regular people did? First of all, who the hell wanted to be ordinary? Isabelle had worked her whole life *not* to be. She didn't do social media because she had no need to stay in touch with people she'd gone to high school with. Still, she knew other people lived and breathed it. Because, like her sister, they had nothing else to do. She picked up the phone and typed in her sister's name.

There were hits for modeling, a few acting gigs, LinkedIn, Instagram, Twitter. "TikTok, Elaina? Seriously?"

There was little to no information on where Elaina came from, her family, definitely no mention of Isabelle. *You don't like what people say about you.* What was there to say? She'd written her own damn bio more than once.

Isabelle Duprees was a thirty-three-year-old self-made woman,

MIT graduate, designer of several lucrative apps as well as the creator of Fit for You, a fashion app that paired a woman's body with clothing to accentuate and flatter her features. An investor with an aptitude for great deals and timing, a member of New York's elite, a woman who commanded a boardroom, a real estate magnate. A multimillionaire. What the hell could Google tell her that she didn't already know? She purposely kept her romantic connections—not that there'd been any outside of Jonathan—intensely private.

Then do it. Check. She let out a low growl of irritation and tossed her phone onto the bed. Why did she let Elaina do this to her? It'd always been this way. Her sister was probably sound asleep. She should march in there and kick her out just for the pleasure of it.

Chicken.

Of course, it was Elaina's voice in her head. What was she scared of? Nothing. Maybe someone had made some speculations about her life, personal or otherwise. Maybe someone had photographed her coming out of The Met last week when she'd taken a day to clear her head after a particularly brutal deal had fallen through.

Picking up her glass, she drained what was left of the champagne but it swirled in her stomach like an oncoming storm. Setting the glass down, she picked up her phone again.

She typed her name into Google but her finger hovered over the search button. Pressing it, she exhaled sharply. There. Done.

Isabelle scrolled down the page, up again, her brows pinching in confusion. She typed her name into the search again and came up with two clearly linked results. How was that even possible?

Facebook

https://ms-my.facebook.com > public > Isabelle-Duprees

LinkedIn

https://www.linkedin.com/in/isabelle-duprees
-9c87465/-Isabelle Duprees

Manager, The Book Stop - Poppy, Pennsylvania.

Born: Isabelle Carolyn Duprees, June 5, 1990 (age 33), Ashland, Tennessee.

A picture of her came up when she clicked on the link—one she'd never posed for or taken.

Ignoring the tightness in her chest, she pressed the back button and typed her information in again, even putting "New York" in the search bar. How much had she drunk? The champagne bottle was still almost half full. But she'd had a fair amount at the event. *Her* middle name was Carolyn, after her father's mom. *Her* birthday was June 5th. *She* was thirty-three, almost thirty-four. What she wasn't was a freaking manager at a The Book Stop. Was that supposed to be some sort of clever play on *The Book Shop*? Maybe her phone was messed up. She typed in The Book Stop and saw that not only was it real, but it also had an interactive website with cutesy virtual book pages that turned. Isabelle scoffed, tapped on the picture in hopes of finding something useful but all that did was make it bigger. Isabelle blinked, her stomach and her vision swimming in unison. She'd never lived in Pennsylvania. *It's obviously not you.* Someone had paired her picture with the name. *With your birthday and middle name?* Phone clutched in her hand, she stalked to the windows, pulled the blind away from the glass to see the usually calming view of the city. It didn't settle her in any way. Forcing herself to take a deep breath. She could make sense of this.

She turned, typed the search into Google again. Okay, not

to be all the way on the side of arrogant, but shouldn't there be thousands or at least hundreds of hits about her that were actually true? Even her sister had more search results.

Elaina. Had she . . . ?

What? Hacked her phone? Google? The internet? It was a ridiculous notion and Isabelle immediately disregarded it.

Her hands shook as she walked back to the bed, sat down on it, took a few deep breaths. She was exhausted and emotional. The day, her sister, and the scene with Jonathan had caught up with her. She was, after all, human. Everyone had a moment here and there. She tried the search again. *Pennsylvania.* An unhappy laugh escaped. No, thank you. Her finger hovered over the Facebook link for several seconds before she pressed. Nausea roiled. It was a good thing she was sitting down.

Even if she had a Facebook account, she wouldn't post that many pictures of absolutely nothing. Who the hell cared if someone made bagels from scratch? Who even *makes* bagels from scratch? What was the point of that? It was a time suck. More photos of wildflowers than anyone ever needed, for God's sake. Landscapes, books, bookmarks, fucking selfies with flowers in the woman's hair, her head tipped up to the sky.

Isabelle shut her phone down, paced for a full five minutes, then turned it on and tried again.

When the same results came up, she jumped off the bed and hurtled toward the door, which bounced against the wall with the force she used to yank it open.

"Elaina!" she yelled, barrelling down the hallway.

There had to be an explanation, and like most of the inexplicable, unpleasant pieces of her life, she'd bet anything her sister was at fault.

Somehow.

SIX

Before everything had changed for them, young Isabelle used to let herself into Elaina's room whenever she wanted. Sometimes, like when their parents fought or her mother cried, Elaina would let Isabelle crawl into bed with her. Other times, when Isabelle was just lonely and wanting some company, her sister would throw pillows and stuffed animals at her instead of letting her anywhere near the bed. Isabelle could only remember a handful of times after their father died where anyone in her house offered her comfort. Or remembered she existed. She'd lain in her bed listening to the sounds of the television, her mother and sister murmuring, quiet laughter or tears. No door on the living room but Isabelle always felt like she was on the outside without a key to get in.

But this wasn't Elaina's bedroom. It was Isabelle's house, and she could do whatever she wanted.

Elaina slept through Isabelle charging into the guest suite. Though smaller than her bedroom, it was still a wonderful space with its vanilla cream walls, dark wood four-poster bed, and a comfortable sitting area that overlooked Central Park. The space was ironically inviting considering Isabelle never let anyone stay over. Her sister was tucked under the plush navy comforter—she'd gone for neutrals in here—surrounded by pillows. Elaina hated sleeping alone so she'd always surrounded herself when she slept.

Isabelle stomped over, slapped the base of the lamp so it'd wake her sister.

Elaina winced when Isabelle said her name.

Blinking, she put a hand over her face and offered a muffled, "What?"

Isabelle shook her sister's shoulder. "Wake up!"

"Oh my God!" her sister shouted, rolling away only to get stopped by her own pillow barricade. "What's wrong with you?" She pushed up on one arm, her face wrinkled with sleep.

"I googled myself," Isabelle said, as if that would explain everything.

Even half-asleep, her sister was an expert eye roller. "Incredible. Way to go. Maybe you are human. Manic but human. Can I go back to sleep now?"

Isabelle crawled up onto the bed, perching awkwardly. "Why do you have so many pillows around you?" She had no idea why she even asked but Elaina looked smaller, more vulnerable among them.

Elaina shot her a *what-the-hell* glare. "They're *your* pillows." It sounded like an accusation.

"They look pretty. They're for decoration. You're not supposed to sleep on all of them."

"I was too tired to read the room rules. My bad. Get off." Elaina pushed her away.

Swatting at Elaina's hand, Isabelle shoved her phone in her sister's face. "Something's wrong with my search. It doesn't make sense."

Another eye roll. "You're a bazillionaire and you can't do a Google search? Typical."

Frustration, fatigue, and other feelings she didn't want to address made Isabelle's pulse quicken. "You made me do this."

Elaina gave a short laugh. "Did not."

They stared at each other. How did they always fall back into the same habits they'd had as children?

"Stop being grouchy and look at my screen," Isabelle said after another moment of their staring contest.

Huffing, Elaina shuffled into a seated position, then yanked the phone out of her hand, her brows furrowing, nose scrunching in a way that made Isabelle's breath catch. She was looking straight at her sister but seeing the young girl she once was. "What is this?"

Rubbing the spot on her chest that suddenly ached fiercely, Isabelle said, "It's what came up when I googled my name."

Elaina went to the search bar, typed in her sister's full name, and the same result popped up instantly. She repeated the process, this time typing in Isabelle's birthday and birthplace as well. Nothing changed.

Her head snapped up and she locked her gaze on Isabelle's. "Am I awake?"

Isabelle reached over, pinched the underside of her sister's biceps. Elaina swore, fumbling the phone.

She rubbed her arm, sending daggers Isabelle's way. "Son of a bitch."

"You're not dreaming. What is this?"

She continued to rub her arm, frowning. "How would I know? I didn't invent Google. Maybe we're both drunker than we thought. Did you click the links?"

"Of course I did. The Book Stop sounds like somewhere a high schooler would work. But I googled that too. It's real. There's a Facebook page. My face in hundreds of stupid photos with people I've never seen. All my details are there but that's not my life."

Elaina picked up the phone again, clicked Facebook, her frown deepening. "Huh. No surprise there."

Isabelle leaned in. "What? What did you find?"

"This version of you doesn't have any proof of my existence either. Not one fucking picture."

Blowing out a harsh breath, Isabelle tried to ignore the pinpricks of worry stabbing against every inch of her skin, the strange sensations volleying around in her chest. Her mouth was dry. Her heartbeat felt like an incessant, obnoxious knocking. "This isn't a joke."

When Isabelle went to pick up her phone, Elaina put a hand on her trembling arm, stopping her. "Hey. Look at me."

Isabelle glanced at Elaina.

"We're both a little off. You smell like you crawled inside the bottle. I'm still a little buzzed myself. This is weird but let's leave it until morning."

Isabelle threw an arm out, gesturing at nothing. She hated her own lack of composure. "So, I should just go to sleep?"

Elaina nodded. "Sure. Why not? This is some *Twilight Zone* shit that neither of us can address right this second. Sleep. We'll check it in the morning."

The morning was coming far too fast. "I have a meeting first thing."

"Of course you do. No such thing as a weekend in your world."

Just like that, tension settled between them again. "I won't apologize for working hard."

Elaina simply stared at her, like she wanted to say more but didn't. Why that made Isabelle feel defensive, she wasn't sure but she sure as hell didn't like it. That seemed to be the night's theme: things Isabelle did *not* like. She moved off the bed, grabbing her phone as she did.

"Fine. I'll just go to sleep." Her words came out like a threat and her feet didn't follow through.

She stared at Elaina, her stomach tightening like someone was pulling a corset around her waist. Rubbing her knuckles along her breastbone, she tried to box breathe but couldn't inhale deeply enough. There wasn't enough room inside of her for all of this.

Elaina waited, her gaze steady, one side of her mouth tipping up. Isabelle had always envied her full lips, the barely-there beauty mark at the corner of the right side. Her sister, even pulled from sleep, was beautiful.

"Want to crawl in?"

The urge to say yes was so strong, Isabelle snapped, "Why are you so irritating?"

"Part of my charm. Crawl in or get out."

Turning, she didn't bother saying goodnight and walked out of the room, closing the door behind her. She thought of going to the kitchen for something to eat but what she really needed was sleep.

In her room, she dimmed the lights, crawled into her own bed. Her mind raced with thoughts she didn't want to have. Jonathan. Pennsylvania-Isabelle. Elaina in her guest room. Jonathan.

Sleep came but it provided no comfort and even less clarity.

SEVEN

Ingrained routine trumped hangovers. Even bad ones. The stench of alcohol seeped out of Isabelle's pores as she completed the fifth mile on her treadmill. Her lungs ached as the machine came to a stop. She chugged her water even though she knew better.

Shower, meeting, deal with life. That was her immediate schedule. She hadn't been back on her phone, and the need to check it made her skin crawl. Which, in turn, made her feel out of control, one of her least favorite feelings. To prove she could, she'd avoided her devices all morning. She wasn't controlled by these things. The previous night was clearly just some kind of technological glitch.

When she descended the steps, she wasn't surprised by the quiet of her living area. Elaina had always been a late sleeper. Their mother was the same. Or had been. Isabelle had no idea what their mother was like anymore.

Padding into the kitchen, wiping her forehead with the end of the towel around her neck, she thought about her mom. It wasn't something she spent a lot of time doing. Certainly not on a typical morning while she did her post-coffee workout.

Catalina Duprees was a force of motion and energy. Isabelle and Elaina's dad, Charlie, always said that getting Cat to fall in love with him was like catching a shooting star. He loved his wife and their family more than anything on earth.

The ache settled back under Isabelle's rib cage when she thought of him.

Their mother hadn't wanted children. She loved her daughters but their dad was the nurturer, the caregiver, the provider. He was everything. For all of them. They'd lived in a small, basic, one-level home in northern Tennessee, not far from the Kentucky border. Isabelle's father worked for the electric company. He made decent money—enough that if his wife wanted to stay home and be with her children, she could. She definitely wanted to stay home but Catalina liked it better when the girls were at school rather than eating up precious moments of her day.

When Charlie came home each night, she'd come alive. She sat on the countertop, chatting about reality show characters like they were her closest friends. He'd prepare dinner, chat with the girls while they did their homework at the table—not that they had much at young ages. Sometimes Isabelle and Elaina just colored or drew while their parents shared their days. All of them together.

They'd eat as a family. He'd clean up, help the girls plan their lunches, get them ready for the next day. Read to them, put them to bed. Tell them they were safe and loved and wonderful. He held them together.

And then he was gone.

They'd all fallen apart. The difference was Catalina and Elaina had each other, and Isabelle had nothing. No one.

Elaina stumbled into the kitchen like a very attractive zombie. "Coffee."

Isabelle prepared her a cup, not saying anything because all her words felt jagged, like they could cut her on the way out. She took her own coffee and went to shower.

She felt more herself when she donned a pair of black Prada dress pants and a pale-pink Dior sweater. Taking her time with her makeup, she used all the strategies at her disposal to keep her brain uncluttered. Focused. She'd owned enough companies, funded enough employee wellness retreats to know the tricks to mindfulness inside and out. Her phone would have dozens of messages. She couldn't remember the last time she woke up and *didn't* check her email immediately.

She was in her home office, ready to deal with her life, when 9:00 a.m. hit. With Zoom, she had the home-field advantage. Plus, she really wanted to prove herself.

An hour later, she hung up as a part owner of Bayer Hotels. The Moores likely wouldn't invite her to their next cocktail party but that was a consequence she could live with. The urge to call Jonathan, to share the news with him, to hear his voice and, undoubtably, his pride, was like a wave—nearly strong enough to knock her over.

Unable to put off looking at her phone any longer, she returned to her room to grab it off her bedside table. Kaia had, of course, texted over a dozen times. The last text simply said: EAT.

Once again, she found herself in the kitchen, this time putting together a small meal, reminiscing. But there was nothing pleasant about the memories she had of her mother, who she hadn't spoken to in ten years, after her father's death.

But there were some good ones around meeting Kaia. In her fridge, Isabelle found clear-topped containers, each with food choices she liked. She took her time making up a board of Rouge River Blue cheese, rosemary flatbread bites, some figs, and a handful of hazelnuts. She contemplated a glass of wine to kick the final dregs of the hangover out of her system. If it weren't Sunday, she'd be at her office on Water Street. Kaia would bring her lunch or she'd meet with someone, pick at an overpriced salad at a restaurant someone else chose in hopes of softening her up across the table.

"You willing to share that or are you still ignoring me?" Elaina asked, showing up again without any warning.

Isabelle tamped down on the small gasp of surprise. "There's enough for two. If you want something different, there are other options in the fridge."

Elaina opened the fridge, selected a soft drink, and cracked the top. She helped herself to a glass, pouring the soda in a long stream, moving her hand up as the can emptied. Always a show with her sister.

She took a sip of the soda and leaned against the counter, staring at Isabelle. "I know pretending things don't exist is your specialty—I forget, did you actually major in that at Harvard?"

Isabelle's skin tightened. "MIT."

"Whatever. Same thing. But no, you majored in being too good for the general public, right?"

Isabelle wiped her hands on a napkin, happy with the presentation of her board, then turned her gaze to her sister. "Yes, while you attended the 'school of life,' working toward your *how to be a bitchy sister* degree, I excelled in everything else."

Elaina's brows rose, the faintest hint of amusement in her gaze. She picked up the charcuterie board and walked away with it. Refusing to take her sister's bait, Isabelle grabbed a soda for herself, poured it into a glass, and took both drinks into the living room. By the time she sat down on the sofa, noting that Elaina had already selected some cheese and crackers, she'd smoothed herself on the outside.

"You've gotten much better at smack talk," Elaina said with a bite of cracker in her mouth.

"Which is all the more impressive because I don't practice on anyone but you," Isabelle said, selecting a cracker and taking a small nibble over a napkin.

"If you need more practice, you could always do something radical and call Mom."

Keeping her jaw unclenched was no easy task. "I'm good. We said all there was to say after you two skipped my graduation."

Elaina shook her head. "Jesus Christ. Do you let anything go? It's the strangest dichotomy, I swear. You hold a grudge and pretend we don't exist at the same time."

Lifting her brows, Isabelle held her sister's gaze. "I minored in how to do that."

The smallest laugh left her sister's lips and it reminded Isabelle of her mother with a razor-sharp pang. "Last night was no dream, Iz." There was a softness in Elaina's voice that pulled at a longing Isabelle had buried years earlier. "I keep refreshing Google."

Her throat felt thick. She didn't know what was bothering her more: the desire to let go of her anger or the whole Google thing. It was easier to focus on her default. Work. "I have a phone interview soon. How long are you planning on staying?"

Elaina shrugged. "Hadn't thought about it, really."

Of course she hadn't. Forethought wasn't one of her sister's strengths. Isabelle tried to remember the last time her sister had visited and wanted nothing. Money, a signature, to help their mother, the house needed repairs, they needed a better car, she was out of work. "Do you need money?"

Elaina's jaw tightened even as she picked up a couple hazelnuts, tossed one and caught it in her palm. Isabelle had to restrain herself from telling her older sibling not to play with her goddamned food.

"Do you use me as a write-off? That's a thing, right? Richie Riches like you get a tax break for charitable donations, no?"

Inhaling deeply, Isabelle then breathed out slowly. She'd bought in on a chain of hotels before noon *with* a hangover. She could have a civil conversation with her sibling. "Can we stop? Please?" One more question sat on her tongue like an anvil. Only pride and determination not to be a coward pushed it out. "Is Mom okay?"

Elaina stared for a minute, her gaze full of words Isabelle hoped she wouldn't say. "For someone so smart, you're acting like an idiot. I came to see you. Not get money, not because someone's sick, not wreck anything or make it worse. I came to see my sister. But now," she said, loading up another cracker. She was supposed to use the ingredients sparingly, not glob them on the cracker like that.

"Now?"

"Now, I'm thinking we do a road trip."

Isabelle worked not to crumple the napkin in her fingers. She'd lost her appetite. "Excuse me?"

Her phone rang. A pair of earbuds were on the coffee table. She put them in, opened her phone in practiced motions.

"Isabelle Duprees," she said, standing to walk to the windows.

"Hello, Ms. Duprees. It's Sabrina Kote from *People* magazine. Your assistant gave me your number and arranged for us to speak."

Glancing back at her sister, she played with the napkin in her hand. "Yes. I'm aware. I've got about fifteen minutes."

The reporter laughed. "Of course, you're a busy woman. I've got five questions for our Fast Five. The first is how do you spend a typical day? Just the bones are good. Whenever you're ready."

Walking the length of the window and back, Isabelle gave the woman a rundown of a typical day. Up at five, check emails, prioritize them, work out, shower, begin answering emails while sending messages to her assistant for her schedule. She checked in on each of her investments, spent some time looking over the markets, seeing how she was impacted, had meetings for upcoming or existing investments, spent some time writing—she planned to do a book someday—a lunch meeting, more time with emails, more meetings. Midday, she liked to stretch her legs, get out for a walk. If the weather was off, she'd take a car to The Met, walk the exhibits, spend some time with her thoughts. Back to work until midevening. Late dinners at home if she didn't have meetings. Some reading and a glass of wine or tea as the night wore on. A bath and bed. Pretty standard but definitely no time to squeeze in bagel baking.

"That's a lot packed into one day," Sabrina said.

"I suppose." Isabelle wasn't trying to be moody but her brain felt off. *Hangovers will do that to you.*

"What did you want to be when you were a child?"

An innocuous question. Only one answer sprang to mind. "An adult."

Sabrina laughed like Isabelle had told a wildly funny joke.

"Women you admire," Sabrina said, laughter still in her voice.

"Michelle Obama, Emma Watson, Mackenzie Scott."

"Powerhouse women. Impressive. Is there something in particular you admire about them as a collective?"

Isabelle pinched the bridge of her nose. "Is that one of the five questions?"

The silence told her she was being snappier than she meant to be.

Question three asked her about her favorite place in the city. Easy. The Met. Question four was about her love life.

"No comment." She didn't have one anymore anyway. What bothered her more than Jonathan walking out the night before was how much it upset her to think about the fact that they were over. It was a clear indication she'd let it go on too long.

"Okay," Sabrina said, exhaling a sharp burst of air into Isabelle's ear. "Last question and it's one we ask everyone: What's the strangest result you've ever found when you google your name?"

Isabelle's chin snapped up, her hand dropping. Her gaze met Elaina's, who must have already been looking her way.

"I don't make a habit of googling myself. The purpose of a search engine is to provide answers. I don't need answers about myself."

"Thank you for your time, Ms. Duprees. The article will be in next month's issue." Sabrina's brusque tone was punctuated by her hanging up.

Isabelle removed her earbuds, chewed on her bottom lip.

"It's shocking that you've never won any awards for your charming personality," Elaina said, finishing the last of the crackers.

Forcing her teeth farther into her lower lip was the only thing that stopped the rude retort fighting to get out.

Undeterred, her sister finished off the hazelnuts. "Anyway, you lied."

Sitting on the edge of the couch, Isabelle didn't look at her sister when she responded. "Until last night, it was true."

"For someone who loves power, you're not very brave." Elaina leaned back, chewing, put her sock-clad feet on the coffee table. Near the food.

Isabelle stared straight ahead, gripping the napkin in her fingertips. "You don't know me." Her sister had no idea how brave she was or how hard she'd fought to sit in this very spot.

"Izzy. Look at me."

Isabelle turned her head, her posture stiff. The softness returned to her sister's gaze and this time, it almost pulled her under. She blamed the moment of sentimentality on her hangover. She needed to go to bed for twelve hours, reset herself like she would her phone.

"I don't know what the hell is happening but that woman we found online? It's real. I called. I talked to her."

"What?" The word came out as a whisper.

"She sounded exactly like you. The universe is fucking with us. We need to figure it out because as much as you think *I* don't know you, I'm worried you might not know yourself."

EIGHT

Isabelle stood up, staring at her sister.

A road trip was the exact opposite of what she needed. Elaina smirked, knowing the silence was making her sister twitch on the inside.

"Some of us can't drop everything and take off," Isabelle finally said, crossing her arms over her chest.

Elaina leaned back into the plush cushions. Isabelle had gone through weeks of painstaking research to choose her couch, wanting the perfect blend of comfort and class. Her sister looked like she belonged there as easily as she would in a wicker chair. Of the two of them, Elaina was more adaptable. *That comes from having love and support.*

"You own your own company. From what I've read, you own other people's companies too. There's got to be some perks, Izzy-belle."

"Call. Me. Isabelle."

Elaina smiled. "You are so easy to rile up. It's actually a comfort to know some things don't change. Like I said last night, it surprises me you're such a chicken. All that money and power, you'd think you'd have some backbone."

Squeezing her biceps so she didn't reach out and squeeze her sister's neck, Isabelle paced. "I'm not pledging a sorority, Elaina. I don't *do* road trips. I do business trips. Vacations."

Elaina scoffed. "Bullshit."

There was no point arguing that one.

Elaina stood up, blocking Isabelle's path. "Doesn't it weird you out that some other version of you is out there?"

A lump lodged itself shakily in Isabelle's throat. "Don't say it like that. Lots of people have the same name. Same birthdays. Same middle names. It's not that weird."

Elaina nodded, pulled her phone out of her pocket. She tapped on the screen, pressing some numbers before dialing.

It picked up after the third ring. "Thanks for calling The Book Stop. Izzy speaking. How can I help you?"

The lump in Isabelle's throat grew claws.

Her sister's eyebrows rose, stayed there.

"Hello."

It was her voice. But it wasn't her.

Elaina hung up.

They stared at each other, and Isabelle had a quick flash of when they were kids, locking eyes across the table, neither of them willing to blink first. *Fuck.* Being with her sister made her feel out of control.

Then take control.

"I have commitments I need to honor. I can't just leave. I'll need the day, at least, to get organized."

"Well, at least you think the people you have in your life *now* deserve that kind of respect. For us, it was just walking away without a backward glance."

Isabelle curled her fingers into fists. How could two people live through the exact same moments and see them *so* completely differently? There was a hint of something in Elaina's gaze, something Isabelle didn't know her sister well enough to identify. That, in itself, tugged at strings she thought she'd severed. Part of her wanted to be honest about that, to blurt out what she was thinking, but she pictured Elaina saying something about her being more robot than human.

Instead, she surprised them both and said, "We'll take the trip. But I'm driving."

Isabelle kept a close eye on the line between caring and needing. She could absolutely run her life on her own. She could definitely take care of herself. But the fact that Kaia seemed to understand her on a whole other level, and liked her anyway, pushed her toes over the line now and again. She cared what Kaia thought. Cared about her. But she didn't need her approval.

"How am I supposed to not worry about you when you've never done something like this?" Kaia's scolding tone was laced with genuine concern.

Isabelle wondered if, like with Jonathan, she'd let this relationship move beyond what she could control and contain.

"You're not being paid to worry. You're being paid to do as I ask."

"You have no idea how much I do for you that you *don't* pay me for and I'm okay with that. In fact, I prefer it that way, so you'll be a little thrown off by how much you need me if you ever decide to cut me loose," Kaia said, clearly undeterred by Isabelle's tone. The clicking of a keyboard punctuated her words.

Isabelle's mouth turned up on one side. There was a lot to like about Kaia. In another world, another time, they may have even been friends. But Isabelle couldn't make her family like her, so she'd given up trying with everyone. She had acquaintances, colleagues, business partners, lovers, assistants. But if ever anyone was going to cross that divide, it might be Kaia. *And maybe Jonathan*, her traitorous mind whispered.

"Update, please." Isabelle packed as if this was a business trip. A couple of days didn't require much.

"Your SUV is waiting. I still think you should've let me hire a driver for you."

As if she sensed Isabelle was about to cut in, Kaia pushed on. "Hotel information has been sent to your email. I've moved your Monday morning meetings to the afternoon so hopefully you'll be able to take a few calls. There isn't much you can't do remotely but I wish you'd tell me what this is about."

Zipping up her Chanel duffel bag, Isabelle found herself wishing for the same thing. *My sister goaded me into googling myself and it would appear there's another version of me out there that I need to check out. Why? Oh, because my sister knows how to get under my skin and my own curiosity is scraping at me.*

She huffed out a laugh. That'd go over well.

"Did you just laugh?"

Isabelle's lips quirked. "Do I pay you extra to be annoying and a little cheeky?"

"No, ma'am. All part of the service."

She went through the check list in her head one more time with Kaia just to ease her growing anxiety about this spontaneous adventure. *No, not an adventure. An information-seeking mission.*

"Isabelle?" Kaia asked when the air between them went silent.

"Hmm?" She grabbed her laptop and phone chargers, wrapping the cords before tucking them into the side of her bag.

"You know I'd do anything for you, right? I'm talking *bury the body* anything."

That brought an actual laugh Isabelle didn't even bother to cover up. "I appreciate you, Kaia. I don't say it and I likely don't show it, but I do. I'm okay. Honestly."

After hanging up, she checked all the outlets, windows, and appliances, making sure everything was safe. Despite Elaina not having lived with her for over a dozen years, her sister waited patiently on the couch like this routine was standard and expected.

Or maybe she was just sleeping.

"You and Kaia are close."

Isabelle looked up from her phone where she was double-checking the route she wanted to take.

"I suppose. She basically manages my life so I don't have to deal with details. That tends to make people close."

Elaina made a sound that was somewhere between an exasperated sigh and a snort. "Most people make friends."

Shoving her phone in the pocket of her jeans, Isabelle did her best to tamp down on a biting retort. She didn't need to share that her assistant was basically her only friend. "I'm not most people."

Elaina shot a small smile toward Isabelle. "On that, we agree. Can we go?"

Pulling in a deep breath, Isabelle counted out her exhale before replying. "Yes. Let's get this over with."

Bouncing up off the couch, Elaina patted Isabelle's shoulder on her way by. "Great attitude, sis."

Isabelle started to roll her eyes and then remembered she wasn't a surly teenager and stopped. She'd faced bigger obstacles than this.

It was just a few days.

They'd show up in Pennsylvania, meet a stranger with the same name who sounded like Isabelle on the phone, and it would turn out to be absolutely nothing. A silly whim she'd followed to assuage misplaced guilt over her sister's words and subtle looks. To prove to herself that there was only one Isabelle Duprees that mattered. The world couldn't handle another. And neither could she.

NINE

They were less than an hour into the drive before Isabelle realized the idiocy of trapping herself in a car with her sister. Unspoken memories, emotions, and words filled the car like water in an enclosed tank. Isabelle was running out of room to breathe, her head barely above the surface, a stitch in her side, legs flailing, lungs tightening with alarming speed.

She'd locked herself into her past willingly and now it was drowning her while her sister ate Twizzlers and hummed along to the radio.

Elaina finished one candy, pulled another. "Want me to drive?"

Elaina's voice, mercifully, pushed the image of Isabelle's head sinking beneath the water from her mind.

"No."

Elaina shrugged. "This is a new record."

Isabelle kept her gaze pinned to the road in front of her but in her periphery, she saw the licorice twirling in her sister's hand. In a couple of swift movements, Isabelle pushed the button to lower her window, ignoring the wind and sound whipping around them, grabbed the Twizzler, and tossed it out of the SUV.

"What the hell?!" Elaina turned her head, staring behind them like she'd be able to see her lost candy hit the ground.

Isabelle raised the window. "Stop playing with your food. It's distracting."

"Well, that was littering. I thought better of you, Isabelle Duprees."

Elaina made a *tsk*ing sound and against her own better judgment, Isabelle laughed. "No. You didn't. You never have."

The twang of the guitar coming through the speakers felt like a toothpick scratching over her skin. She switched the station, and was surprised when Elaina didn't complain.

Leaving it on something that wouldn't make her claw at her ears, she settled back into the drive before curiosity got the better of her.

"*What's* a new record?"

Elaina gave a half laugh. "Us not fighting. Don't worry, you wrecked that. The streak is broken. I'm pissed about my Twizzler."

"You have a whole bag."

"Yeah, but I'm scared to eat them now that I know about your repressed candy hatred."

She didn't want to smile or laugh. She didn't want to pretend that years of hurt and anger weren't simmering between them. But it would be a long ride if she focused only on that. They should have taken a plane.

Adjusting her grip on the steering wheel, she did her best to listen to the music and drown out the sound of her sister's nonstop chewing. Elaina only had two car modes: eating or sleeping.

When her sister grew quiet, Isabelle chanced a look over to

see Elaina with her fingers touching the window, her legs tucked under her, watching the world go by. Something tweaked in Isabelle's chest, pinching right around her heart like skin caught in a zipper.

Turning her gaze back to the road, she ran through agenda items for the meeting she had the next day. They'd hit Poppy, Pennsylvania, in a few hours, stay at the hotel Kaia booked, then go to The Book Stop after the meeting in the morning. They could have wrapped it up in one day, even headed back to New York that night, but Isabelle liked the wiggle room. *He will win who, prepared himself, waits to take the enemy unprepared.* The Sun Tzu quote calmed her. She was, literally and figuratively, in the driver's seat.

Questions would be answered, weirdness gone. Her sister would go home and the things inside of her that had tipped sideways would be righted.

The tension left her shoulders when Elaina, predictably, fell asleep. Sparing her another glance, seeing the way her dark eyelashes rested against her pale cheeks, brought another sharp pang. No one ever set out to ostracize themselves from their own family. At least, Isabelle hadn't. It'd been one of those choices that wasn't really a choice at all: keep them in her life or thrive.

Questions tumbled through her brain but they all led back to wanting to know the real reason for Elaina's visit. The last time she'd seen her, they'd parted on less than amicable terms.

Grinding her back teeth together, Isabelle pushed out of the double glass doors, knowing her sister would follow. The New York sunshine warmed her bare arms. She'd forgotten her blazer in the conference room when she'd been informed she had a visitor.

"Could you slow down? Where are you even going? I've barely said hello and you're mad? How is that possible?" Elaina called out behind her.

Isabelle wove through people with the experience of someone who did this almost every day. She slowed, waited for Elaina, only because she didn't want her personal garbage with her sister spilling all over the sidewalks.

"I'm mad because you show up out of the blue when I've asked you repeatedly not to do that. I'm mad because I asked you not to show up at all. And yet, here you are. I was having an excellent day." She stopped herself from crossing her arms over her chest like a child.

"And I ruined it. Well, at least I'm consistent." There was hurt in the tenor of her sister's voice, but Isabelle was immune to it. "Can we just go somewhere and talk?"

"I need a coffee. You have until I finish it to say what you came to say, ask what you came to ask."

They crossed the street with a horde of people. Isabelle liked the feeling of being lost in the center of a group. Surrounded and invisible.

Starbucks was busier than normal. There were three lines going, all the tables taken. A baby cried over someone's laughter, orders were shouted and names were called. Isabelle didn't like this kind of crowd.

Taking a spot in one of the lines, Isabelle worked to smooth out her temper. Maybe excellent *had been an overstatement. She'd presented her pitch to the multimedia company, assuring them she was the one to help them reach the next level with her investment and guidance. But she wasn't the only pitch of the day and the meeting had ended abruptly. Because she'd been rattled. She didn't get visitors. So, she'd known right away who was in the lobby.*

The line moved like molasses. Across the room, near the window, a dark-haired young woman used her foot to jostle a baby stroller, settling the infant's crying. A young child sat almost on top of the wood table, showing her mother pictures in a book. The woman's hair was pulled back from her face in a ponytail with expert precision, not a strand out of place. She nodded along with a smile while tapping something out on her phone. Another child, probably a little older than the table crawler, reached for the book, knocking over a cup in the process. The woman barely looked up from her text, caught it, righted it, and moved it out of the way. She distracted the child with a different book. Now that *was multitasking.*

It took a few more minutes to get their orders. When they did, the only option for seating was at the far end of the table where the young mom navigated the needs of three people over her own.

"Listen, I didn't mean to make you mad, but I knew if I called, you wouldn't answer."

Isabelle took the lid off her cup while her sister sipped her drink across from her. "That should have been a hint."

"You know what, I get that you don't need us now, but could you put the bitch act away for ten minutes?"

"Language," the brunette down the table said.

"What's a bitch?" the table crawler asked.

Heat traveled over Isabelle's cheeks.

"Nothing, sweetie," the woman said, shooting Elaina a glare.

Elaina shrugged. "He'll find out eventually." She turned back to her sister.

"Seriously, Elaina. Could you at least try to act like you've been socialized?"

"I'm a hell of a lot more socialized than you are. Have you

been anywhere other than work, Starbucks, and home in the l ast year?"

She had. But not many places. She liked her life. It was turning out better than she'd hoped. Except for the occasional disruption.

"What do you want, Elaina?"

Her sister set her drink down, met Isabelle's fed-up stare. "The house went up for auction and we can't match the bid."

Isabelle felt her brows draw together. "I sent you money for the back payments and the mortgage. That should have paid for everything outright."

"Well, it didn't."

Isabelle sighed. What Elaina meant was that she and their mother had pissed it away, assuming Isabelle would pick up the check.

"Some land corporation wants to buy it. They've offered high because of the location."

Her childhood home rested on a large, secluded property. Their father had turned away more than one bidder. The neighbors slowly sold out over the years, surrounding the home with bigger, fancier, modern houses.

"Do you know the company's name?"

Elaina pulled her phone out of her purse, which hung across her chest.

"Just email the information to me. I'll take care of it." By take care of it, *she meant she'd put the house in her own damn name. They weren't losing the only connection she had to her father, even if she couldn't stand to be there.*

Elaina smiled. "Now that wasn't so hard, was it?"

The woman at the table started packing up a bag with the books and snacks. One of the kids complained, asking for more treats. She whispered something quietly and the little boy sank down into his seat. Standing, she told the other child it was time to go and suggested he go to the bathroom.

"I need to get back to work," Isabelle said, overheated despite the air-conditioning.

"I took the bus here. I don't have anywhere to stay." Elaina looked at her sister expectantly.

"There are hotels everywhere. I live in a one-bedroom apartment."

"It'd be nice to visit with you. We could go see a show. That's what you New Yorkers do, right? You probably have fancy box seats or something."

"I don't want to visit with you. I need to go clean up your mess." From her own purse, she pulled out her phone, brought up her banking app, and pressed some buttons. "You have money in your account. Enough for a hotel. Go see a show if you want. Then go home and stay there."

Elaina's chair scraped against the floor as she stood up. "Fine. Stupid me, thinking we could actually spend some time together."

Isabelle could only shake her head. Her sister never showed up just for time. Elaina left her coffee, stalked out. Isabelle picked up her cup and her napkins, looking around for a garbage can. She caught the young mom's gaze.

"If you keep giving in, they never get used to the word no," she said softly. There was no judgment in her voice. Instead, there was a surprising amount of kindness and understanding in her gaze.

Isabelle sighed. "As I'm sure you know, sometimes buying yourself some peace is worth the poor behavior."

The woman nodded, smiling when the little boy came back proud of himself. Isabelle threw the cups away and was walking past them to the door when she heard the woman speak to the older boy.

"We have to go. Your mommy and daddy will be home soon."

She wasn't sure what compelled her to do it, but Isabelle stopped in front of the woman.

"These aren't your kids?"

The woman laughed. "No. I'm a nanny. Well, for now. Their mom is pregnant with the fourth, so she'll be home with them soon." She bobbed her eyebrows as she set a hand on the stroller. "Number four was a surprise."

Isabelle laughed. She did very few things spontaneously. Decisions mattered. But she had no regrets when she slid a card across the table to the young woman and told her that if she ever needed a job, to call her and Isabelle would help her out.

Kaia had called three months later. Elaina hadn't visited again since.

Isabelle smirked as her sister came to, just as she was pulling off I-78. Impeccable timing as usual. She'd worried about the drive but in between napping, snacking, playing on her phone, and singing, Elaina was surprisingly nontalkative. It gave Isabelle too much time with her own thoughts, but it was better than arguing with her sister.

Isabelle's stomach rumbled with hunger. Elaina stretched as much as she could. She glanced around, leaning forward.

"We're here? Why didn't you wake me up? There. Let's hit that diner." She pointed across the street to a restaurant that looked more like a storage unit than a place to eat. The neon sign read Niki's.

"We just got here. I'm not hungry."

"What time did Kaia program you to eat?"

Isabelle bit her tongue.

"I looked up places to eat here online. This one is good."

"The hotel will have room service," Isabelle said. She didn't trust anywhere with a neon sign.

"I don't want hotel food. I want a burger. Fries. A milkshake. From *there*."

The sign for the diner read Burgers, Fries, Milkshakes.

Sighing, Isabelle pulled into the lot, parked at the end of the row. If she said no, her sister would complain that on top of everything else, she was a food snob. Besides, Isabelle really wanted out of the car.

"Wow. You didn't even argue." Elaina unfastened her seat belt, slipped her shoes on.

"Maybe I just want a burger, fries, and a milkshake."

Elaina laughed. "Well, if that's the case, I'm buying. How long has it been since you had a milkshake, Izzy-belle?"

They got out of the car and she hoped Elaina would let it go. Instead, she nudged her hip with her own and smiled at her. "Well?"

Isabelle held her gaze until the smile slipped from Elaina's mouth. The day before he died, their dad had taken Elaina and Isabelle out for milkshakes to celebrate the start of summer. He'd always called her his Izzy-belle.

Elaina cursed under her breath like she actually regretted not remembering. Then, like it'd never happened, she looped her arm through Isabelle's. "Oh. Then, it's long overdue."

Nerves and unease skittered across Isabelle's skin. What was she doing here? Not just at this diner but in this town. With Elaina. Chasing after nothing.

Maybe they'd just go home in the morning. She could call Kaia and arrange a flight. Send her sister wherever she wanted to go and head back to New York.

"Come on. As Dad used to say, there's nothing a milkshake can't fix or make better."

He had said that. As much as Isabelle loved him and missed him, she'd grown up fast that summer. It hadn't taken long to realize that he was wrong. Some things were irreparably broken.

IZZY

TEN

Uncomfortable sensations, something like longing and nostalgia, threaded themselves through Isabelle's ribcage, wrapping impossibly tight. With her sister by her side, the feelings were magnified.

You're just tired.

And possibly still hungover.

The diner was a colorful blur of clichés. Red vinyl booths lined two walls, while the back had a swinging door and an open space between the kitchen and dining areas where the food was passed through. Currently, burgers the size of Isabelle's head sat under a heat lamp. A giant square countertop sat in the middle of the diner, waitstaff serving up dishes and milkshakes to the customers sitting on the red vinyl spinning chrome stools. Isabelle half expected the servers to be on roller skates. Vintage posters hung in cheap, colorful frames on the walls. Music played from a bright-red juke box in the far corner. Over half the booths were full, couples and groups laughing and chatting. It made Isabelle's head ache.

"Wicked vibe. We seat ourselves. Not one of your fancy restaurants," Elaina said in a low voice, scanning the space.

She brushed past Isabelle and headed for an empty booth on the right.

A woman in an aqua blue shirt that read *Niki's* in a white oval across the front smiled brightly as she set a pink milkshake in front of a little girl whose ponytails were so high on her head they had to hurt. When the drink spilled with her first sip, the girl's father passed her a napkin, unfazed by the stickiness as he made the little girl laugh.

The waitress glanced over at them, her smile wide. "Have a seat anywhere."

Isabelle slipped into the booth near the back, across from her sister, who already had the tri-fold menu open. The smell of grease and onions were equal parts inviting and nauseating. Shrugging out of her lightweight jacket, she placed it and her purse on the bench beside her after ensuring there weren't crumbs from the last person's meal.

"You look like you're trying to sink into an ice bath." Elaina bounced a bit in her seat. "Come on. It's comfy, and fun." Her sister tilted her head to one side. "Sorry. *Fun.* That's this thing—"

Isabelle's scowl cut off Elaina's words but didn't hide her sister's smirk. "Our ideas of fun have always been different."

"Amen, sister. Your kind of fun would put me to sleep." She lifted her gaze from the menu. "Though, not the kind you were looking to have last night. Do we get to talk about the James Bond Tux guy?"

Isabelle opened her menu in response.

"Rumor has it, some sisters tell each other everything," Elaina said in a stage whisper.

Isabelle focused on the menu. She wasn't playing this game—pretending there wasn't a reason they weren't close. Or that Elaina wasn't every bit as aware of that reason as she was. She just wanted to eat some food and get to the hotel. The longer she was away from New York, the more she doubted what she was doing. The purpose of this trip was some anomaly she should have ignored.

"Hi. What can I get for you ladies?" The waitress's voice caused goose bumps to freckle every inch of Isabelle's skin. She looked up slowly, worried she was stuck so deep in her own head that she was hallucinating.

Eyes identical to her own stared back. Identical except for the light and happiness in them. Her own dark hair looked softer on this woman, who'd tied it into a braid that hung over her shoulder. Isabelle felt her heartbeat in too many spots on her body. Looking at this woman, whose name tag read Izzy, she felt like she was looking in a mirror before bed. The other her was makeup-free and even though her online information said they were the same age, with the same birthdate, this woman looked years younger than Isabelle felt. Particularly in this moment.

When the menu started to crumple in her grasp, her sister reached over and placed her hand over Isabelle's.

"We'll take two vanilla milkshakes," Elaina said with an eerie sense of calm, and the other woman nodded and walked away.

The menu crinkled but Isabelle couldn't unclench her fingers.

"Shit," Elaina muttered. "Maybe I didn't think this through."

Isabelle shook her head. "You see it, right?" Was that even her voice? She sounded like she was inside of a tunnel.

Elaina looked over to the waitress, but Isabelle kept her eyes glued on her sister, grateful for once, that she was there as a focal point.

Elaina's eyes came back to hers. "I did a little more digging online than you did. I knew she worked here. I thought, you know, the element of surprise and all that jazz."

Like an elastic had been snapped against her skin, Isabelle recoiled, pulling the paper menu to her chest. "What?"

Elaina blew out a sharp breath. "She had some Facebook posts of staff parties here. I thought we'd get it out of the way. Rip the Band-Aid off. I gotta say, I did *not* expect that. Even seeing her pictures. Your pictures. Whatever. Even *seeing* it online is nothing like this. Breathe. Jesus Christ, take a breath."

Isabelle dropped her hands to the table, trying to do as Elaina said, trying to wrap her head around what she'd seen along with the fact that her sister had ambushed her. Elaina reached for her hands immediately, pressed hers against Isabelle's shaking ones. The pressure reminded her that this moment was real.

She shook her head slowly, wishing she could knock things into place, make them make sense. Sweat beaded along her hairline. The diner felt like a sauna. Her stomach rolled.

"What's happening?" The words came out as a whisper.

"I don't know but if you lose your shit right now, we'll never find out. Take a breath, Isabelle." There was zero playfulness in her sister's tone.

It was like ice water to the face. Isabelle pulled her hand free, sat up straighter, and nodded. "You shouldn't have done this. I wasn't prepared."

Elaina pulled back. "You can't prepare for everything."

Shaking off the frustration of having her sister take the choice out of her hands, she tried to explain it. "People have doppelgängers. It's a real thing."

Elaina folded her hands on top of her menu. "Right. And yours just happens to have the same name. How did she not register that she was basically looking in a mirror? Did you make a deal with a sea witch or something?"

Isabelle's mouth dropped open. "You think this is funny?"

Elaina shook her head immediately. "No. Not at all. Strange? Yes. Freaky? A hundred percent. But definitely not funny. This is some sort of messed-up Scrooge voodoo."

Isabelle's brows pushed together and it felt like all her little heartbeats created one giant, heavy beat at the base of her neck. "What are you talking about?" She looked around quickly but no one was paying any attention to them.

Her sister's eyes were wide with some of the surprise Isabelle felt. She leaned closer, subtly pointing her finger toward the counter where *Izzy* was mixing up milkshakes. "That woman there is like your ghost of . . . well, I don't really know. In Scrooge, he has the ghost of past, present, and future."

Isabelle's breath caught. "This isn't a fucking Dickens novel, Elaina."

Elaina waved her hands toward Isabelle, shushing her. "Keep it down. And no, maybe not, but something weird is going on and I think the universe wants you to pay attention."

"I think the universe wants me to take a spa vacation with a crate of champagne. Or get checked for a stroke."

Izzy came back to the table, two creamy, delicious-looking milkshakes on her tray. "Here you go, ladies. Do you need more time with the menu?"

Isabelle couldn't sort through her thoughts fast enough. "I thought you worked at The Book Stop. Why are you waitressing?"

Elaina's emitted a small groan. Izzy frowned as she set the drinks on the table. "Excuse me?"

Her sister cleared her throat. "What my sister means is, we just got to town and we saw you on the book store's website when we were checking out things to do. Or . . . we thought we did. We might have been wrong. It occasionally happens."

Elaina's lie rolled off her tongue in a jovial tone that sounded fake to Isabelle.

Izzy straightened, her easy smile returning. "Oh. First, welcome to Poppy. Second, yes, I'm the manager there. I forgot I put all the staff photos on there. If you haven't been yet, you need to. I personally order all the books and I make sure to have a wide selection. Small but mighty, right?"

Isabelle stared at the woman, listening to the inane chatter come out of what *looked* like her own mouth. "If you work there, why do you work here?"

An almost growl left her sister's mouth at the same moment Isabelle felt a sharp jab against her shin.

"Lots of people have two jobs, Isabelle," Elaina said through gritted teeth.

Izzy grinned, pointed at her name tag. "Hey. Twins! I'm Izzy, short for Isabelle."

How could she not see it? Izzy was looking right at Isabelle with no sign of recognition. No flicker of awareness, surprise, or any of the fear bubbling in Isabelle's veins.

Izzy hooked a thumb in Elaina's direction. "Your sister's right. I work here a couple afternoons a week. I love it though, so it's more like hanging with friends than work, you know? Anyway, what can I get for you ladies?"

Resisting the urge to rub her shin, Isabelle glanced back at the menu. "I'll have the chef salad. Dressing on the side."

When she looked up, Elaina was glaring at her. "Seriously? No. She won't. She'll have a burger and fries. I'll have the same. Thanks, Izzy. Sorry. We're a little tired from the drive. Our manners have clearly suffered."

"Don't tell Niki I said so, but y'all will definitely enjoy the burgers more than the salad," Izzy said, leaning down to grab the menus. "And no worries. Let me get your orders in and I can give you a couple sight-seeing destinations if you're here for a few days."

Before Isabelle could respond, Elaina nodded. "That would be fantastic."

When Izzy walked away, Elaina shook her head. "You have the social skills of a piranha. What is wrong with you?"

Isabelle leaned in closer, careful to keep her voice low. "Oh, I'm sorry, did you just run into yourself in a seedy diner in the middle of nowhere? Excuse the hell out of me if I'm a little thrown."

Elaina leaned back, a smug smile on her face. She tapped her nails on the tabletop. "I didn't know the great Isabelle Duprees could be thrown off her game."

Panic grew wings in her chest. "This is *not* a game. I have no idea what this is."

Maybe it was her tone, maybe the look on her face, or maybe the fact that despite the buried anger and years apart, they did recognize each other's tells, but Elaina lost the smirk, gave her a gentle smile.

"It'll be okay. We'll figure it out. Just let me do the talking. You're too wound up. You come off bitchy."

Isabelle closed her eyes and counted to ten. She wouldn't be able to figure out what was happening if she strangled her sister in this booth.

When she opened her eyes, the look in Elaina's told her she knew exactly what she was doing. Pressing every button Isabelle thought she hid so well.

She felt the buzz of her phone vibrating in her purse but ignored it. She thought her threshold for dealing with stress was a hell of a lot higher but apparently it went into freefall when faced with—as her sister phrased it—Scrooge-like voodoo.

"I'm a friendly person. Let me talk with her. I'll get her to open up a bit."

"I'm friendly," Isabelle said, her spine stiffening.

Elaina snorted. "Yeah. Like I said, friendly like a piranha. The last *Newsweek* article I saw called you a cross between a great white shark and the Grinch."

Isabelle frowned. She purposely didn't read articles about herself. She didn't care what anyone said but that didn't mean she was without feelings entirely. "That seems harsh. And somewhat childish."

"Yeah, well, you probably stole someone's company or fortune, and most people don't like that much. It's the grown-up version of kicking over a sandcastle."

Isabelle rubbed the knot of tension on the side of her neck. "I don't bully people to get what I want." Maneuver? Sure. Play them like chess pieces? If necessary. Since when was that bad? Did Elaina really not understand how hard she worked?

Her sister's brows arched. "Yeah. I'm sure you send them home with goodie bags after you level them."

Before Isabelle could defend herself, Izzy returned with a toothy smile. It was disconcerting, to say the least, seeing this bubblier, *lighter* version of herself.

She's not you, Isabelle reminded herself. *Doppelgänger at best. Same name. Weird things happen all the time.*

"Okay. Let me give you the rundown on Poppy. First, not a whole lot of folks land here for good. We're one of the smallest towns in the state but what makes us stand out is, despite that, we have a Target. It's a long story that went our way since who doesn't love Target?"

Isabelle. Isabelle had no great love for the chain store. She felt nothing one way or the other. But this woman lit up when she talked, like she was proud of the mundane facts she was sharing. "There are some gorgeous hikes if you're into that sort of thing. There's a delicious taco stand by Plaza Park. Best tacos ever. And of course, The Book Stop. It's got a coffee bar and touristy trinkets. Oh! Speaking of trinkets, if you're looking for . . ." Izzy's chipper tone and misplaced enthusiasm made the words jumble in Isabelle's brain to the point that she couldn't decipher them over the buzzing in her head. A new song came through the speakers, louder than the previous one, jolting her back into the moment. Isabelle felt like she was being squeezed from the inside.

This wasn't her. This wasn't a different version of her. She wanted to stand up and shout. Not that she ever would but she wanted to stand up on the booth seat and yell that she knew the universe was messing with her and she was not down for it.

Instead, she interrupted Izzy. "Do you think we look alike?" It didn't make any sense. It was right there in front of her. If Isabelle and Elaina saw it, why weren't others freaking out over their likeness?

Elaina muttered a curse, barely under her breath.

Izzy stopped talking, stared at Isabelle with her mouth open. "I'm sorry?" The confusion in her gaze, the sudden stiffness in her stance told Isabelle that whatever this woman saw when she looked at her, was not herself. She didn't see it and damn if that didn't make it freakier. *Keep it together, Isabelle.* Her phone vibrated again like a lifeline to the real world.

Elaina laughed too loud, delivering another kick to Isabelle's shin. "She means me and her. We're sisters and everyone says we look so much alike but we just don't see it."

Everything about Izzy softened in a split second. To be so easily disarmed seemed like a flaw. "Oh." She tilted her head, really inspected the two sisters. "Same nose. Same eyes. For sure. Definitely. Uh, I should check on your orders."

Isabelle stared after her, confusion making her chest tight. Something hit her in the cheek. Turning, she glared at Elaina while she picked up the crumpled straw wrapper and set it aside.

"How old are you?"

Elaina scoffed. "Old enough to know how to have a conversation with someone without weirding them out. You're sending major creeper vibes."

Isabelle inhaled sharply and tried to keep a handle on her frustration. Frustration led to mistakes. "You understand how insane this whole thing is, right? It doesn't make sense."

Her sister studied her for a moment as she sipped her shake. When she set it down, there was something that looked a lot like pity in Elaina's gaze. "It's weird. You're right. I don't have any answers other than, not everything wraps up nice and neat. Some things are messy, inexplicable even. Let's do this: instead of trying to make it make sense in that big brain of yours, just let it happen. Let's see where this leads."

"Leads?"

"Yeah. Did you not hear anything she said? There's an open market tonight on Main Street. Poppy is known for it. According to Izzy, there's nowhere better to listen to live music, eat street food, and buy anything you need. She'll be helping run a booth after her shift tonight. Seems one of the guys she's seeing owns a hobby farm with fruit trees."

Isabelle's eyes narrowed. "One of?"

Elaina's smile grew. "Yep. Looks like *other you* has a way better social life."

Isabelle picked up her milkshake, the cold glass settling her in the moment. "You know nothing about my social life." And yet, Elaina wasn't wrong.

That cleared up some things in Isabelle's mind. This woman looked like her, talked like her, shared her name and her birthday. But the similarities ended there, because the life Elaina just described sounded like Isabelle's personal version of Hell. Even aside from the diner and working two jobs, there was nothing about Izzy that made her want to take another look at her own life. If anything, it just motivated her to get back to it. As soon as possible.

ELEVEN

Isabelle's phone continued to buzz as the bellman—or more accurately, the front desk clerk who she'd insisted carry their luggage up to the second floor—and as it so happened, the top floor—let them into their room. If this is what Kaia booked, she was certain it was the best the town had to offer. Which said a hell of a lot about the town.

She tipped him without looking, the action second nature, while pulling her phone from her pocket. She'd started reading through texts, prioritizing while Elaina wandered across the room and flopped down on the bed by the window without even inspecting it. Isabelle wished she had a black light, but that would probably make the whole experience worse.

"Jesus," Elaina said in a long drawl, kicking off her shoes, one landing with a thud on the floor, the other on the flower-patterned bedspread. "You ever shove that thing down the front of your pants? It vibrates non-fucking-stop. Might put something other than a sour look on your face."

Isabelle's chin snapped up and without warning, a laugh burst from her chest. It was rough and almost rusty but what shocked her more was her sister being the cause. The smile lingered, her body relaxing slightly.

Elaina jackknifed into a sitting position, pointing at Isabelle. "Did you just laugh? Out loud?"

Lips twitching, Isabelle shook her head. "It was an accident. I need to make some phone calls."

The smile her sister gave her somehow loosened something in her chest while tying another knot in her stomach. Elaina pushed up off the bed. "I'm going to shower before we head to the market."

Again, the idea of staying, learning more, caused sweat to dot the back of Isabelle's neck. Though she prided herself on having one hell of a poker face, Elaina must have caught a quick glimpse of her reservations.

Walking over, she stopped when they were nearly toe to toe. "You're not backing out. Don't be such a wimp."

Isabelle didn't let out the breath she was holding until the bathroom door closed. She shut her eyes for a brief second and tried to regulate her emotions. It shouldn't be that hard. She'd been locking down her feelings for years.

Her phone buzzed again, this time with a phone call from Jasper, one of her junior assistants. He was excellent at his job—efficient, knowledgeable, and able to recite client details like a computer.

"Jasper." She toed off her shoes, sat on the squeaky swivel chair by the scuffed-up desk.

"Evening, Ms. Duprees. I understand you're out of town on business, but I thought you'd want to know that Esther and Oscar Moore have put a bid in on the Destiny Ridge project. I believe it's a direct retaliation for the Bayer Hotel purchase."

Isabelle moved to the bed, sank down, perching on the edge of it while pinching the bridge of her nose. "We'll see how that plays out. They won't know what we bid, plus Donovan Westbrook wants to join forces. Reach out to him and see if he's serious. If we work together but each make a bid, we'll be in a better position." They'd turn the run-down motel into midrange condos.

"Will do."

She had no doubt. Her throat tightened with her next thought. "Have you checked the stadium properties like I asked?"

Of course he had.

"I emailed you earlier today."

"I haven't had a chance to get to all of my emails. Listen, can you do something for me outside of the rest?"

"Of course, Ms. Duprees. Always."

The genuineness of his tone lightened the weight on her shoulders. Her sister had plenty to say about her personality but the people who worked for her were loyal and happy.

For more than just a paycheck.

She hoped.

"I'd like you to see who owns The Book Stop in Poppy, Pennsylvania. I want a breakdown of the past five years, sales, management, ownership. Cross-reference it with any other locations." She didn't think it was a chain, but it was worth checking.

"Got it. Shall I contact Mr. Fairbanks regarding the stadium properties?"

The little stitch in her heart was probably nothing. Certainly not a reaction to just his name. He'd wanted to get her input and thoughts on buying into housing surrounding some of the bigger sports stadiums. She'd been reluctant to dive too deeply into business with him because she was too busy thinking about other things when they were together.

"I'll do it myself."

"Understood. I'll forward you the prospectus for Destiny Ridge for you to survey."

"Thanks, Jasper."

Isabelle disconnected, tossed her phone on the bed. She could hear Elaina singing in the shower and tried to block it out with her to-do list. But the only thing coming into her mind was the look on Jonathan's face when he'd left her apartment. The defeat in his shoulders had etched itself in her brain. She'd done that.

She hated being a cliché. Business. Pleasure. Two entirely different things. He was the only one she'd ever blurred the lines with and worse, she'd never let herself analyze the reason why.

Before she could change her mind, she dialed his number, her breath hitching when the call connected. She resisted the urge to wipe her damp palm on her jeans.

"Hello, Ms. Duprees. Mr. Fairbanks is unavailable at the moment. Can I give him a message for you?"

Isabelle bit down on her bottom lip.

"Ms. Duprees?" the voice repeated.

The metallic taste of blood touched her tongue, making her release her lip. "No message."

She hung up.

Elaina opened the bathroom door, leaned against the frame as steam followed in her wake. "I saw your scrunchy face when we walked in. You can say what you want about this hotel."

"Motel," Isabelle muttered. There was a clear difference.

"Whatever. That showerhead is magic."

Isabelle felt like her clothes had shrunk. Hell, like her skin had. She needed out of this room. Out of this town.

Walking to her suitcase, her hand on the knot she'd created in the towel, water droplets dripped down Elaina's slender back. An intricate tattoo wove from her right shoulder, over the bone, down into the towel. Petals fell from the center of the flower, leaving it almost bare. One-handed, Elaina tossed the suitcase on the bed, unzipped it, and pulled out some clothes. Like they were teens in a locker room, something Elaina had always been more comfortable with than her, she dropped the towel, pulled on her clothes while Isabelle stared at the wall.

"Change your clothes, Izzy-belle."

Isabelle moved because she needed to do something, not because Elaina told her to. She took a turn in the bathroom, cleansing her face, using the routine to settle the unrest buzzing around inside her chest. The bathroom mirror was cracked in the corners, faint streaks of cleaner slashing the center, making her face look distorted.

Seems fitting.

It felt like a waste of time to add makeup. Instead, she tucked her things away, changed her clothes to something more open-market suitable.

Her phone buzzed as she set her suitcase alongside the bed. Jonathan had never put an intermediary between them. Not once.

"Why don't you leave that thing here?" Elaina used a compact to apply some lipstick, snapping it shut then putting it in the purse she'd slung across her chest. The spaghetti strap tank top showcased tanned, toned skin. Her sister hated the gym, but she'd always been athletic. It gave Isabelle a strange sense of peace to know that Elaina continued to take care of herself.

Isabelle grabbed her own purse, picked up her phone, shooting her sister a glance through lowered lashes. "You think so little of what I do."

Without warning, her sister was in front of her. She whipped the phone out of Isabelle's hand, shook it a little. "Who dies if you don't answer a goddamned text? Does the sky fall? Does the market crash? Does your life or anyone else's actually fall apart?"

Showing anger gave her sister the upper hand so Isabelle

kept her expression bland, didn't grab for the phone. "No, Elaina. Absolutely nothing happens if I don't answer my phone. I make so little impact on the world with what I do, nothing will change if I don't respond."

Elaina rolled her eyes. "You're such a drama queen. I wasn't worried about what you do for the world. I was more thinking you could use a break from it."

Before Isabelle could respond or process that, Elaina threw the phone on the bed. "Let's go."

Picking up her phone, putting it on silent as an unsaid concession, Isabelle did something she hadn't in more years than she could count: she followed after her sister.

TWELVE

Isabelle hadn't known what to expect from the market. She hadn't actually thought about that piece of it since she was too busy trying to figure out what to say to her other self to find out more information. Like, why the hell did you settle in a sleepy little town when Philadelphia was only an hour away?

Instead of setting up the event on Main Street where the motel and several businesses were located, vendors apparently set up several blocks over, offering items at booths, tables, and tents in the middle of residential streets. Large wooden sawhorses cordoned off streets. Handmade signs with arrows pointing the way were stapled to poles. Isabelle half expected some of the signs to point in opposite directions.

This way to Wonderland.

Music pumped through the air from somewhere Isabelle couldn't see. As they crossed one street to enter the market, a man on a bike whipped past, shouting out a hello.

When Isabelle jolted, Elaina laughed. "You okay?"

Some New Yorker she was. She hated the way her nerves had taken up residence in her brain and her gut. She nodded, glancing around, taking in the houses, the mowed lawns, and the tic-tac-toe games drawn in sidewalk chalk on the cement.

"These kinds of things can be great for small towns. Socially and economically," Isabelle murmured.

"Is that so?" Elaina's tone was dry, but Isabelle ignored it.

She didn't like entering unknown situations, and focusing on what she knew helped ease the uncertainty. "It seems odd for this to be on side streets rather than the main drag. Those shops are missing out on a valuable opportunity to engage foot traffic."

Elaina looped her arm through Isabelle's, pulling her around one of the wooden blockades. "Maybe you can enlighten them."

Isabelle resisted the urge to yank her arm away. Instead, she took note of an older couple sitting on a front porch, watching people walk past their home in search of entertainment and food. Though there were others on the street, it seemed fairly quiet and uneventful and, so far, there were no vendors. The woman, a pair of knitting needles in her hands, a blanket over her lap, smiled at her.

"Enjoy the market!" she called.

Elaina waved back as they continued walking. All the houses seemed small, tidy, and cared for with small bursts of flowers lining some of the windows. Some homes had wooden signs on their lawns with business names: Netty's Fabrics & Sewing, Paw's Clipping & Dog Grooming, and The Beauty Booth were just a few.

Elaina moved like she knew exactly where she was going. Isabelle kept pace easily but not nearly as enthusiastically.

Answers. She wanted answers. They turned left at the next corner and the little area transformed. People filled the street, chatting and laughing. Each side of the street was lined with small, canopied booths. People sold their wares, socialized, gathered. This was probably the entire population of the town. Picnic tables were set up on sidewalks under the blooming branches of trees. Packs of kids raced around, played makeshift games, or got their faces painted. Others bounced in one of those ridiculously ugly blow-up contraptions.

The scent of grilled meat and cinnamon filled the air and even though they'd eaten not that long ago, Isabelle's stomach rumbled. The source of the music stood in the center of it all: a round stage with mounted speakers facing in all directions. People chatted over and around it unbothered. Happy. A couple of male guitarists bounced on the balls of their feet, facing each other as they played. A woman crooned into the microphone, her fingers tapping against her thigh.

Moving slowly through the crowd, Isabelle noted the bulk of vendors sold homemade craft items—blankets, scarves, hats, carved decorations, painted wooden signs. Things Isabelle had no need for, but still, it was impossible not to feel the sense of community.

It made her think about—

Elaina nudged her arm. "Remember the carnival Dad took us to? I thought that was the most amazing thing I'd ever seen. All those lights? God. It was incredible. It wasn't until I went to Coney Island years later that I realized what a puny excuse for an event it was."

That.

It made Isabelle think about that same memory. It'd been tucked away in the recesses of her brain like a file she'd lost access to years ago. The strength of the memory made her feet unsteady. The images were so strong she wasn't sure if the scent of French fries was from now or then. The lights, the midway, games that cost five dollars for a fifty-cent toy. Greasy food in paper cones, corndogs, and mini donuts. The Ferris wheel standing like a sentinel in the center of the church parking lot in downtown Ashland, Tennessee. It was like Disneyland had come to their tiny hometown.

"Still. It was one of the best nights of my life," Elaina said on a sigh.

The wistfulness in her sister's tone got lodged right under Isabelle's breastbone, like a sliver, poking into her heart. "You spent about five years' allowance trying to win a pink teddy bear with blue eyes."

Elaina stopped so suddenly, Isabelle thought something was wrong. She looked around for a threat, something that had alarmed her sister.

"You remember that?"

The look on her sister's face made Isabelle's heartbeat feel more present. Stronger. Too strong. "Yes." She held her stare.

"It wasn't all bad," Elaina whispered.

Isabelle bit the inside of her cheek to stave off the emotion swamping her. Not all bad, no. But not enough good either. "Let's do this."

Pushing everything else aside, she considered tonight her self-care for the week. She made time for yoga, working out, and meditation. This could somehow be lumped in with that and if she felt out of place, out of touch with herself . . . well, too bad.

Being uncomfortable made a person grow. There was nothing comfortable about how she'd made it to the top. Nothing comfortable and safe in her history. She couldn't even hate those pieces of herself because they were part of the whole.

The band started up, the woman's voice surrounding them like a soulful hug, an apt soundtrack to an inexplicable experience. Conversations provided a steady hum that let Isabelle block out her thoughts as they looked through soap scrubs, homemade candles, and other things people had created with their own two hands. Isabelle chatted with a couple of vendors. She liked small business. Everyone started somewhere. Not everyone knew how to take it to the next level, but she'd purchased more than one start-up company, and those had paid off nicely.

She took a few business cards, ignoring Elaina's efforts at teasing her, waiting for her sister when she added purchases to her large over-the-shoulder bag. Isabelle tried to relax, enjoy herself, but the underlying reason for their being at this place hovered over her like the clouds rolling in.

It wasn't until they were halfway down one side of the street that she came face to face with herself.

Izzy smiled when she saw them, like they were old friends. She stood behind a table set up with a couple vases of bright flowers in between weathered crates turned on their sides, displaying jars. There was a banner along the front of the table that simply read: *Tucker's.* Izzy waved. Isabelle was certain she'd never been so open and trusting. Not even when she'd had no reason not to be.

Izzy had tucked her brown hair into two braids. If she was going for country chic, between the hair and the checkered off-the-shoulder shirt, she'd found it.

"Tuck, these are the women I was telling you about," Izzy said, pulling on the arm of a man who was bent over something behind a table, his face hidden.

He unfolded his body to show a beard-covered face, sharp green eyes, and considerable height. He looked like he should star in a Western. Isabelle absolutely could not see herself with someone like him. But, more than a little curious, she held his gaze, waited for any hint of recognition, any sign of shock, surprise, utter disbelief that his girlfriend's doppelgänger was standing in front of him.

She gestured to both of them. "Isabelle, obviously not going to forget your name. And Elaina, right? This is my friend, Tucker."

Before anyone else could say anything, Izzy asked. "You want another freaky fact?"

Elaina leaned in. "Always."

"I have a sister named Elaina."

Elaina looked at Isabelle who could only stand there like she was watching a weird skit.

She turned back to Izzy. "That is absolutely freaky. Are you close?"

Her smile dimmed and Tucker stepped closer, smiling at Izzy like she was responsible for putting the sun in the sky.

He extended his free hand. "Nice to meet you both. Izzy says you're tourists. Just passing through?"

The fact that Izzy didn't answer the question of whether or not she was close to her own Elaina felt like an answer in itself. They all shook hands.

"We are. It's a cute town," Elaina said.

Isabelle stopped staring at herself, stopped trying to see inside the other version of her own mind, and stepped forward, her fingers dancing over an assortment of jam lids.

"It's definitely a cute town." When had she last used the word *cute*? "Have you lived here long?"

Tucker ran a hand down Izzy's bare arm and Isabelle shivered. Did she want someone to look at her that way?

Not someone. Not just anyone.

"I've lived here my whole life."

Izzy's furrowed brow smoothed out. "Not me, but I'm a townie through and through. Nowhere else I'd want to be." She smiled up at Tucker, and Isabelle recognized the longing in the woman's gaze. She clearly wanted more with this man but she'd introduced him as a friend.

How would you introduce Jonathan?

Isabelle shoved thoughts of him aside. “What made you settle here?”

Elaina stepped closer. A warning not to push too hard.

A few people stopped by the table, picking up the jams and gift baskets to check them out.

“Aside from the cute factor? Actually, I was on my way to Boston. I was eighteen, planning on going to school. Bus broke down and I was waiting right in Niki’s diner and felt like there was no reason to go any farther. You ever get that? A feeling you’re so sure about, you just follow it even though life had been leading you another way entirely?”

Isabelle swallowed, trying to gather moisture in her inexplicably dry mouth.

Elaina wasn’t so easily phased. Of course, it wasn’t her the universe was messing with. “Isabelle went to school in Boston. She doesn’t do much without thinking it through.”

Izzy stared past them, like she was trying to see something that wasn’t there. “I was here two months before I remembered I’d been here once before when I was little.”

Something shook inside of Isabelle’s brain, rattling loose. Izzy met her gaze, held it. “My dad had a job out here. He brought me with him. He didn’t travel for work much but when he did, I always tagged along. It was like our own little adventures.”

Isabelle rubbed the aching spot in the center of her chest, images flashing in her mind like sparks, too fast to capture.

She was eight. He’d died a month later. He’d been doing some electrical work for a friend of a friend who was building a house. She’d slept most of the way in the backseat. Every time she’d woken, he’d been singing, snacking on chips or popcorn. That memory had been buried like a deleted file. It hurt to reopen it.

Elaina gripped her hand. "Isabelle lives in New York. She loves it . . . don't you?"

She turned, looked at her sister, realizing she'd missed something by zoning out. Elaina continued, keeping her fingers locked around Isabelle's. "Sorry. We're a little out of it today. A combination of hunger and fatigue, I think. Your jams look amazing."

Jams. Safe topic. The switch centered her in the moment. Tucker picked up a small platter with little pieces of bread, each with a dollop of jam.

"There's mixed berry, pear, and apple."

Elaina dove in, taking one of each. "Oh, apple jam? That sounds delightful." She popped one in her mouth then grabbed another and pushed it toward her sister. "Mixed berry. Try it."

Isabelle tried to rear back but didn't have the room. "Stop—" Opening her mouth gave her sister the opportunity to shove the bite into her mouth. Isabelle ground her teeth together for a second before chewing.

She licked her lips. "It's delicious." She wasn't lying. That was damn good jam.

"Thanks. I'm pretty proud of it," Tucker said.

Izzy picked up a business card, passed it over. "He's selling online now because the demand is so high. Tuck donates half the proceeds to the local shelter."

Elaina picked up a jar with a cute, homemade label, turning it to read the back.

Isabelle was stuck on what Izzy said. "That's very generous. You both work very hard. You must have a secondary source of income, then? Or primary, I suppose," she said to Tucker.

Izzy scrunched her brows but Tucker seemed to take the question in stride. Elaina mumbled under her breath, dug through her purse for her wallet.

"I run a hobby farm but construction pays the bills. This takes up a lot of my time. But I love it."

That didn't make sense. "You must be very profitable if you're able to use the income as a donation."

She could clearly see she was making Izzy uncomfortable and it struck her as strange that the woman didn't say anything. There were any number of responses she herself would offer to someone overstepping. Maybe this was her with no backbone?

"I apologize for my sister. She works for a big corporation. When she closes her eyes, she sees dollar signs, so she doesn't always understand those who don't," Elaina said, stepping firmly on Isabelle's toes.

Isabelle cursed, pulled her foot from beneath Elaina's. "Ouch. Knock it off. I'm sorry. She's right. I'm overstepping but I am surprised, as a successful businesswoman, that you wouldn't take those profits and capitalize on them. Especially if you can afford to donate them. You could scale your business. The jam is delicious. If it wasn't, it wouldn't matter how well you were doing because quality matters, even in today's market."

"Tucker's happy with the way he lives his life." The protective edge in Izzy's voice once again made Isabelle wonder why this other version of her didn't label her relationship with this man.

Pot, meet kettle.

"I wasn't suggesting otherwise," Isabelle said, softening her tone. Maybe her purpose was to make their lives better? Offer some advice? "Regardless of how happy both of you are at your current jobs, no one avoids success, right? I mean, you clearly like what you do and that's a benefit but if you didn't want to make money, you'd just give your product away."

Tucker's green eyes sparked with something that she couldn't read. "Ma'am, I appreciate what I think are your good intentions but you don't know me. Or Izzy. You have no idea why I started my business or why I run it the way I do."

Shit. She was wrecking this—whatever it was. She held her hands up. "I'm sorry. You're right. I get wrapped up in the business piece. The jam is delicious and clearly you know what you're doing."

Both of them softened while Elaina made herself busy looking at the gift packages featuring the different flavors of jam.

"Aren't you on vacation? Maybe you should just enjoy the market. There's excellent food here tonight," Izzy said.

"My sister doesn't take vacations," Elaina said, setting down another jar.

Isabelle frowned at her. "I'm here. I'm doing what you asked. Cut me some slack."

"I'll do that when you figure out how to have some fun," Elaina said, a wide smile on her face.

"You want fun, you ought to stick around. I'm playing with the band later," Tucker grinned.

"A man of many talents," Elaina said. "Musician, jam maker."

"He's good at everything he does," Izzy said with obvious adoration just as the tempo of the music changed. Her gaze lit up and she hurried from around the table. "This is one of my all-time favorite songs."

And just like that, Izzy Duprees danced in the street, ignoring the people who moved around her like this was just something to expect, something she did all the time without care or thought. A few people called out greetings as they passed her, telling her she looked good. The band did a shout-out, calling her by name. All the while, Izzy raised her hands over her head, her body moving in a way Isabelle was positive she herself had only ever moved in the privacy of her own bedroom. The delight on Izzy's face as she tipped her chin up to the sky was something both familiar and hauntingly unknown to Isabelle.

For a moment, Izzy was all Isabelle could see and in those endless seconds, she both hated and envied herself more than she ever thought possible.

Tucker appeared at her side. “She’s beautiful, isn’t she?”

Isabelle turned her head to look at him, watching the way he watched the other her. Like he couldn’t look away. Like he didn’t want to.

“Being near her is like getting close to the sun,” he said, his voice gravelly with emotion.

“Sounds painful,” Isabelle said softly.

One side of his lips tipped up under his beard in a self-deprecating smirk. “A little pain never killed anyone.”

Isabelle nearly laughed. Truer words. “You’re not . . . exclusive?”

Tucker gave a laugh that held no mirth, running a calloused hand over his beard. “She’s scared.”

“Of?”

His eyes came to hers and again she wondered if he’d *see.* “Of needing me too much. Anyone, really. She’ll love you with her whole heart but she’s scared to give it away.” His gaze returned to Izzy.

Isabelle blinked rapidly, unsure how to absorb this information.

“You’re okay with that?”

“I don’t need words to know what I can see in her eyes,” he said as Izzy crooked a finger, beckoned him forward.

Tucker moved toward her like he had no choice or desire to do otherwise. His hand seamlessly grasped the one Izzy lifted over her head and he spun her, pulled her into his strong arms. Izzy’s laughter rang out over the music like it was part of the song.

Isabelle lost those moments, caught up in watching this other version of herself. She wasn’t sure how long she stood there before Elaina joined her, standing so close their arms were touching.

"I forgot what you looked like when you're happy," Elaina whispered.

Isabelle's gaze snapped to her sister's profile watching Tucker and Izzy, and now several others, dancing in the street. There was a sheen in her sister's gaze she didn't understand.

"I'm happy," Isabelle said, the words weightless even to her own ears.

Elaina turned her head and Isabelle bit her lip to keep from saying more when she saw the unshed tears resting on her sister's lower lashes.

"Whatever else, it's good to know some version of you is."

Elaina slipped her fingers around Isabelle's wrist, tugged her gently in the opposite direction.

Neither of them spoke as they wandered past the next few tables, looking at them without seeing them.

"Do you think they know they're in love with each other?" Elaina asked as she ran her fingers over a beautiful, handmade cerulean scarf.

Isabelle looked back to where they'd left Tucker and Izzy dancing but couldn't see them through the crowd and the curve in the road.

"I don't know how someone could feel something and not *know* it. Ignore it? Deny it? Sure. But they must know."

Elaina's fingers paused. "You'd think, wouldn't you?"

"That color would be striking on you," an older woman said as she pushed up from a lawn chair behind the table.

"It's gorgeous. Did you make it?" Elaina asked.

While her sister chatted with yet another stranger, Isabelle wandered forward, unsure what to make of anything. What the hell was she supposed to make of any of this? Why was this happening? Had she been here before? A déjà vu sort of feeling made the hair on her arms stand up. Her bus had driven through this place, that much she remembered now. But she hadn't gotten off. The bus hadn't broken down. She'd gone to Boston, just like she planned. Accepted the full ride and worked on her degree while putting her past behind her.

Isabelle pushed the heel of her hand to her sternum, trying to relieve some of the pressure. It didn't help. Elaina came to stand in front of her, the bright blue scarf around her neck even though it wasn't cold.

Without warning, Elaina put her hand on Isabelle's arm, rubbed in circular, soothing motions. "Let's grab some street food and make our way back to the hotel."

Isabelle met her gaze, saw something there she barely recognized. Compassion.

"That color *does* look good on you," Isabelle said as they walked.

"Thanks. I bought you one too." She dug through her suitcase-bag and pulled out an infinity scarf in a slightly paler blue, passed it to Isabelle.

Emotions warred in her chest. She couldn't remember the last time Elaina had given her *anything.* "Thank you."

"Of course. It's the least I could do since you're paying for the trip."

Isabelle arched her brows at her sister's dry humor. "Gee, you're so sweet." Elaina didn't need to know she was fighting a grin.

Elaina shrugged, a subtle smile tugging at her mouth. "We all have our talents. The good news about all of this is, with how you're acting, I'm starting to suspect you might be a real girl after all."

Isabelle's lips twitched without permission but she held back the bark of laughter. Hard. Mostly. Unfortunately, Elaina knew it.

THIRTEEN

The soft sound of Elaina breathing evenly in and out was oddly soothing. Sleeping next to her sister in the same room felt like diving firmly into the past and forgetting she'd worked her whole adult life to avoid exactly that.

Atypical restlessness made her hyperaware of her surroundings. The feel of the scratchy sheets against her bare legs and arms, the heavy heat of the air, even with the fan blowing almost directly on her. She kept her phone clutched in her hand while she stared at the bumpy, off-white ceiling.

Her thoughts ran on a loop: Izzy, Tucker, Elaina, her dad, Jonathan. Her mom tried to sneak in but Isabelle held strong, forced those images and memories out. Tomorrow, she needed to go home. New York City.

She needed to refocus and remind herself of what mattered. Isabelle Duprees had created one hell of a life for herself and she didn't need to waste it in a low-budget motel room in Nowhere, Pennsylvania.

Her hand buzzed. Or more accurately, her phone *in* her hand vibrated and the sensation on her skin, in this quiet stillness, made her think of Elaina's vibrator joke. It'd pissed her off in the moment, but right now, it made her smile with a soft shake of her head. Turning it over, she blinked when she saw his name, irritated by the surge of her heart. Was that even a thing? Your heart didn't move around in your body. It beat, pumped blood, but it couldn't *surge.* But there was no denying the increase to her pulse.

> I couldn't talk today. I need some time to transition from what we were to what we'll become.

God. Talk about robotic. That was it? He was putting her firmly in a category of . . . what? Past mistakes? Transgressions? Never really fucking mattered?

You have zero right to be offended, she reminded herself. *Less right to be hurt. And absolutely no reason to be this happy to see his name.*

Regardless, she was all of that and more. Isabelle didn't believe people could be unaware of their feelings but at this moment, she knew they could choose to be blind to them. Unwilling to *see* them for what they were. She was the only person on earth who could be right next to someone—even if that someone was sleeping one bed over—and feel utterly fucking alone.

By design. She'd told herself being alone, the proverbial island unto itself, meant she'd never feel what was bubbling up inside of her at that exact moment. Sun Tzu said in the midst of chaos, there is also opportunity.

Her fingers hovered over the screen. If she left it, let the time pass, they'd find a new space. Space to be something else to each other. Space for her to pretend she didn't feel all of the things she did. For him.

I'm not close to my sister. Any time I spend thinking about her is spent on thinking how not to think about her.

She pressed send before she could change her mind.

Way to go. I doubt Sun Tzu meant for you to take an opportunity to embarrass yourself.

He responded quickly. Some things—people—could be counted on.

What do you think about when you're with her?

She smiled in the darkness as she typed out a quick response.

You, apparently.

Oh, you think maybe Tzu meant take the opportunity to be vulnerable and have someone walk all over your heart. Sure. That makes sense.

She cringed, squeezed her eyes shut like she used to do when she was little and something scared her. Can't see it? Then it's not real. Her phone buzzed.

You like perfectly stored boxes. No overlap. That was fine at first.

She was on a roll now—even though part of her knew she should stop.

The lids appear to be off now. There's not only overlap but a fucking disaster all over the floor.

His response was instantaneous.

I think that means you're doing life right.

Isabelle's hand trembled but she made herself type.

I think I don't know what I'm doing at all.

She watched the three dots pulse, disappear, reappear. Her nerves danced for every second it took for him to respond.

I'm in love with you.

She sucked in a sharp breath, held it. Breathing it out, she didn't give herself time to think.

Well. Good thing the lid was already off. That just blew the entire box up.

His next response came fast again.

Nothing ever goes back in the box, metaphorical or otherwise, the same way. You need to think about that.

Like she'd be able to *not* think about that?

How? How can you know you love me?

Even as she typed it, she knew she'd already felt the truth of his declaration. Ignored it but felt it all the same. And if she'd ignored his feelings for her, she'd buried her own under cement. Built an empire on top of it and stayed on the highest floor as far from them as she could.

Sometimes there are no answers
to the questions you ask, Isabelle.
Sometimes you just feel something.
Even if you wish you didn't.

Isabelle's throat felt tight. Her eyes stung. She typed five words.

Do you wish you didn't?

This time she didn't breathe in between.

That's not what I'd wish for, no.

She exhaled, her pulse slowing to a dull thud.

Don't forward my calls to
your secretary.

His response took longer than usual.

Isabelle. I can't hear your voice
right now. It might kill me.

She hated that she hurt him. It scared her that she wanted to fix it because she figured she'd just make a bigger mess out of things if he let her.

Then I won't call. I'll text. I don't want you to stop wishing. I just need a bit of time to unclutter the mess from all the boxes spilling open. Can you do that?

She had no right to ask him anything.

I can. You asked me how I know. You told me once that the best moment of your day is slipping off those mile-high heels you wear all day. You said there's few things that feel better than that. That moment, that simple split second of utter fucking relief. It's how I feel when I see you. When I'm with you.

Maybe her heart couldn't surge but it was possible her lungs could overinflate, creating a tightness in her chest that was impossible to breathe around. She typed one last message, figured that would be the end of it for the night.

We're not done.

But she was wrong. He had one last thing to add.

Then the boxes have to go.

She set her phone on the nightstand, rolled to her side, nearly let out a scream when she saw Elaina was on her side, hands tucked under her cheek, staring at her.

"Jesus. I thought you were sleeping." Surely this day counted as bonus cardio the way her pulse kept scrambling.

"Why was it so hard for you to accept that Izzy is happy?"

The blanket felt heavy even though it was thin. "I don't understand when people don't want more. How can she be happy with . . . less, when there's more available?"

"What's the more?"

Isabelle leaned up, smacked the pillow a couple times, then lay her head back down.

"They could do so much with that business. I mean, if they're in it together. Good product, decent branding and logo. She's thirty-three and works a retail job."

"She's the manager."

"Of a bookstore. Trust me, there's more."

"You'd know," Elaina said softly.

That's right, she would. And did. And she didn't feel guilty about it because every bit of her *more* came from working her ass off.

"There's nothing wrong with wanting more. You can buy a base model car. It'll get you from point A to point B. But if you can afford an upgrade that includes heated seats, superior safety features, and a sunroof, what are you achieving by saying, 'No thanks. I'm good with the bare minimum'?"

"Sometimes people don't realize there's more to want."

Isabelle rolled onto her back, stared at the ceiling. "That can't be true. No one lives in a bubble. She goes to work every day. You're telling me she's never thought about making more money? If she lives in an apartment, she's never thought about having more space? She knows. She might be scared of more but she knows it's there." Fuck, why did talking about the other her feel so much like talking about herself when there was nothing the same about them.

Elaina was quiet for a few minutes. "Maybe a base model isn't so bad. If it works. Does what you need. All those extra options mean more chance of things breaking down. Failing you."

"It surprises me when people are happy with *good enough*."

"Are you?"

"Happy with good enough? No. Didn't I just say that?"

"No, Izzy-belle. Are you happy? Full stop."

Isabelle blinked. She could lie. She could brag. She could tell her sister that, if she wanted to, she could never go to work another day in her life and still live a life few could imagine. She had every possible thing she could ever want right at her fingertips. What she didn't physically have, she knew how to get.

Inhaling slowly, letting herself feel the air fill her lungs, she breathed out just as slow because the truth lodged a sharp object through her ribs that she had to breathe around. "I don't know."

FOURTEEN

Isabelle held her breath, giving her sister's sleeping form one last glance, letting the motel door close quietly behind her. She'd answered a dozen emails and rescheduled meetings after waking with the sun. Elaina slept like she'd been drugged. It'd always been that way. Once she was out, you had to put effort into waking her up and then were usually sorry for doing so.

The air was cool even with the sunshine as she walked across the parking lot. She hoped walking the mile or so to The Book Stop would help her get her head around what she was doing.

Indecision and uncertainty made her skin itch. In New York, she was certain of who she was and what she wanted. Out here, she wasn't sure of anything.

A few cars passed by as she walked the main strip and she wondered what kept this town, and so many others like it, afloat.

Closer to the big city, it'd be feasible for people to commute for their jobs, but the town itself was unremarkable. Elaina would tell her there was nothing wrong with that. Maybe there wasn't. It wasn't *wrong.* Just not something Isabelle wanted.

A man in a baseball cap gave her a strange look as he passed her but Isabelle didn't care. She lived in New York. Strange looks were standard.

She saw the bookstore from across the street. It was nestled in the middle of a row of shops—a dress store, a convenience store, a dry cleaner, and a coffee shop. At home, her walk to work from her apartment filled her with her energy and ideas. It breathed life into her, made her eager to start her day. But this? What would this give her? The same small shop day after day, likely the same customers, the same people. Work at the diner. The night market every now and then. Tucker and maybe a few others. On repeat. How could that fulfill her?

Stiffening her spine, she crossed, walked through the empty parking lot, and stopped in front of the store. There were window displays on each side of the double doors.

On the left, an overstuffed armchair was angled toward the window. Picture books were stacked on a side table to its left. A little circle of stuffed animals was set up, several books spread out in front of them like they were taking turns reading to each other. In the other window, posters advertising new books and a local author signing hung from the ceiling on almost invisible strings.

"Choose a book, Izzy-belle."

Six-year-old Isabelle looked up at her father. He was so tall, his smile so warm. He squeezed her hand, giving her that little nudge that filled her with happiness.

"Which one should I choose?"

He knelt beside her, gestured to the picture books, to the chapter books, and around the store where a few other families browsed.

"What kind of adventure do you want to have?"

Isabelle curled into him, her arm around his neck as she looked at the shelves in front of her, tapping her index finger to her chin.

"I'm not sure."

"Then let's grab a few. That's the great thing about books, Izzy-belle; you can have as many adventures as you want without even leaving the house."

Sucking in a breath, Isabelle suddenly knew, before she pulled the door open, before the little bell signaling her arrival chimed, why Izzy worked at a bookstore. But she still didn't understand why that was enough.

Jasper had emailed everything he'd found on The Book Stop.

The space was fairly small, with a path down the center of the store that led to a checkout counter. To her right and left, freestanding shelves took up every inch of available floor space. Floor-to-ceiling shelves lined the walls. A couple of tables were wedged in between smaller shelves. In the corner, closer to the window, a little area had been set up as a reading nook for kids.

Signs labeling sections hung from the ceiling. Closer to the checkout desk, there was a table with kitschy gifts: bookmarks, *What should I read?* cards, and notebooks. Behind the counter sat an open doorway with one of those beaded curtains that made obnoxious noises when a person passed through.

They'd had one covering the pantry doorway in her childhood home. Isabelle had gotten her hair caught in the beads once when Elaina dared her to sneak some cookies. She'd gotten in trouble for taking the cookies and had to have a chunk of her hair cut because her mother hadn't had the patience to work it free.

Their mother had given Elaina the cookies as a way to show Isabelle poor choices led to poor results.

The beads behind the curtain parted, hands dividing it down the center. "Sorry about that. Good mor . . ." Izzy stopped in her tracks, a dash of uncertainty in her smile, the strands of beads click-clacking back to their spots. "Oh. Hi. We didn't see you again last night."

"We were tired, so we went back to the motel. Did Tucker sing?"

See? I can socialize.

Izzy's gaze lit up. "Boy, did he. I swear, even if he didn't look like he does, I'd have fallen for him the first time I heard him sing. He thought you guys were a hoot."

"Oh. That's . . . nice." She couldn't stay here much longer. The need to get back to her life was pulling at her like an anchor. "He's nice. You seem happy with him." In general.

Izzy tilted her head to the side. She wore her hair loose today, making her look younger. She came around the counter. "He is and I am. Why do I feel like every time you talk to me, you're looking for a secret I don't know?"

Isabelle arched her brows. It was the first time she'd recognized a trace of herself in Izzy.

"Because I feel like you do know."

With a softness Isabelle didn't possess, Izzy reached out and squeezed Isabelle's arm. "Is this because we have the same name? Because our sisters do? I'll admit, that coincidence is a little out there even for me."

"Why do you live here?"

Izzy yanked her hand back like Isabelle had slapped her. "Not that it's any of your business. But I love it here."

"Why? You like . . ." she stopped herself. "You *seem* like you'd like the big city. Somewhere with the kind of light and energy you have inside of you. New York, Boston. God, even LA. Why here?"

Isabelle wasn't sure she'd answer but she gave her other self credit for not looking away, not even blinking.

"I'm not into chasing happiness. I'm more about finding it right where I'm standing."

Fucking riddles. What the hell was that supposed to mean?

It doesn't matter. Get on with it.

She had a purpose and, as usual, a few different routes to getting what she wanted.

"I'm an investor, Izzy. I looked into this company and there's potential. If I opened a store in Philadelphia, there'd be more traffic. What would you say to running that store?"

This was just part of the more.

"That's an hour and a bit away. That's a lot of commuting."

"It is. But there'd be an increase in salary, benefits, and vacation time." None of which were offered to her now. She made an hourly wage. And not a great one.

Izzy leaned against the counter, twisting her hands together. Isabelle recognized the motion because it was one she did when she was unsure about something, weighing a decision.

"Why me?"

"I see something in you." *In myself.*

"I don't want to commute."

Isabelle smiled. "So, move."

Izzy's eyes widened. "It costs a lot more to live in the city than it does here."

"What if there was a housing allowance?"

Pushing off the counter, Izzy closed the gap between them. "What do you want? Why are you doing this?"

Taking a deep breath, Isabelle held her composure like a bomb that could blow at any moment.

"I'm an investor. I told you that. I'm trying to see exactly what it would take for you to want *more*."

A laugh bubbled out of Izzy. "More than what?"

Isabelle shook her head, gesturing with her hands around the store. "More than this." She dropped her arms. "Surely this is a stepping stone. You can't want this at sixty. Seventy. How will you retire? Where do you want to be in the next five years? Ten?"

The other woman moved back behind the counter and Isabelle knew it was because she needed the space. *That's right. Wanting more isn't comfortable. It means uprooting your life.* She'd personally never let that hold her back.

"I don't know what you're after but I don't need or want your advice. Or your money. I don't want to live in the city. I like my life here just fine. It's easy and I'm happy. Do you know how rare true happiness is?"

Before Isabelle could scramble for an answer, Izzy continued, irritation flashing in those familiar eyes. "I come here every day, and when I'm not ordering or stocking books, I'm reading. I love reading. I'm surrounded by adventures. By love and mysteries, other worlds, monsters and heroes. When I leave here, I go to another job where I can sing along to the songs playing on the juke box. An actual juke box . . . not Pandora or Spotify. There's simplicity in that. I like that. No, I fucking *love* that. And I've got a man who's willing to wait for me to stop being scared and jump in with both feet. A man who will love me no matter where I work or how much money I make. Maybe he'll strike it rich with his jams, maybe he won't, but his feelings for me are like diamonds—shiny, beautiful, and indestructible. I don't know where I'll be in five years or ten. And I don't care. The only thing anyone ever has is right this minute. Why would I waste it chasing after maybes?"

Isabelle blew out a breath, squeezed her fingers into fists. "Because for minutes to turn into something, for them to matter, you have to have a plan. A way to get there."

Izzy shook her head, like she pitied Isabelle. "All the plans in the world don't stop life from happening. When it does, all your plans disintegrate. So, why not just enjoy the ride?"

Isabelle threw her hands up. "*Enjoy the ride*? Jesus Christ. You're like a Zen cartoon character. This can't be all you want!" She didn't mean to yell but for fuck's sake. This was ridiculous.

"You've got about thirty seconds before I call the police. I don't know what you want from me but my life is none of your business." Izzy's voice shook.

Isabelle stomped forward. "How can you not know what I want. *Look* at me. My name is Isabelle Caroline Duprees. I was born in Ashland, Tennessee, on June fifth. I'm thirty-three."

Every ounce of color drained from Izzy's face. She picked up her phone from the counter, her hand shaking. "How do you know those things?"

She really didn't see it. This woman was terrified. She looked close to tears and Isabelle didn't want that. She was strong. Determined. Bold. But not intentionally cruel.

"I'll go. I'm sorry. I'm sorry." She truly was. She'd come in here not liking the other version of herself very much but it paled in comparison to how she felt about who she herself was in this moment. As she backed up, hoping to make Izzy more comfortable, she asked, "Can I just ask one more thing? Just one. Please."

While she would have refused, the other version of herself sighed, gave in. "Fine. What?"

Navigating around the shelves, trying not to cause more damage than she already had, she kept moving toward the door.

Isabelle swallowed past the lump in her throat. "Are you close to your mother?"

Something passed over Izzy's features, hardening them, turning them to something Isabelle saw each day in the mirror and was sorry to see in this softer, sweeter, more hopeful version of herself. "My mother loves two things: my sister and cheap beer. Now go."

Isabelle nodded, left the store. At least, in both lives, their mother was consistent.

FIFTEEN

Isabelle held the coffees and bag of pastries she'd picked up in one hand while opening the door with the other. Elaina was sitting on the bed, legs crisscrossed, watching something on the television.

Moving into the room, letting the door shut behind her, Isabelle saw it was a talk show.

"Bless you. I needed coffee more than my next breath," Elaina said, jumping up and meeting Isabelle in the middle of the room.

"There's instant." She jutted her chin toward the little tray of cups and tin of coffee on the desk. A sign said hot water was available from the tap. High class, this hotel.

"Don't be gross."

Isabelle shook her head, tossed her purse on the bed, passed her sister the bag, and sat with her own coffee.

"So? How'd it go?" Elaina took the lid off her cup.

"What?"

Blowing on the steaming liquid, Elaina watched her over the rim, then risked a sip. She sighed in pleasure, closing her eyes. "Mmm. You're my favorite sister."

Isabelle sipped her own coffee, ignoring the statement.

"You obviously snuck out to go visit Izzy. What happened?"

For some reason she couldn't explain, she didn't want to meet her sister's gaze. "She doesn't care where she's at professionally in five years. In twenty years. I offered to open a second store, let her run it. Told her there'd be a housing allowance, benefits, anything she wanted."

Elaina sank down on her own bed, her legs hanging off the side. "You're a stranger. She'd be stupid to take you at your word. Especially if she's you. You're a pain in the ass. A know-it-all. An egomaniac."

Isabelle's chin snapped up as she gave her sister a dry glare. "Do you have a point?"

Elaina smiled. "Yeah. You're a lot of things but you're not stupid. Why would she trust you, a stranger who for some reason doesn't see you're her. She's you. Whatever." She shrugged like this wasn't the most bizarre conversation ever.

"That's just it. She didn't care who I was or if it was legit. She just doesn't want it. She's not making plans to enhance her career. It's not a priority. She's happy with her life the way it is right now. She truly doesn't want *more.* She's not looking for anything other than enjoying the moment."

"A lot of people work so they can live rather than the other way around."

"Then what's the damn point? Every single day is the same. I'm not sure if you'd pray harder for retirement or death. I mean, what the hell does she look forward to?" Isabelle took a gulp of her coffee, burning her tongue and throat in one go.

"There's twenty-four hours in a day, Izzy-belle. Maybe she's more focused on the sixteen she isn't at work."

Isabelle sighed. "I want to go home." What she wanted was to tell her sister about Izzy's comments on their mother.

She wanted to ask if both of those things were still true. She'd stopped looking through her financial records when they had something to do with her sister or her mom. She knew Kaia had paid for more than one stint in rehab. In business, knowing every detail put her on top; made her fierce. In her personal life, knowing the truth felt like admitting failure; it made her feel weak. Helpless. And she hated it so she didn't dig too deep. Perhaps she compensated for taking the easier route in her personal life by pushing herself so hard with her work.

Elaina sipped her coffee in silence for a couple of blissful moments.

If they left now, she could possibly make the meeting at the Waldorf tonight, but it'd be tight. She needed Kaia to reschedule it to be safe.

"Do you think if we google you from here, the New York you would be the only thing that shows up?"

Isabelle groaned. "I don't care. I like the New York version of me. We need to go back to our lives." She stood up and caught the look of hurt on her sister's face. "What?" What the hell had she done now?

"Nothing. But I'm curious so I'm going to look."

"Ever heard of Pandora's box?"

Elaina smiled. "Yup. It killed the cat."

Isabelle laughed, resisted the urge to flop on the bed and curl up under the scratchy covers. "You're an idiot. I'm going to freshen up and we'll get on the road." She set the near-empty cup on the dresser, looked back at Elaina.

Her sister sat on the bed, staring down at her coffee like it had the answers. She looked sad. Alone. Isabelle pushed aside the emotions stirring inside of her chest. They'd made their choices. She might not know if she was happy in a purely emotional sense but she was happy with the path she'd chosen. Elaina chose her own. Isabelle hadn't put the distance between them by herself.

Guilt tugged at her as she changed her clothes into something more comfortable for a long drive. When she left the bathroom, hair and makeup refreshed, feeling more like herself as a result, she was determined to get home as quickly as possible.

Elaina had set her suitcase on the bed, her purse on top of it. She stood at the end of the bed staring at her phone.

"We good?" Isabelle asked.

"Define good."

Rolling her eyes, Isabelle grabbed her Chanel bag, tucked her makeup inside. "Are you ready to go?"

"I am. But we aren't going to New York."

She set the bag down on the bed, looked at her sister. "Want me to drop you off somewhere?"

That would be best anyway. The sooner she could return to her regularly scheduled programming, including Elaina being somewhere other than with her, the better.

"Virginia Beach."

"Jesus Christ, Elaina. You might have flunked geography but surely you've seen a map."

Elaina's gaze was steady when she held up her phone. "There's another you in Virginia. Izzy isn't listed anymore. No New York you. Just this one."

Isabelle's stomach twisted. "Stop it." She pushed her hand to her stomach.

"Your choice, Isabelle. Be a coward, go back to New York. Or face whatever the hell is going on. That answer is south."

She closed her eyes, wishing that when she opened them, she'd be in her own bed, in her own home, living her real life.

When she opened them, Elaina was staring at her. Through her, really.

"I have to reschedule a meeting."

To her credit, Elaina simply nodded. She didn't act triumphant for getting her way. In fact, if Isabelle didn't know better, her sister almost looked like she truly cared.

SIXTEEN

Her sister may have changed over the years, but many of her tiresome habits stayed exactly the same. Elaina complained when they stopped in DC for a quick bite to eat and to stretch their legs.

"It's not a road trip, Elaina."

They walked along a cobblestone street toward a quaint diner by the water—no neon signs—in Old Town Alexandria. The ocean air washed over Isabelle's skin, reviving and waking her up. She wasn't used to driving for long stretches of time. Even when she had a meeting outside of Manhattan, Steven did the driving. It was strange to realize she'd missed the act of doing so. Of getting behind the wheel and navigating the path. But she was about ready to let her sister drive now, even if she hadn't planned on doing so.

"All I'm saying is we stay one night. We'll go see a few sights, do a little shopping, and leave for Virginia Beach in the morning. Your precious schedule can handle a tiny delay."

Stopping outside of the restaurant, Isabelle looked out to the water, trying to find calm in the waves. People walked the street, some chatting, others clearly visiting. In the distance, a city cruise liner was being loaded with passengers.

"We're not here to sight-see. I just want to get where we're going." Isabelle tried to keep her tone even.

"I've never been to Washington. Not all of us have traveled the world," Elaina said.

Isabelle brought her gaze back to her sister's. "I'm sorry that my need to figure out why the universe is fucking with me is putting a damper on your impromptu vacation. I know you don't think so, but I have a life to get back to. Deals and meetings. People waiting on me."

Elaina gave a sarcastic half laugh. "Right. Important people. People who actually matter to you."

Sighing, Isabelle opened the door, let her sister go ahead.

They kept going two steps forward, eight back. They shared a moment, something passed between them, then one or both of them slashed each other with razor-sharp claws for little to no reason. The seesawing was giving Isabelle a headache.

They didn't talk while they waited to be seated. The server offered them a wine list, promising to be back with waters.

"Do you mind driving for a bit?" Isabelle asked, looking at the list.

"The all-mighty Isabelle Duprees is willing to relinquish control?"

Isabelle set the drink menu down with a quiet deliberateness. She leaned forward. "Can we stop? Please? I have a headache. I'm tired. I don't want to fight with you. What I want is a glass of wine and an hour to close my eyes. Will you drive or not?"

Elaina regarded her carefully then picked up the menu. "No problem. You're insured, right?"

Isabelle wasn't even surprised by the laugh this time.

They each ordered the soup of the day, sandwiches, and salads. Elaina asked for a Coke while Isabelle treated herself to an expensive glass of wine. She didn't actually drink all that often for obvious reasons. Their mother's trouble with alcohol had started when they were in their late teens. When Elaina stopped being their mom's security blanket and Isabelle just wasn't good enough, Catalina turned to beer. Whatever they could afford with Isabelle's part-time jobs.

She didn't realize she was staring at her wine more than drinking it until Elaina said her name.

"Hmm?"

"She's been dry for eight years."

Isabelle didn't look up, couldn't chance looking into her sister's eyes right now.

"I'm glad. I hope it lasts."

"She's turning sixty."

Taking a long swallow, Isabelle moved her glass in soft circles, making the liquid move as she stared out the window. "I know how old she is."

"She met someone," Elaina said in a voice that pulled at Isabelle's heartstrings.

Turning, she looked at her sister. "Someone?"

"She's getting married. She wants you there."

"There's the other shoe. I was waiting for it to drop," Isabelle said, surprise and confusion swirling like her wine. She set the glass down.

"She can't say sorry if you never answer your phone. If you never visit or let her come to you."

The soup arrived. Both women leaned back, let the waiter add some pepper to the tomato and basil bisque. Elaina stirred hers, staring at the liquid.

"Sorry won't fix anything. I'm not angry at her anymore. I don't need her apology. You can tell her I wish her well. And happy birthday." She picked up her spoon, let liquid burn the rest of the words off her tongue. Her phone buzzed in her purse.

She wanted to close her eyes during the drive while Elaina took the wheel, but she knew she'd more likely catch up on everything she was missing instead.

"*Sorry* might not fix anything but it might make both of you feel less broken," Elaina said, dipping some bread in her soup.

Blaming the steam for the dampness in her eyes, Isabelle shook her head. "I'm not broken."

Neither of them said the obvious: Their mother was. Had been for twenty-five years. Since she was the exact age Isabelle was right now.

Back in the car, Isabelle stretched her legs, put the seat warmer on, and angled the air vent. Elaina set up the mirrors and her phone so she could use her own playlists for the rest of the four-hour drive.

Kaia had booked them into a waterfront hotel that she promised would be better than the previous night's. How had that only been last night? Isabelle felt like she'd lived a lifetime in two days.

As her sister used the navigation system to find her way back to the interstate, Isabelle did something she'd never done before. She texted Jonathan on a weekday about something that had nothing to do with work.

The box labeled family is full of things I don't want you to see.

She stared at the phone, wondering if she wanted him to text back more than she worried he wouldn't.

After a moment, he responded.

We all have things we're scared of uncovering. Scared of revealing.

She kept going, part of herself wishing she wouldn't.

YOU don't.

His next message came as fast as usual.

I would say I upended my own personal box of emotions last night.

She felt the smile tug her lips the way his words tugged at her heart.

I'm headed to Virginia Beach.

He sent a surprised face emoji, and then:

Spring Break is over and so are your college days.

Elaina's off-key singing muffled her laughter.

I can't explain it right now. Just something I have to do with my sister.

Understood. How are things going?

Isabelle glanced at her unaware sister, then back at her phone.

Neither of us are in jail for murder yet so I'd say well.

She waited for the next message to appear.

Any other siblings you're hiding?

Isabelle thought about Izzy, then shook the memory—or whatever it was—away.

No. No other siblings. Just Elaina. She's two years older. More fun and far more relaxed than I am.

God. She hadn't compared herself to her sister in *years.*

Your life doesn't leave much room for relaxing.

Take a chance. The only thing anyone has is right this minute.

She typed her next message carefully, mind casting back to what seemed like a simpler time in her life.

Maybe it's time to change that. A few months ago, you mentioned a beach. White sand, blue water, and ice-cold drinks.

When he'd brought it up, she'd shut him down hard.

"I want time with you, Isabelle. Hours. Days. More than stolen moments. Let me take you somewhere. I have a condo in Barbados. One week. Give me seven days of nothing but you."

She'd smiled coyly, her heart flipping over in her chest like a fish desperate to get back into the safety of the water.

"You'd get tired of me. Seven days in a row, twenty-four seven, would be too much for anyone."

Jonathan stroked her slightly damp hair off her forehead, pressed his lips there.

"Then how come it feels like it wouldn't even start to be enough?"

"You going to just sit their looking all doe-eyed and dreamy?" Elaina reached for the soda she'd bought and sipped it, her gaze flashing to Isabelle's phone before moving back to the road.

"Shut up."

Elaina snort-laughed. "Good one."

Her phone buzzed again.

We can't run away from what I feel. We can't bury it in the sand.

She thought about that for a moment, then replied as honestly as possible.

I'm not trying to.

Her fingers clenched around the phone, her breathing shallow. *Even this is making me want more. You've never had more to give.*

She looked out the window, decided she would just type exactly what she was thinking. At this point, she no longer had control.

Until now. Until I realized I'd rather have more with you than nothing at all.

Those three little dots mocked her as she waited.

How long will you be gone?

She wished she was surer of the answer.

At least a couple more days

His response was instant.

We'll talk when you get home

It felt like too long to wait and admitting that, even to herself, was humbling.

You'll see me?

Almost a full minute went by and she suspected that he had been caught up in an unexpected moment of work. And then her phone buzzed yet again.

That's the problem, Isabelle. Even when you're not here, you're all I see.

She sucked in a sharp breath but the look on her face must have cautioned Elaina not to comment.

You're the only one I've ever been willing to let peek inside the boxes.

His reply was brief.

Then it's a start.

Which even her unromantic heart knew was better than an ending.

BELLE

SEVENTEEN

Refusing to be blindsided by her sister again, Isabelle insisted on going straight to the hotel. They ordered breakfast at nearly midnight. Elaina showered first and fell into a soft-snoring heap on the bed closest to the window.

Isabelle made better use of her time by doing what Elaina had called a "deep dive" on Isabelle—Belle—Duprees Longworth. Married three years earlier. Thirty-three years old. Her husband owned and operated a residential and commercial real estate business. While her husband, Brett Longworth, was conventionally handsome with a strong jaw, short hair, and happy brown eyes, Isabelle stared at his photo unable to feel anything other than curiosity.

No attraction. No spark. Nothing. What had made a version of herself marry this man? Was she in love? One of the videos on his real estate website had him doing a walk-through of a house. His voice was quiet and firm, but nothing special. It didn't sound familiar or comforting. It made her wonder, again, what the hell she was doing. Was this even real?

Elaina moaned a little in her sleep, turned onto her side.

None of it made any sense but it was definitely real. Poking around the couple's website, she did her best not to roll her eyes at the tagline: *Live, Love, and Work in a Longworth Property.*

She couldn't risk asking Kaia or Jasper to look him up or dig into him. It would be too weird and too much to explain.

Like she sensed Isabelle was thinking about her, a text from Kaia buzzed on her phone.

> You should be sleeping.

Isabelle held in a quiet laugh.

> So should you.

Her response was almost as fast as Jonathan's.

> My boss is high maintenance. Too much to do and then she takes off on an impromptu getaway. I'd be happy for her but I know Mr. Fairbanks is still in town.

Her assistant knew too much.

> I think I may need to redraw some boundaries with you.

Kaia sent a winky face, and then:

> Good luck. Better women have tried and failed.

Isabelle laughed out loud this time.

BUSINESS boundaries

She watched as the three dots flashed for a long time.

Business, pleasure, life's about blurring the lines. You have a two o'clock phone call with The Economist. They want to talk to you about your recent award and your thoughts on where the economy is headed. They're doing a feature on powerful women. A representative from NBC contacted me about a business-based reality show. I told them no but it's got an interesting premise.

Isabelle thought this over for a millisecond.

Go with the first answer. No.

She smiled in anticipation of her assistant's response.

I figured.

Isabelle's fingers hovered over the screen, itching to fill Kaia in. To talk it out with her, to keep pushing this particular friendship/employee boundary. She looked over at Elaina, who now slept soundingly. Peacefully, like nothing weighed her down. But Isabelle knew that wasn't entirely true. Regardless of how she felt about her sister, she hadn't had the easiest road either. They were in this together. Just them.

Her phone buzzed again.

How long will you be there?

She tapped out a quick response.

Hoping to leave tomorrow night.
Next day at the latest.

Kaia's response speed was just one of many assets the woman possessed.

Quick turn around. Good. Check
your email in the morning for
updates. Now sleep.

Isabelle smiled, then responded.

I'm your boss not the other
way around.

One final message lit up her screen.

Absolutely. Night, boss.

Tossing her phone to the other end of the bed, she flopped down on the pillows with a sigh. Maybe trying to figure things out wasn't the answer.

Maybe there are no answers.

She ignored the urge to wake her sister up just to have someone to talk to. She didn't *need* people. Or useless conversation to fill her brain.

Without meaning to, she drifted off to sleep without getting under the covers.

When she woke, her sister was standing over her at the side of the bed. Isabelle let out a sharp squeal, her hand flying to her chest.

"Jesus. What the hell, Elaina?" She sat up, searched for her phone, saw it at the end of the bed.

"What? I was just making sure you were breathing." She said it with a smile in her voice.

Clearly, Isabelle had slept hard. Elaina was dressed and looking beach-model ready in a sundress and strappy, flat sandals. Her hair was soft around her face, just a touch of lip gloss on her pouty lips.

"I'm hungry. Let's go eat on the beach."

Isabelle shoved up from the bed, resisted the urge to grab her phone because she knew her sister would give her shit for it.

"We'll grab something to go. Brett has an open house this morning. I want to go. It starts at ten."

"So, no tourist stuff here either?"

She pushed past her sister, who didn't even attempt to move out of the way. "I'm not here on vacation, Elaina. I have a life to get back to."

Isabelle was almost to the bathroom door when she heard her sister say, "One I'm not part of."

When she shut the door, she leaned her forehead against the coolness of the wood. Yes. A life that Elaina and their mother weren't part of. Because they'd all made that choice long ago. Actually, Catalina had made it. Isabelle had never had any say in anything that happened after her father died.

By the time she was ready, more questions filled her brain but one nagged steadily.

They waited for the elevator to take them down to the lobby, all their belongings with them. Isabelle had no intention of staying another night. She'd see this through and then go home.

When they stepped into the elevator, they were alone.

Pressing the *L* button, she asked what she couldn't stop herself from wondering. "Do you think, if we went back there, right this minute, Izzy would be opening up The Book Stop, getting ready to start her day?"

Elaina's eyes met hers in the distorted chrome reflection of the wall. "I don't know. I really don't. Do you want me to go there? Find out?"

The doors slid open on the lobby floor. Elaina waved to the front desk clerk, smiled at the bellman who opened the door for them. The sun was warm, the breeze welcome. The idea of the beach didn't seem so bad to Isabelle now, if they had time.

When they got to the SUV and loaded their things in, Isabelle took the driver's seat. "What do you mean, do I want you to go there?"

She backed out of the spot while Elaina dug through her purse. "Simple. You go see Brett and Belle—isn't that funny? Total reality show–couple name. Anyway, you go there, I'll rent a different car and go back to Poppy." She opened up a pack of Milk Duds.

"Jesus, Elaina, we haven't even eaten breakfast yet."

She shook the box. "Milk is good for you." She offered Isabelle one.

Turning into traffic, Isabelle headed for Starbucks. "You would drive all the way back to Poppy? Then what?"

"Then I'd report back."

An uncomfortable ache settled under Isabelle's rib cage. "Why would you do that for me?"

"Why would you pay off our mortgage? *Twice.* Pay for rehab for Mom? Make sure Kaia never forgets our birthdays. Send flowers on the anniversary of Dad's death. We're family, Isabelle. Neither of us chose it. But we can't run fast enough to escape that truth."

Isabelle. The ache in her chest eased.

As she pulled into a Starbucks parking lot, Isabelle looked over at her sister. "We should both be here. We'll do this and then figure out what's next."

Elaina looked over, unspoken words clear in her gaze: she wanted that too.

After grabbing a couple of coffees and muffins, they drove through Virginia, toward a quiet residential area.

The houses were similar, but each stood on its own with unique characteristics—the color, pops of brick, cobblestone pathways, porches, and windows. It was clear they'd been designed by the same person but they had their own personalities. Their own charms.

"Reminds me of home," Elaina murmured.

Isabelle said nothing but her stomach churned with the words. New York City was home for her now and this was nothing like that. Brett's face on a sandwich board greeted them before she pulled up to the house. Over his head was a speech bubble that read Come On In!

"I can't see you marrying someone so . . . jovial," Elaina said, releasing her seatbelt.

"Or corny?"

They shared an amused glance—there and gone before Isabelle could appreciate it.

The house was pale green, like an almost-ripe Granny Smith apple. It had a beach vibe even though they'd left the water behind them several miles ago. Flowers bloomed in a rainbow of colors in painted boxes attached to the windows. The wide, tall front door was propped open, a screen allowing them to hear the soft music coming from inside. The porch was big enough to easily hold the two-seater wooden swing hanging from the rafters. Definitely charming. She liked her penthouse but it didn't mean she couldn't appreciate something like this.

They let themselves in. Isabelle's heart hammered like an overcaffeinated woodpecker. Voices traveled from down the hallway right alongside the pleasant scent of vanilla. An old trick—enticing people with the scents and sounds of a real home. Elaina's shoulder brushed Isabelle's and she realized a little part of her, a hair-width sliver, was grateful she wasn't doing this alone. That she was doing this with her sister.

"Nice place," Elaina said.

They stopped when they reached an oversized, rounded archway that opened into the cheery, yellow kitchen. In front of them, a tall, broad-shouldered man danced with a woman. Isabelle could only see bits of her: hands on the man's arms, long brown hair swaying back and forth and glimpses of legs between his. He sang to her, his head ducked, one hand low on her back, the other up, probably touching her face.

His suit jacket stretched across his back. Isabelle noted the clean-shaven hair line, the manicured, perfectly painted fingernails that gripped his arm when he lowered his head for a kiss. The unseen woman laughed softly as he leaned closer. His head went one way, the woman's another, and her gaze came to Isabelle's.

She'd determined not to be blindsided but that's exactly how she felt staring into her own eyes.

Get over it, she instructed herself. *You were hoping this would happen. That she'd*—you'd—*be here.*

"Oh, my goodness. Honey, we have visitors."

Honey? Isabelle had never called anyone by a term of endearment.

He turned his head and the handsome man from the sign laughed, smiling at them. "Sorry, folks. I dance with my beautiful wife whenever I get the chance."

He hadn't stepped away from her yet so his body still hid most of the woman. Most of herself.

Not yourself. Another version of her. Some distorted other-world her who had apparently fallen in love with a man who danced in the kitchen in the middle of the day.

This new Isabelle had a different kind of happiness in her gaze than Izzy. Her long hair was soft and straight, her face slightly rounder, her laugh light and fun.

"He's a cornball. Welcome to what we call the Cottage Close to the Sea," she said.

The man turned as he spoke. "We name all of our listings."

Elaina smiled so naturally that Isabelle almost envied her but remembered that despite being in this with her, she was simply looking at an alternate version of Isabelle, not herself. That smile wouldn't appear so easily if Elaina were in her shoes. "How quaint. Even the commercial ones?" she said.

Brett stepped to the side of his wife, staying close. He said something but Isabelle didn't hear him. How could she hear anything over the buzzing in her ears, the erratic tempo of her pounding heart. Little dots danced in front of her gaze and she blinked rapidly, clearing them, but nothing about what she saw changed. The other version of her ran a hand over her rounded belly and Isabelle's knees nearly buckled. This version of her was . . .

"Pregnant," Isabelle whispered, the words like fire in her mouth.

EIGHTEEN

Elaina bumped Isabelle's hip with her fist and though it brought her out of the haze, back into this moment, it didn't change what she saw or the way her heart tried to climb out of her body through her throat.

"You're pregnant," Isabelle said again, unsure how to reconcile seeing a version of herself in a way she never imagined. A way she never even let herself entertain.

The couple didn't seem to realize what she'd whispered. Instead, they were lost in each other.

Brett's hand came to his wife's very rounded belly. "Belle's eight months now. This is our first." There was no mistaking the excitement in his tone or body language.

Isabelle's stomach roiled and she worried she might throw up. Right there. She fought the wave of dizziness, feeling like she was swimming upstream in a storm. She reached out, put her hand on the wall. Elaina moved closer, grasped her other hand.

"You're absolutely glowing. Congratulations," Elaina said, her tone even, unbothered, her fingers a vice around Isabelle's hand.

Isabelle couldn't form words or take her eyes off Belle's

stomach, rounded and full, her left hand resting on it protectively. Maternally.

"Thank you," Belle said glancing down at herself.

Brett stepped forward. "Sorry. Let's start over. I'm Brett Longworth. This is my wife, Belle."

Elaina used her other hand to shake Brett and then Belle's. "I'm Elaina. This is my sister, Isabelle."

Isabelle heard the intake of breath from her doppelgänger but couldn't look away from a sight she'd never thought she'd see. Her stomach rounded with *life.*

Not yours. Not you.

"What a small world," Belle said. "My name is short for Isabelle, and I have a sister named Elaina."

No shit.

Elaina squeezed Isabelle's hand until her fingers pinched together and while usually she'd pull her arm away, the move centered her, put her squarely back in the moment. As long as she didn't look at her stomach.

Belle's stomach. Not her own.

The urge to settle her hand over her own abdomen burned inside of her twitching fingers. She pulled a deep, slow breath through her nose. In seconds that felt like days, she stiffened her spine, pulled away from her sister, and offered her hand to both Brett and Belle.

Brett and Belle. Separate yourself. They're a married couple. Focus on that.

"The square footage isn't ideal," Isabelle said.

When Elaina shot her a what-the-hell look, she turned to Brett.

Play to your strengths. Sun Tzu stated that the supreme art of war is to subdue the enemy without fighting. She just never imagined herself as the enemy.

"You have several properties. I'm looking for both personal and commercial space."

Intrigue and happiness lit his gaze. She'd done some digging on him as well. He was a reasonably astute businessman. He'd attended Old Dominion, right there in Virginia. Had two sisters, parents were both lawyers. He'd gone the corporate-assistant-to-the-VP route at a large company before meeting Belle and striking out on his own.

Belle stepped forward. She was dressed in a gauzy black blouse that clung to her belly, accentuated her breasts. She stood a few inches taller than Isabelle and for a moment, Isabelle was lost in the surreal paradox of admiring herself for being able to pull off some kick-ass heels while also carrying a human.

Something *this* Isabelle would certainly never do. Or at the very least, could never have imagined herself doing. Before this moment.

"We pride ourselves on finding what our clients want. Let's show you the space and you can tell us what it's lacking in terms of your needs." She gestured toward the hallway off the kitchen.

While Brett was clearly the *face* of the operation, Belle did the talking, knew the details like she was reading from a file.

"Tell us more about the commercial space you're looking for," Brett said as he took notes on his phone, trailing behind them through the house.

Elaina joined them and despite the strangeness, Isabelle didn't miss the way her sister's gaze settled on certain pieces of the home: the window seat in the spare bedroom, the generous claw foot tub in the en-suite. There was a wistfulness in her older sister she hadn't anticipated. She'd done everything she could—from a distance—to make her family's lives easier. She'd sent money, paid for the house, sent cars and lavish gifts. There was no reason for Elaina to look like she was so . . . lost.

"Are you okay?" Belle asked.

Isabelle started, snapping back to the moment. She realized she was pressing the heel of her hand to her breastbone. It was an unconscious habit she'd worked hard to correct years ago. It was a tell. A weakness.

Brett was showing Elaina the walk-in closet and Isabelle almost smiled at the excited exclamations coming from the recessed space.

"I'm fine. How are you? Your pregnancy has gone well? Those heels are gorgeous but they must hurt," Isabelle said, finding it difficult not to just ask what she wanted to know.

Belle pushed a strand of hair out of her face. Little lines crinkled around her eyes when she smiled and Isabelle couldn't help but wonder if her own did the same. She'd never smiled into the mirror. "Some things are worth the pain. I wasn't sure I ever wanted kids. This was a surprise, to say the least."

There I am, Isabelle thought, finally recognizing something of herself in this other person.

Belle looked toward the closet where Brett and Elaina were still chatting. "I'm not easy to surprise. But falling in love with Brett," she said in a quiet, unfamiliar tone before looking back at Isabelle, "and this baby caught me off guard. I figure if my whole life is going to change in a way I can't predict, I'm in charge of the shoes."

Isabelle's laugh felt dry in her throat. Forced. "It's something." Not nearly enough.

Belle's smile grew. "I never thought it would be enough."

Isabelle sucked in a sharp breath at the woman's honesty. "Then how is it?"

Belle's brows arched up, her smile slipping just as Elaina and Brett joined them.

"How is what?" Brett asked, coming to his wife's side.

"Isabelle wants to know why only having control over my shoe choice at the moment is enough for me." There was a not-so-subtle acidity in her tone that felt all too familiar to Isabelle.

Elaina, picking up on the vibe immediately, shot her sister a disgusted glance.

Whatever. So I'm not Miss Congeni-fucking-ality. Sue me.

"My sister is big on control. In her personal and professional life. She doesn't have the same basic needs as the rest of us like interaction, socialization, and relationships. Please excuse her rudeness. Though, your shoes really do kick ass."

Some of Belle's smile returned.

Brett put an arm around her. "My wife is the driving force behind everything we do. She's brilliant as well as beautiful. She's had control of my heart since the second I saw her."

Something ached in Isabelle's chest. Something she absolutely did not want to feel. Longing. Jonathan's face danced in her mind before she could stop it.

Belle laughed, her posture relaxing. "See? Cornball." She said it like it was a compliment, leaning into his touch.

The tension eased as they left the room, but Isabelle's panic ratcheted up. They were heading toward goodbye without learning anything. She needed to know *something.* How did she end up here?

Despite her sister being a pain in her ass, she could have kissed Elaina for her next question.

"Y'all are so cute. I need some of what you two have. Where did you meet?"

They stopped in the sunken living room, Isabelle's heart racing, her mind spinning with reasons to extend the visit.

"It's a funny coincidence, actually," Brett said.

Belle picked up the story. "I was working for a major marketing company in New York. My boss asked me to join him here to pitch to the company Brett worked for."

Isabelle couldn't silence her shaky breath as the moment thrust forward in her brain at the speed of light. Gateway Media and Marketing.

Randall Siege stared at Isabelle from across the boardroom table, his gaze taunting and predatory in a way that made her uncomfortable and angry. He'd asked her to come to Virginia with him as his companion. Isabelle crossed her arms over her chest, the jacket of her tailored suit pulling tight, her fingers digging into the fabric covering her forearms. She'd politely declined. When he'd said it would be good for her career if she was looking to be fast-tracked, she'd stopped herself from slapping him.

"I'm not sure speed is the bonus you think it is, Randall," she said, her rigid body all but vibrating with implied violence.

Irritation flared in his gaze even as he stepped closer. "I'd like to see you in another environment. Away from here," he said in what she was sure he thought was a seductive and enticing tone.

Isabelle let her lips tip up but stopped short of baring her teeth. "And I'd like to tell your wife what an asshole you are, but something tells me she already knows."

Before he could say anything else, Isabelle held up her hand. "Don't say anything else. I'm going to walk away. We're going to pretend this didn't happen. And you are going to recommend me for the promotion to head of marketing." It would get her away from him and she'd be damn good at the job.

Like a wounded animal that lashes out as a last resort, Randall hissed. "Why the hell would I do that?"

Isabelle stepped even closer, pleased when he stiffened. Not so cocky now. "First, because I deserve it and there's not one person who could say otherwise."

He started to argue but she shook her head.

"And second," she pulled her phone from her pocket. "I don't

trust anyone. Particularly when they stray from the norm. Which is why I pressed record when I walked in here. Who do you think would be more interested in your intriguing offer to share a hotel room with you, Randall? Your wife? Or our boss?"

His face went a shade of red that nearly worried her out of her bluff. In the end, he'd slammed his way out of the conference room. She'd received her promotion and Randall took early retirement.

Belle and Brett were arguing over a detail Isabelle hadn't caught. Her stomach revolted, bile rising in her throat.

"You went? You came here with your boss?" Isabelle didn't care that she was standing right in front of herself—this wasn't her. There was nothing that would have made her compromise her integrity in that way, and it sickened her that the woman standing in front of her, proud as a fucking lion earning its place as king of the jungle, had.

Belle's smile flatlined when she looked at Isabelle, whose hands were actually shaking. The two women held each other's gaze and maybe Belle didn't see *herself* standing right in front of her like Isabelle did but the woman clearly recognized something between them. She *knew* Isabelle was somehow aware that there was more to the invite than she'd said or likely even shared with her husband.

"Actually," Belle said with a cold smile and a tone Isabelle herself had also perfected. "He came down with some sort of stomach bug at the last minute. I came alone."

Isabelle's breath whooshed out of her lungs. Relief made her dizzy.

"Some things work out exactly like they're meant to," Brett said.

Elaina murmured her agreement. Feeling like she needed to lay down, Isabelle looked at her sister and for once, she was at a loss of how to proceed. How to dig deeper. If she kept going, she might end up buried alive.

"Hello," a voice called out from the doorway.

Two men came through the door holding hands, their smiles happy and what Isabelle called untouched. They apparently hadn't faced the realities life so harshly threw at people when they least expected it.

Or maybe they have and are just better at dealing with it than you.

"Hi. Come on in," Belle said, disconnecting from the sisters.

Isabelle knew herself, even other versions, well enough to recognize the woman's need for a break.

"Belle and I host a cocktail party once a month to showcase our listings. Mostly the commercial ones. Your timing is excellent. I'm sorry this house isn't what you're looking for but the location of tonight's party has a lot of the elements you listed on our walk-through." Brett opened his phone again, read from the list. "High ceilings, close to the water in the downtown core. Lots of windows and flexible space. It's the third floor of an already-established retail building, which means you'll have some built-in traffic if that's something that appeals to you."

Jesus. She'd forgotten she told him she wanted a commercial property. If nothing else, it was an excuse to spend more time with Belle. Figure things out.

But at that exact moment, she just wanted to hop on a plane and go home.

"That's fantastic. We'll be there. What time?" Elaina asked before Isabelle could say anything.

Goddamn it, Elaina.

Brett smiled. "Eight o'clock. Let me get your number and I'll text you the location. There'll be other prospective buyers but sometimes those sorts of mixers lead you to something else, so you never know."

Elaina bumped Isabelle's hip with her own. "You really never know."

They said their goodbyes, Isabelle's barely audible. Belle didn't spare her a glance on their way out the door. She had Isabelle's patented dismissal down.

"I'll drive," Elaina said when Isabelle pulled the keys out of her purse.

"I'm fine."

She stopped when Elaina blocked her path. "Of course you are. You're always *fine.* Nothing rattles you. Tell me, do you malfunction if you show too much emotion in a short period of time? Short circuit? Shut down?"

Isabelle ground her teeth together hard enough to hurt.

"Give me the keys, Izzy-belle," Elaina said, her voice soft and coaxing.

The keys in question dug into her palm. "I want to go home." If she'd felt weak before, admitting this to Elaina, of all people, nearly knocked her to the ground.

Plucking the keys from her grasp, leaving a sharp sting on Isabelle's skin, Elaina shrugged. "If I remember correctly, you once told me just wanting something isn't enough. You need to be willing to fight for it. See it through, even if it tears you apart from the inside out. We came here for a reason. If you really want to go home, fight for it. Figure out whatever the universe is trying to tell you and we'll go."

Isabelle didn't even realize her sister was leading her to the passenger seat until she opened the door.

"Get in. Turn your brain off for five minutes. The world won't fall apart if you feel something without thinking it through."

She put on her seat belt, leaned her head back. Maybe the world wouldn't, but Isabelle's real worry was that *she* would.

NINETEEN

From where she sat waiting for her phone to ring, Isabelle could see Elaina walking up the pathway from the beach back to their hotel. She'd spoken to their mother when they returned to the hotel. Of course, Isabelle didn't know that for sure but the conversation and her sister's body language made it likely. She hadn't fully processed everything she'd seen only hours ago. Whether Elaina sensed her need for space or just needed some herself, she'd changed and headed for sand.

Isabelle had changed as well but nothing she did, none of her usual routines—checking emails, following up on contracts, returning phone calls—pulled her far enough out of her own thoughts to escape the image of Belle's swollen belly. The idea that in a month or so, in this life, wherever she was, there would be a baby.

The phone rang just as Elaina let herself back in. Their gazes locked. Neither said anything as Isabelle pressed accept on her phone, putting it on speaker so she could work on her laptop at the same time.

"Isabelle Duprees."

"Good afternoon, Ms. Duprees. It's Jenaya Davis calling from *The Economist.*"

"Yes. I was expecting your call." Her sister moved around behind her. Isabelle did her best to separate what felt like too many overlapping pockets of her life.

"First, congratulations on your latest achievement."

She thanked her, nerves making her antsy. Not about the interview but also not something she could easily identify.

"Tell me what it takes to stand in your shoes," Jenaya said.

She *felt* Elaina's gaze on her but refused to fidget. Instead, she stared at the ocean, breathed slowly. "Focus. Determination. Hunger to succeed."

"All excellent answers. But lots of people have those things."

"And still fail," Elaina murmured.

"I'm sorry . . . ?" Jenaya said.

Isabelle's head whipped toward her sister. She sent her an angry glare that she hoped communicated, "Shut up."

"I apologize. My sister is in the room."

Elaina simply shrugged.

"Oh, hello. May I ask your name?"

To her credit, Elaina searched Isabelle's gaze for approval. She gave it in a subtle nod.

"I'm Elaina Duprees. I didn't mean to interrupt."

"I would imagine relationships with family, friends, and even colleagues are heavily impacted by the kind of drive and hunger you mentioned, Ms. Duprees. Isabelle. Would you say that's true in your case? That you've sacrificed your personal life for your business achievements?"

She wouldn't have said so because it never occurred to her that she did. She'd simply put her head down and done the work.

"I think any time we're hyperfocused on one area of our life, other things take a backseat. That happens to business deals when one is more pressing than the others. It stands to reason that personal relationships and desires would feel . . ." She stared at her sister, wondering for just a minute what it would be like if they'd stayed close. Would she have been able to find balance? Would her portfolio of successes have been diminished by trying? "Strained. I don't think anyone has the perfect recipe for work/life balance. Certainly not me."

Her sister's brows arched with surprise and something that looked almost like respect.

"You're laying groundwork for women in a world that is still largely dominated by men. How do you do that without letting it get to you?"

Looking back to the ocean, she answered honestly. "How do you know I don't?"

"Do you?"

Jonathan's words sprinted to mind. *I'm so tired of pretending at these events, Isabelle.*

"Success in any area of your life requires commitment and sacrifice. Does it bother me that I can't bring a date to the Met Gala without it ending up in *Page Six*? Does it piss me off that any show of passion about what I do is printed as me being overemotional? Yes. Those things bother me. They *get to me.* I've had men shout and rage at me in meetings that didn't go their way. None of them were labeled ballbuster, ironheart, or Business Bitch of the East."

"Ouch," Elaina muttered behind her.

"There's still a large gender chasm. Do you see it changing?"

The question felt so much bigger than what Ms. Davis was asking. Isabelle turned slowly to see Elaina staring at her.

"Changing? Yes. Closing? No. Women still make up only a small percentage of the richest people in the world despite steadfast and extraordinary contributions to politics, science, business—everything." She paused, unsure why her thoughts wouldn't line up in the way they typically did. It was as if they were bouncing off one another, little Ping-Pong balls impossible to hold still. "I'm surprised by how much I wish my answer was different because hope isn't typically one of my attributes. I prefer the tangible. But in this case," she said quietly, holding her sister's gaze. "I'd say we'll never know if we don't try. And keep trying. Nothing changes without effort."

They talked for a bit longer, and Isabelle got caught up in the details of a program Jenaya brought up. It focused on exposing young girls to the business world as early as middle school and showing them the impact their words and ideas could have.

When they hung up, Elaina was laying on her bed, eyes closed. Isabelle got up, intending to splash some water on her face. Her emotions felt like jagged edges of glass running over her skin.

"You sounded intrigued by the Young Women in Business Mentorship Program," Elaina said with no inflection. "Volunteering isn't usually your jam."

Because her sister couldn't see her, Isabelle rolled her eyes. "My jam? I'm not a teenager in a garage band. This isn't volunteering, though I most certainly do offer my time, thank you very much. It's an opportunity to help pave the way for young women. If we want change, we have to work toward it."

Elaina's eyelids fluttered open. "Ain't that the truth. How about you? Do you want change? Are you ever going to forgive me? Forgive Mom?"

Fire flashed in Isabelle's chest. "I wasn't talking about us."

Elaina got up off the bed. "I am. What's it going to take?"

"I don't want to do this right now. If you haven't noticed, I'm dealing with some other emotional landmines at the moment."

"Maybe it's all tied together. All of it. Your choices. Your past. Your future. The lives you could have led."

Swallowing past the dryness in her throat, Isabelle didn't respond.

Elaina lowered her gaze, shoulders losing their stiffness. When she looked back up at Isabelle, there was a vulnerability there that erased some of the anger between them.

"I keep thinking . . . in this version of your life, I'm going to be an aunt," Elaina said in a voice so low, it was hard to hear.

The words twisted something inside of Isabelle's chest. Questions rushed forward in her brain: Did Elaina want children? Had she married? Come close? What was still missing from her life?

Elaina let her off the hook. "I didn't bring a cocktail dress. Did you?"

A breath of relief left her aching chest. It hurt to feel this much. Of course, if she told her sister that, she'd make some crack about her being a robot. "No. I'll ask Kaia to have something sent up to the room."

Elaina's gaze widened and she looked around the room like Isabelle's assistant might materialize out of nowhere. "Is she magic? She's not even in the same state."

Lips twitching, Isabelle grabbed her phone from her desk. "She definitely shows signs of having some sort of mystical power. I'm not sure how she does everything but I'd be lost without her."

The look in Elaina's eyes shuttered like a heavy curtain had dropped down. "Right. Of course you would."

When she walked away, Isabelle swore under her breath. *This* was why she focused only on work. Anything else was too fucking hard.

TWENTY

It turned out the listing Brett and Belle were showcasing wasn't far from the hotel. Kaia had performed her magic, having two gorgeous gowns, enviable heels, and even jewelry sent to the hotel. As she and Elaina rode the elevator up to the third floor of the Boulevard Building, the silence between them scratched at her skin. Her sister was stunning in the midthigh-length, aqua-green Vivienne Westwood scoop neck with delicate swirls of embroidery. With the elevator lighting and the mirrors surrounding them, the triple-loop diamond Harry Winston earrings created a halo of sparkles around Elaina's head.

Knowing Isabelle's tastes and her preference for supporting female designers and businesswomen, Kaia had selected a knee-length Ellie Saab dress in the palest of pinks. The layered, scooped neckline added body to the simple, elegant cut of the dress. They'd dressed in silence, helping each other zip up, doing their makeup side by side in the mirror. A ritual many sisters shared that they never had before. In truth, Isabelle had never shared that ritual with anyone. Neither of them went to the fall formals or their proms. There'd been no late-night gossip sessions over boys.

When the elevator doors slid open, they both stepped out, but Elaina stopped, glanced at her sister.

"Why didn't you go to your prom?"

It was strange after all these years apart, and having not been close to each other since they were young children, that their thoughts overlapped.

"I had no interest. I was a year and a half younger than all my classmates. I didn't have any friends. I just wanted to be done."

Done. Gone. She'd taken online courses to accelerate her graduation. She'd left almost immediately after the school year ended.

Elaina nodded, her fingers gripping the small clutch that Kaia had sent. "I ended up going to Marcus Carroll's. He was a year younger than me."

Isabelle could vaguely picture the boy who'd brought her sister clutches of wildflowers. Back then, Elaina was loved by everyone. Her vibrant personality charmed even the hardest of hearts in their small town. Between her outgoing nature and the pity their family inspired, Elaina had never lacked for companionship.

Music flowed over laughter and conversation. It trickled out to the small entryway that opened into a large, warmly lit space dominated by windows and a gorgeous view of the sun sinking down into the ocean. Pinks, oranges, and subtle blues twisted together where the water met sky.

"Nice place," Elaina said under her breath.

"It is."

Isabelle scanned the crowd of dressed-up strangers who sipped on champagne and nibbled on hors d'oeuvres. Not quite the elite crowd she'd socialized with the other evening, but as a general rule, these things all ran the same way and she'd been to enough of them to understand the way they worked. Everyone wanted something. Conversation was a currency, a way to gather information that would best suit the individual. It would surprise people to know how much intel and leverage could be gained at these mixers. If she asked the right questions, someone would be able to tell her more about Belle.

"You look like you're planning an attack. Lighten up, Izzy-belle. This is a party. Let's have some fun." Elaina looped her arm through her sister's.

"I'm not here to have fun," Isabelle reminded her, failing to keep the edge out of her tone.

"That should be your motto." Elaina did some scanning of her own, smiling at people who looked their way. "If I forget to say it later, I had a really good time tonight."

Isabelle sucked in a sharp breath and turned her head to see Elaina grinning at her like quoting one of their favorite movies, *Pretty Woman*, wouldn't unearth emotions she had no time for.

"Really?" She covered the ache in her chest with a dry tone.

Elaina bounced her eyebrows. "Not often I get to dress up in designer duds and mingle with the important people."

Her sister started to step forward but Isabelle pulled her back. "Money doesn't make people important, Elaina."

She wasn't sure what made her say it, wasn't even sure she fully believed it but she didn't want Elaina thinking any of these people were better than her because of their financial status.

Elaina studied her carefully to the point Isabelle wanted to fidget under her gaze. "Money gives you power. Power makes you important."

She was doubtful they'd ever close the valley of mistrust between them but if nothing else came from the strangeness of all of this, Isabelle hoped her sister would at least see her more clearly.

"Again, no. What you do with the power makes you important." And saying it, she realized maybe she'd overinflated her own sense of importance, because if she really thought about it, what had she done? What legacy would she leave?

"Let's mingle. See what people have to say about Belle. Don't ambush her or push her buttons," Elaina said, snapping the moment closed.

They parted ways, each of them weaving through a sea of expensive colognes and perfumes.

Isabelle saw Brett by the bar and headed toward him. He grinned, waved.

"Hey. You made it. You look great," he said, offering his hand for her to shake.

"Thank you," Isabelle said, using the hand-to-hand connection to check for even a hint of a spark or recognition. She felt nothing and saw no trace of anything in his gaze. Surely, if she could love him in one version of her life, she'd feel something in this moment.

She pulled back, met his gaze. His wavy, dark hair had been styled into submission with product and he wore his suit well but she couldn't imagine herself being pulled to him physically or emotionally.

"This is quite a turnout," she said.

"We do really well at these events. I'm sure, in whatever your line of business is, you understand the value in networking." He placed money on the bar top. "Let me buy you a drink?"

"I'll have a gin and tonic with a splash of lime."

The bartender, tall with a little too much facial hair for Isabelle's liking, smiled appreciatively at her. "Yes ma'am. And you sir?"

"Hell, why not? Give me the same."

Brett smiled at her as their drinks were made. "So, tell me more about what you'd use the space for."

She didn't want to talk business. The thought sucked the air from her lungs. She *always* wanted to talk business.

"I'm an investor, primarily. I also work with companies to find their trouble spots, help them fix them, maximize their strengths. I own a number of properties that I rent out to a wide range of businesses. I'd utilize this space for something like that. I like the windows."

How would Elaina navigate this conversation? She had a way of pulling secrets from people. Isabelle didn't see her sister in the crowd.

The drinks were set on the bar but Isabelle pulled a bill from her own clutch. "Allow me."

Brett smiled, pulled his own money back. The bartender slipped a napkin toward her and Isabelle saw the number he'd written on it, met his gaze, took only her drink, and turned away.

She and Brett walked toward the windows, him saying hello to various people. It had been a very long time since Isabelle had been an unknown at an event, even a small one like this. There was a freedom in it, she realized. Casual conversation and chit-chat were not her forte but Brett wouldn't know the difference.

When she turned away from the stunning view, she saw him staring at her and nerves squeezed her heart.

"There's something familiar about you," he said.

"Hmm," Isabelle murmured against the rim of her glass. "You and Belle must do very well if this is only one of your listings." They would have only received a percentage of sales but even small portions of millions added up nicely.

He nodded, sipped his gin and tonic, scrunched his brows at the bitterness, which nearly made Isabelle laugh. Rather than try to impress her, he should have ordered what he wanted.

"Our office is close to here, actually, but much smaller, less extravagant. Belle's a firm believer in being far too busy to spend a lot of time in the office. If we're always on the go, our space can be fairly basic. Now, our house, on the other hand—it's something else. She designed it herself with every creature comfort you can imagine." He scanned the room, searching for his wife.

"A home should be a sanctuary. The more comforts and pleasures you have at your fingertips, the better," Isabelle agreed, turning slightly so she could people watch and seem less interested in learning something of value.

"You sound like Belle."

Her jaw clenched. "We probably have a similar business outlook. Did you both grow up well off?"

He shook his head, took another swallow of his drink. "Not at all. My parents were both teachers. They did okay but we were certainly never wealthy. And Belle . . . well, her family didn't have a lot of money. I would have done well, *was* doing well career wise before I met her, but she's got a gift for turning very little into something extraordinary."

At least some things transferred from version to version of herself. "Are you close to your families?"

Don't push too hard.

A man in a strikingly well-cut suit approached them, gave Isabelle a once-over before reaching out a hand to Brett.

"Longworth. Good to see you. This space is fantastic. We're doing so well at the last location you found for us, we're expanding."

Brett shook his hand then gestured to Isabelle. "I'm glad to hear it. You'll have some competition for this place. Isabelle, this is Gavin Cromwell. Gavin, this is . . ." Brett trailed off. "I don't even know your last name."

Her throat constricted. She couldn't say Duprees. He'd know her mother's maiden name. "Fairbanks," she said, refusing to read into why Jonathan's last name had rolled off her tongue so easily. "Isabelle Fairbanks." She reached out a hand. "Cromwell . . . as in Cromwell and Company? Sporting goods giants?"

His smile suggested she'd impressed him. "I'd say the one and only but the truth is, I have four brothers."

She'd read a particularly interesting article in *Time* magazine on his family and their enterprise.

Elaina showed up at Isabelle's side. "Who do we have here?"

Brett leaned in, greeted Elaina the same way he had Isabelle. "This is Gavin Cromwell. He was just telling your sister about his many siblings. Gavin, this is Elaina. Fairbanks? Is that correct? I didn't even ask if Fairbanks is a married name."

Elaina's brows arched and a quick glance at Isabelle told her she wasn't going to let that go.

"No. My sister would never marry. Why, then she might have to share the remote," Elaina said, easily making Gavin laugh.

Isabelle sent her sister a sharp glare but Brett pulled Elaina's attention by asking if she was having a good time.

"Absolutely. It's wonderful. I don't attend many events like this. I love an excuse to get dressed up."

"You certainly do it well," Gavin said, a rather heated gaze moving over her.

Did she have someone at home? Isabelle didn't like the little dig about her own personal life but she knew nothing of Elaina's. She'd worked hard over the last dozen years to push that piece of her past into a sealed box. Kaia didn't even bother to give her updates anymore unless it was something pressing such as *Your sister is in town*.

"I could use a drink," Elaina said, looking around like one might appear.

"Let's take care of that," Gavin said smoothly, offering his arm to her.

She saw her sister's second of hesitation and wondered

again about her personal life. But then she placed a hand on his arm, keeping enough distance between their bodies to not truly answer the question.

Brett shook his glass. "I should grab another and mingle. Listen, check out the rest of the space. Get a feel for it. I'll touch base with you tomorrow afternoon. I have several other residential properties I think might meet your needs."

"Thank you," she said, unable to think of any reason to detain him.

She stood by the window, watching people laugh, talk, dance. Her gaze wandered to her sister who had her head tipped back in laughter at something Gavin said. Elaina had always navigated personal connections well. She was a natural flirt with a palpable energy. People were drawn to her, just like they had been to their father.

Fatigue rolled over Isabelle unexpectedly. More than just tired from travel or lack of sleep. A bone-deep exhaustion that came from her brain spinning at alarming speeds and her own inability to find an answer to anything. Then again, how could she get answers when she didn't know the questions? The only one that kept running through her mind was: What the hell is happening to me?

She swallowed down the rest of her drink but her throat remained dry. A headache started at the base of her skull, beating in time to the music that people were dancing to. Despite the sleeveless dress, she felt overheated.

Searching for air, for space, for a little bit of logic that would somehow make things make sense, she left the room.

The quiet hallway off the main space led to restrooms and what Isabelle assumed would be a staff area. She pushed through the door and nearly collided with the very pregnant version of herself.

TWENTY-ONE

Belle's hands immediately wrapped around her stomach, clearly a natural instinct.

Isabelle had always been fairly certain that pregnancy and motherhood weren't for her. The idea of having a baby, nurturing it, raising it, seemed foreign and entirely too demanding. There'd been a brief period between nineteen and twenty when she'd fallen for one of her professors and thought herself in love. She'd had more than a few thoughts about a future with him. Maybe a family. But she'd pointed out an error in his financial plan during a large group lesson and his ego couldn't handle the fact that she'd been right. He'd given her the cold shoulder for a week or so before she called him on it. Isabelle figured if you could walk away that easily, it wasn't love.

"Are you okay?" Isabelle asked.

Belle was somewhat pale under her expertly applied makeup. Her long hair had been tucked into a loose chignon. She wore a gorgeous, gauzy dress with a halter-style top and flowing skirt. It shimmered like a glittery river.

"Yes. Thank you. I just needed . . ." She paused as though her professional and personal self were opposed.

This was some alternative-world/multiverse version of *alone time* that Isabelle couldn't quite wrap her head around. If she tried, everything went out of focus and became harder to understand.

"Space? Some air?"

Releasing a soft laugh, Belle nodded. "Yes. Exactly."

She backed away from the doorway, moved into a room set up with round tables, chairs, a couple of couches, and a small kitchenette. Definitely a staff area. Opening the mini fridge, she grabbed two bottles of water and passed one to Isabelle before taking a seat at a table.

Grateful for the opportunity, Isabelle joined her.

"Brett loves these events. I often tease him that he should have 'the more the merrier' tattooed on his arm." She took a long drink of her water, one hand resting on her stomach.

It was probably normal to wonder what Belle felt like. What it would feel like to go through all the phases of pregnancy. But having a child didn't guarantee a bond or even love. In her case, it hadn't even meant comfort, protection, or guidance from her own mother past the age of eight.

"Oh," Belle said, laughing as she set her water down.

Isabelle stared at her, a bit lost as to what was funny until the other her reached out, took Isabelle's hand. "The baby is moving."

Too surprised to do otherwise, she put her fingers on Belle's stomach. Something nudged her hand, rolled beneath it. A small sound escaped her. Shock. Surprise. Awe.

Looking up through lowered lids, she met Belle's gaze. Held it. "Are you scared?" Her words unintentionally came out as a whisper. They felt thick in her throat.

"Of the baby?"

Leaning back, Isabelle opened her water, took a small sip.

"The baby. Being a mom. Loving it enough. Losing your focus for work. Hell, even your marriage."

Belle sighed, then spoke quietly. "Not of those things. For me, fear has always been about the unknown. Once I'm in a situation, I can deal with it head-on. It's the thinking ahead, coming up with *what if* or worst-case scenarios that really throws me off, so I try hard not to do that. I focus on the moment. In this moment, I'm pregnant and happily married. I've been in other situations where my happiness was snatched from me. Where the outcome wasn't in my control and things didn't go the way I wanted them to."

Isabelle watched as the other version of herself looked past her shoulder, like she was being pulled down by the weight of memories. She couldn't help but wonder which of them brought sadness to her eyes. The sudden death of her father, the way her mother collapsed into herself, only coming out of her fog long enough to latch onto Elaina and pull her into the cocoon of grief. Was she picturing the little girl she'd been, putting herself to bed, making dinner for the three of them, riding her bike to get groceries because no one else would? She was eight. Heartbroken and alone.

"Why are you crying?" Belle asked.

The words shocked Isabelle. Raising her hand to her cheek, she realized a couple of tears had fallen. She started to laugh it off, make a joke, dismiss it. But it felt wrong to lie to herself.

"I was thinking about moments in my own life where happiness was fleeting. Where the times when I felt truly happy seemed more like a movie I'd seen than moments that actually happened."

Belle nodded. "It changes you . . . but we get to decide how."

"Brett credits you with all of his success."

It was like the sun rose in her eyes, in her smile, just from hearing his name. The intensity of emotion shining from the other woman made the strings around Isabelle's heart cinch tight.

"I'm definitely the business brain in the relationship. I never thought I'd find someone to balance me out because I didn't know I was off-kilter."

Isabelle clenched her jaw, fought back the immediate denials that sprung to mind. She wasn't *off-kilter.* She was just fine. Her life was the way she wanted it to be, the way she'd chosen. Every damn step of the way.

"I grew up sooner than I should have had to," Belle said quietly, both hands now on her stomach. "It gave me a hard exterior. When I lived in New York, I needed it. Hell, living in Tennessee, I needed it. Brett softens me. I tease him that I'm the brains and he's the heart." She looked up, met Isabelle's gaze. "Without both, you're not really whole."

She boosted herself up, ignored Isabelle's attempt to help her. "I think I'll go find my husband. I hope you enjoy your night, Isabelle. Let us know if the space works for you."

Belle walked away, leaving Isabelle alone, wondering if she knew herself at all.

Determined not to get bogged down by irrational feelings and the spiraling questions making her dizzy, she went back to the party. It was in full swing and she sincerely hoped no one was signing any paperwork that evening.

The sky had gone dark but lights danced in the distance, sparkling like stars through the many windows. The dance floor had grown, the music pumped, and waiters wove discreetly through the crowd with beverages. Brett and Belle chatted animatedly with a small group of people.

Loud laughter she'd recognize in her sleep pierced through the room. Elaina, always the life of a party, spun in a circle,

Gavin watching her. *Everyone* watching her. If Isabelle had built a wall around her heart, her life, then Elaina had built a bridge.

Isabelle pulled out her phone, requested an Uber, and texted Elaina she'd meet her back at the hotel. Staying here would only make her feel like more of an outsider in her own life. This wasn't her. She might not have all of the answers but she knew enough to know that *Belle* wasn't her.

Back in the room, grateful for the quiet, she took a long, hot shower, doing her best to scrub the moments off herself. Some of them were stubborn, clinging to her heart like the water on her lashes. She didn't know how to make sense of anything. Wrapping herself in a towel, her hair tucked into another one, she grabbed her phone.

Staring at it, she tried to think of what she could text that would help her feel less alone but not make Jonathan think she was straight up losing her mind.

I feel like I'm standing in front of a mirror and don't recognize myself.

The three dots popped up immediately and she wondered if the burst of energy, of happiness, she felt in her heart was reflected in her gaze. The way Belle's had been.

What are you hoping to see?

Pulling the towel off her head, she set it on the nightstand, then sank down onto the bed, grateful for the faceless interaction that gave her just a touch of bravery.

Someone strong who hasn't let the past define her when the entire goal was not to. Someone who is more than the sum of the profits they make. Someone important.

She swallowed past the lump in her throat as she awaited his reply. She'd held him at arm's length this entire time but he hadn't let it stop him from finding a way in—working his way under her skin and creeping into her bloodstream.

I think at some point, everyone fails to see what's right in front of them. You're the strongest woman I know, professionally.

The mild insult had her huffing out a breath.

Just professionally?

A smiley face appeared on her phone.

She laughed. "Jerk."

Another message popped up seconds later.

I believe personal strength comes from knowing that leaning on someone, letting them all the way in, doesn't make you weak.

Maybe it was the memory of a baby moving under her palm or the look in Belle's eyes when she spoke about Brett but Isabelle suddenly felt very alone. She'd, of course, felt this before. The difference was, in this moment, she didn't like it. She didn't want to be. She'd put all her focus into her work, worried that anything less was not enough. But with every deal she'd made, there'd been a little clutch in her gut. An *Are you sure?* in her mind. In those moments, the ones that led to success, she'd jumped anyway. Taking a deep breath, she held it. And typed.

I miss you.

She waited, her breath whooshing out of her lungs. The three dots appeared and then disappeared, and her hands shook with the regret of having revealed too much. She knew better. What was she thinking? How could letting someone in make her strong when it gave them the upper hand?

All of this was messing with her head, making her think she wanted something other than the life she'd poured her heart and soul into creating. When the phone rang in her hand, she nearly dropped it. Seeing Jonathan's name on the screen made her pulse hiccup.

"Hello?"

"I had to be sure it was you," he said, his deep, soothing voice moving over her like a welcome embrace.

She frowned. "Is that supposed to be a joke?"

"Isabelle, in all of the time we've been together, not once have you shown your cards the way you just did with three words."

"It's not a poker game." She didn't mean to be snappy but hearing his voice settled something in her and she realized he might have had the upper hand all along. Which was why she'd kept her distance.

"No? Then why do I feel like I just won the whole pot?"

Despite the smile his words brought to her face, she kept her tone even. "Because you're an easy mark."

His laughter wrapped around her in the dim glow of the hotel room. "There's my Isabelle."

His Isabelle. She hadn't been anybody's anything for longer than she could remember. Which was good. It was what she wanted. Easier not to be left behind. Forgotten. Leaning back against the headboard, she pulled one of the overstuffed pillows onto her lap, let her hand rest there, and her mind went back to Belle's stomach.

"Are you okay?" he whispered.

She closed her eyes, listened to his breathing, tried to figure out how to put all the emotions running through her into words that made sense.

"I'm tired," she said. It was as close to the truth as she could give him.

"I miss you too."

His words felt like finding something treasured that she'd long ago forgotten she'd lost.

"I bought into the Bayer Hotel. Majority shares." Business was easy compared to emotion.

"I read Kaia's press release. I think it's great. It's a boutique hotel in a great location."

Words she'd dismissed dozens of times danced through her head. "I want to open multiple locations."

"You'll need investors."

She pulled in a deep breath. Her life. Her choice. "I only want one."

He grew so quiet, she wondered if she'd lost the call. She even pulled the phone away from her face to make sure she hadn't.

"Jonathan?"

"What are you thinking?"

Okay. He wasn't saying no to something that would link them indefinitely.

"You buy in and help fund a second location. Bayer becomes a sister hotel, less upscale but more affordable under the Fairbanks umbrella."

"So, you're looking for the name?"

Isabelle Fairbanks. She hadn't played pretend like that since before her father died. And even though she'd only done so earlier that night to make things less awkward, it had felt like something close to right.

"It's a good name," she said softly. "One I'd be proud to put mine next to."

His silence unnerved her, wound knots in her stomach that she suspected she might not ever untangle.

"Come home, Isabelle."

She smiled. "Soon."

TWENTY-TWO

Isabelle timed her inhales and exhales to the ebb and flow of the water, allowed her eyes to close as she moved through a handful of her favorite yoga positions on the sand. When she opened them, gazed at the bubbling whitecaps as the waves broke softly against the shore, she felt a peace she hadn't felt in days. They'd go home mere hours from now.

Well, Isabelle would return to New York. She wasn't sure what Elaina would do. Her sister hadn't returned until the very, very wee hours of the morning. She'd fumbled around the hotel room, making noise in her attempts not to.

Part of Isabelle had wanted to ask about the evening. About Gavin. Had she spent the evening with him? It occurred to her as she lay there in the darkness that she didn't know how to engage in that kind of "girl talk" conversation. Not with her sister. Not with anyone, really.

She'd sidestepped all those opportunities out of a desperate need to prove herself and perhaps the misguided idea that getting close to anyone would put her at risk of failure. Folding at the waist, she let her breath leave her lungs, relaxed her spine, tried to clear her head again. But in the back of her mind, she wondered if she had missed opportunities for friends she had feared were just out to use her?

Rising, she lifted her hands high over her head, then pressed her palms together, lowered them in front of her heart. Didn't matter now. She could do things differently. This strange whirlwind had opened her eyes. Mission accomplished. She could open the door for Jonathan a bit more, maybe make a friend or two. Not avoid every single one of her sister's phone calls. Growth.

A couple of runners passed in front of her, heavily engaged in their conversation. The beach would fill up soon but it was still early enough to avoid dealing with people.

"Do you ever sleep in?" Elaina asked, coming up beside the towel Isabelle used in place of a yoga mat.

"I don't like missing the day." She glanced at her sister who held two take-out cups of coffee. "One of those mine?"

Elaina's lips curved. "Since I don't know anyone else here, yes."

She took the one her sister offered with a laugh. "I'll take it."

Isabelle sank down onto one-half of the towel, leaving room for Elaina to sit beside her. They drank their coffees, stared at the water. It wasn't a bad way to start the day.

"I have to say, I enjoyed that party a hell of a lot last night," Elaina murmured after a long sip.

"I'm glad. Did you learn anything?"

Turning her head, Elaina studied her over the rim of her cup. "Staying out dancing all night with strangers isn't as easy as when I was younger," she said, smirking.

Isabelle rolled her eyes, looked back at the water, let the coffee and the breeze wake her all the way up. "Not exactly what I meant and definitely more than I needed to know." Still, questions scratched along the surface of those upended boxes, begging to be asked. Was Elaina happy? Single? Doing something that made her want to get up every morning? Was she really healthy?

"According to my subtle sleuthing—and can I just say I would have made an excellent detective?—Belle and Brett are a well-respected couple. While he's definitely the social one, the face of what they do, her strength and business prowess, like yours, are recognized and coveted. Gavin said she's had several head hunters approach her for a variety of positions. Again, like you, when she sets her mind to something, she's got a focus that makes tunnel vision look like a panoramic view. Her focus now is Brett, their business, and soon, their baby."

Several thoughts tumbled around in Isabelle's head even while unfamiliar emotions did the same in her chest. She focused on the most surprising piece. "It almost sounds like you complimented me there. Twice." She lifted the cup to her lips.

Elaina's shoulder nudged hers. "You're a pain in the ass but I'm not oblivious."

Isabelle lowered her hand, angled herself toward her sister. "*I'm* a pain in the ass?" Her voice rose over the seagulls chattering in the distance.

Her sister's grin widened. "I know. But I forgive you."

She could only shake her head and fight the smile. "You. Are. Unbelievable."

"Aw. You're not so bad yourself. Sometimes."

Isabelle groaned and turned away. The silence, the proximity, and the location wrapped around her, and she realized it might have been the nicest moments she'd spent with her sister in more years than she could count.

"Why are you crying, Izzy-belle?" Eight-year-old Elaina crawled into the fort Isabelle had made in her closet by stretching her clothes from one hanger to the next. Isabelle clutched a little brown bear,

its ears worn from years of rubbing them absently. At six, Isabelle's entire world was made up of that bear, her big sister, and her dad.

"Mommy said she'd done her share. She said she had me even when she didn't want to. For him. And now it was her turn to have a life and he promised to give it to her."

Elaina's arm snaked around her little sister, pulled her tightly into her side, nudged her messy-haired head onto her shoulder. "Grown-ups say things they don't mean. Mommy's just mad because Daddy has to work instead of taking her away this weekend like he planned."

"She only likes you." Isabelle sniffled, irritated with herself, even at six, for crying.

"That's not true. Don't say that. She loves you."

Isabelle pulled out of her sister's comforting embrace. "I'm going to run away." The idea had crashed into her and set her in motion. She scurried out of the closet, accidentally pulling down three of the shirts that made up the loose roof of the fort. Her backpack hung on a hook by the door. She grabbed it, stuffed Bear into it, went to her dresser to get some clothes.

Elaina was beside her before she could pull the first drawer open. "Stop it, Izzy-belle. You're not going anywhere." She yanked the backpack out of Isabelle's hand, tossed it by the bed.

Anger rose inside of Isabelle and she pushed Elaina as hard as she could. "You're not my boss. You're dumb and I'm leaving."

Instead of pushing her back, Elaina grabbed her by the shoulders, yanked her close, and hugged her, trapping her arms. Isabelle fought the hold but her sister was stronger. The fight left her with a deep sigh and more tears fell.

"You're not leaving. You can't go. We're a team. I need you. And it's my job to take care of you. I can't do that if you run away."

Isabelle sniffled, wiped her face on Elaina's shirt, and her sister must have really been worried because she didn't even yell at her for it or call her gross.

"Mommy doesn't like me."

"That's not true. She loves you. She just says dumb things when she's drinking."

"She didn't want me." Her voice shook with pure emotion.

Elaina's arms tightened around her, her head resting on the top of Isabelle's. "Because she knew, even before you were born, that you'd be so special we'd all love you the most."

Daddy had said something similar the last time Mommy hurt Isabelle's feelings. She rubbed her back, whispered, "We're okay. It'll be okay."

"I love you the most." Isabelle squeezed her sister with all the strength her little arms could muster.

"Then don't go," Elaina whispered against her hair.

"Hey," Elaina said, giving Isabelle a small nudge with her hand. "What's wrong? You look like you're going to cry."

Isabelle straightened her spine, caught off guard by the strength of the memory. She rarely recalled things from before her father died. Her life had easily snapped in two pieces like a piece of spun sugar, so delicate and fragile. Before and after.

"I'm sorry I left," Isabelle said, her voice quiet to keep the quiver hidden.

Elaina's mouth opened and closed. She blinked rapidly. "I'm sorry we didn't give you a reason to stay."

Isabelle nodded. It was enough. The contents of her life boxes had been shifted around, sorted through, and now she could put the lids back on. Move forward with this new organization system. She stood up, offered a hand to Elaina.

Her sister stared up at her outstretched arm, squinting because of the sun. A small smile touched her lips when her palm slid against Isabelle's.

When they were both standing, they stared at each other

somewhat awkwardly and Isabelle wasn't sure how to close the physical gap between them. As usual, Elaina took the choice from her by throwing her arms around Isabelle's neck. One quick squeeze and her sister pulled back, grabbed the towel, and shook off the sand.

The rest of the world was waking up. Little shops along the boardwalk were coming alive, people surfacing for the promise of coffee and sweet pastries, some on their way to work, some with just a day of sand and sun on their agenda.

"Not to wreck this, and I won't push, but I brought an invitation to Mom's wedding," Elaina said as they walked the worn path back to the hotel.

Isabelle swallowed the sudden dryness in her throat. "Why would she want me there?" She felt Elaina's gaze on her like the intense sun on her back.

"You're her daughter."

That never mattered in the past, Isabelle thought but refrained from uttering it out loud.

"Sobriety brings clarity?" Elaina continued. "Jesus. I don't know. But he's good for her. You'd like him."

They stopped for a woman jogging with a stroller, let her pass before crossing over to the hotel.

"Just because we're somewhat okay doesn't mean I'm ready to let go of the things she did." The boxes were reorganized in her head and her heart, but they weren't fucking magic. Still, she wouldn't say that to her sister because she really didn't want to throw away this tentative new bond between them.

Elaina stopped at the entrance to the hotel, turned to Isabelle. "If you can forgive me, you can forgive her."

Isabelle looked into her sister's eyes, hoping this was the last time they'd ever have this conversation. "You were a child when she fell apart. The same as me. You can blame her drinking, the grief, immaturity, it doesn't matter. Her husband died, she curled into a ball and never came out for me. She pulled you in with her and it left me alone." Her chest grew tight, making it hurt to pull in a breath. "It was the two of you, watching movies, crying, laughing, hugging, fucking *healing*, while I stood on the sidelines. Alone."

Elaina looked around them with a grimace. Isabelle could feel a few people around her but she didn't *see* them. Elaina grabbed her arm, yanked her into a shady, slightly removed spot by an enormous potted plant.

"You think I wanted to be there with her? In a fucking cocoon of grief? I didn't know what to do because like you said, I was a goddamn kid. And quite honestly, even at eight, you could take care of yourself better than she could as an adult."

Isabelle shook her head, her breath increasing, her lungs shrinking. "No. No. It's not okay. Don't let her off the hook. She's a selfish, self-absorbed woman who only ever thought of what she wanted. If she hadn't whined so much about being able to go on a girls' trip, he wouldn't have been working overtime. He wouldn't have died."

She couldn't do this. She couldn't have this conversation. A few minutes of humor and decent conversation scattered over a few days couldn't erase everything. Not when Elaina still stood up for Catalina.

"I know. She knows. We know, Isabelle. Stop fucking punishing her for it."

She wasn't even aware she was backing away until her shoulders hit the glass of the hotel. "No. She didn't want me and she got her wish."

Elaina crowded her, fury flashing in her gaze. "For someone who hates her so much, you're a lot like her. Selfish. Self-absorbed."

Her hand came up without warning and would most definitely have struck Elaina if her sister's reflexes hadn't been quicker. She gripped Isabelle's wrist, her nails digging into the skin.

"She was a drunk and a shitty mom. He loved you enough for all of us. He made up for whatever she didn't give *you.* Do you see me resenting you for that? Parents aren't supposed to have favorites. But *they* did. They fucked up. They fucked us up."

"Excuse me, ladies, is everything okay here?" A tall, wide-shouldered bellman in a dark-blue suit stood in front of them.

Elaina dropped Isabelle's arm. "Fine. Just a sister spat."

He nodded, folded his arms in front of him. "I understand. If you're guests of the hotel, I'll ask that you take the conversation inside. If not, I'll have to ask you to leave the property."

Isabelle turned her gaze to him, rubbing the raw spots on her wrist. "We *are* guests at the hotel, thank you very much."

He nodded, clearly unmoved by her tone. "You're drawing a crowd, ma'am. I'll need you to take your argument somewhere more private."

Isabelle's teeth ground together even as she steeled her shoulders and looked at her sister. She was digging deep to find words that would clarify her feelings but there weren't any. There were absolutely no words to define how she felt.

Elaina backed up, her hands lifted in front of her, palms out. "Trust me, this argument is over. And so is this trip."

She walked away without a backward glance, leaving Isabelle alone on the sidewalk. Isabelle clasped her hands together in an effort to deny, and hide, their shaking. All these years, *she'd* been the one to walk away. From everything. Family, friends, acquaintances, jobs, opportunities. Cutting ties was fine when you were the one leaving, when you were the one with the power. But the opposite, being the one left behind, was entirely different.

"Ma'am?" The bellman stepped forward, crowding Isabelle. Or maybe it just felt that way. "Are you all right? You seem like you're having a bit of trouble breathing."

The compassion in his tone tugged at the already tenuous strings holding onto her control.

"I'm fine. Can you have my things brought down from my room?" She mumbled the room number.

He nodded, still watching her carefully. "Of course."

When he left, she did her best to pull in a shaky breath. She was fine. If she kept telling herself that, there was a chance she'd actually believe it.

TWENTY-THREE

Elaina didn't text. She didn't come find her sister like she had all those years ago in the closet and so many other times that Isabelle didn't want to think about. Isabelle dealt with the unsettled energy making her foot tap, making her feel like she'd had too much caffeine, by doing what she always did—she worked. They'd been in each other's space for days. A little distance wouldn't hurt.

In the quiet of a tiny conference room just off the hotel lobby, Isabelle waited for the Zoom meeting to start. Kaia had done her best to move meetings and engagements around but there were things in the works that couldn't just be ignored.

Especially not if all you have in your life is work. You might want to keep a firm grasp on that since you keep fucking everything else up.

She shook her head, trying to rid herself of that thought. It wasn't all a loss. She and Jonathan would be on stronger footing when she returned. Plus, now she knew, firsthand, that her mother and sister were okay. Maybe the guilt that had called shotgun since Elaina's appearance would take a backseat. Or get lost all together.

This little break had opened her eyes to a few things, refocused her with a better understanding of what she wanted. The legacy she wanted to leave behind. *Google results are hardly a legacy.* But weren't they? In today's world?

The computer pinged with an email a second before the screen filled with C. J. Rowland's face. Her brain shuffled facts like a Vegas card dealer.

Cedrick John Rowland was fifty-eight, in excellent shape that he credited to the internationally renowned fitness centers he owned and operated around the world. Drafted by the NFL in the second round at twenty-two, he'd had a long, successful career, two high-profile marriages, and two even-higher-profile divorces. When he injured himself before his team made it to the Super Bowl, his intense workout routine started as rehabilitation, an attempt to get back on the field. When that didn't happen, he channeled his energy in a different direction, opening gyms and making triple what he had as a top earner in the NFL. What he hadn't done was endear himself to the public—particularly those of the female persuasion.

Getting the niceties out of the way, Isabelle cut to the chase.

"I'm not sure I want to be in the fitness space, C. J." Honesty was best but that didn't mean she couldn't, or wouldn't, push the truth in an effort to not overplay her hand.

"I understand that, Isabelle, but I'm not asking you to buy into or support my already-successful empire." One of his hands swept through his slightly too-long salt-and-pepper hair. He smiled like a man who thought he was charming.

"What are you asking?" Normally, she'd have Kaia or Jasper or one of her other assistants research the details, get them to her upfront to find out if she was even interested in having a conversation. However, in this particular case, C. J.'s businesses were universally strong, and he'd phoned her, personally, several times to leave messages about connecting. Curiosity might lead down dark paths, but then again, it could also make her richer.

Money doesn't make people important, Elaina.

She clenched her jaw when her own words flitted through her head. Maybe not. But it sure as hell didn't hurt to have it.

"I need to widen my market. Eighty-four percent of our gym memberships are held by men," C. J. said, leaning closer to the screen, making it easier to see the wrinkles around his eyes.

"As long as the client base and profits are steadily increasing, what do you care which gender works out?"

"I don't like knowing there's a large, untapped pool of potential customers. Especially since I don't think it's because they aren't working out. They aren't working out at *my* gyms. I think we both know garnering favor from the female demographic isn't my strong suit," he added, his smile turning somewhat sheepish.

So, he wanted what he couldn't have? Ego was always part of these things, but was C. J. really looking to soften his image and widen his market or was he trying to make himself look good to downplay a number of very public indiscretions?

Of course, when *his* relationships and missteps were splashed across *Page Six*, *he* didn't get called derogatory names that made his next business meeting rife with discomfort.

C. J. continued, his tone jovial. "I want to change that. And I want your help. I want to partner with you. The time is right. Your name, your boss-lady persona, undeniable successes, and reputation for solid business sense, paired with my already-successful formula for state-of-the-art fitness centers, will make a women-only branch of my gyms a gold mine. For both of us."

It wasn't a bad idea. It was, in fact, quite a good one, and though Isabelle wasn't sure about the fitness space, she was always looking to expand her portfolio. However, she was still stuck on the flippant summary of her that included the words *boss-lady persona*. What the actual hell was that? She was an investor, a real estate magnate, an innovator of adaptable and in-demand technology, and one of the richest women in the United States.

"Isabelle, you're a good-looking woman with an enviable body." C. J.'s words broke through her thoughts like a truck ramming into a wall.

Mild irritation shifted into an anger that had her itching to slam the laptop closed. "Excuse me?"

"Facts. That's the secret to *my* success. You're tight-lipped in interviews, hedging around the secret to yours, but mine is straight up facts. And the *fact* is, you, a gorgeous, successful woman punching her manicured fist through the proverbial glass ceiling while telling people that your body is a result of working out at *our* female-friendly fitness centers, will make us goddamn billionaires and leaders in the fitness industry."

Isabelle glanced at her phone, saw that Kaia had texted. But not Elaina. Her sister had to have calmed down by now.

"Isabelle?"

Moving her gaze back to the screen, she hated that she had to work at staying focused. She didn't let personal issues impact her professional life. And they never got in the way of a deal.

It made her sick to think it, but she didn't want to do this right now. More than that, she felt personally affronted by his commentary and she knew, down to her bones, business was not supposed to be personal. "You have a proposal? Plans? Ideas for starter locations, projections, and possibly some current and former athlete endorsements?"

His eyes lit up, shining through the fifteen-inch monitor. "Of course. My flagship is in New York. There's a bank of buildings in Hell's Kitchen, close to the water. I'm thinking we go all out—gym, spa, an oasis. A buddy of mine bought it off the city years ago. The upkeep was solid but he's looking to liquidate. I think I can get us an excellent deal."

Jesus. Was she this obnoxious in meetings when she wanted something? A memory tapped in the recesses of her brain, but she couldn't pull it forward.

"He's been overseas but he's coming back. Right now, it's home to some community-based programs. It's basically a write-off for him . . . he never had any real plans for it, so I don't think he'll have a problem letting it go."

It suddenly hit her. "There's a Young Women in Business Program in that building. They've had trouble starting up but now that they've found an affordable space, they're looking for female mentors to participate." The reporter from *The Economist* had sounded so excited and energized about not only the space, but the program, the community, and helping young women who didn't always have access to opportunity.

C. J.'s brows drew together. "So?"

Her breath hitched. "*So*, I just finished giving a maybe to someone deeply invested in the program and I don't think the optics of reneging *and* booting them out of their space would be great."

"Come on, Isabelle. We're not exactly running charities in our free time. You own a ton of real estate, and you know as well as I do that it's not easy to snap it up at a decent price. Especially one in good shape that was cared for, in an area that can and has improved. Who the hell cares about a community program? This is a great opportunity to do something valuable and reap the rewards in a big way."

She kept her temper tethered but her hands curled into fists. No, she was hardly running charities. Elaina's words cannonballed into her mind: *Do you use me as a write-off? That's a thing, right? Richie Riches like you get a tax break for charitable donations, no?*

"I think if you're truly invested in this idea and want me to take part, if you're certain about the potential, a different location isn't a big deal. As you said, I have several properties." But she already knew she didn't want to work with this man.

Isabelle made a note on her phone to ask Kaia about the building, its history, and the current owner.

"Potential isn't a big enough word. Since when do you care about community programs? You going soft, Duprees? Becoming one of those mushy-hearted fucking philanthropists?"

Her back stiffened, her stomach pitching as she flattened her palms onto the tabletop. She sucked in a breath, steeled her gaze.

"Thank you for thinking of me. Email me the particulars and I'll review them."

His eyes flashed fire. "Isabelle."

"I'm afraid I have another appointment. Take care, C. J."

She closed the laptop lid, ending the conversation. Letting her hands rest on the smooth chrome of her computer, she took a moment to steady herself. It wasn't as if she hadn't had shitty pitch meetings before. She'd experienced every kind of treatment from adoration to absolute dismissal. Her feelings weren't hurt, and she wasn't mad at C. J.

But she was also absolutely pissed off. Because she hated what he'd said, how arrogant he'd been about his prospects and the severe lack of respect he showed for not only her but a program that could very well make a big difference in someone's life. Many someones.

What bothered her more than all of that was the fact that he'd pegged her correctly when he'd asked why she cared. Because she wondered if, even a week ago, she would have.

Just because she wasn't a philanthropist didn't mean she

didn't care. Did people feel about her the way she now felt about C. J.? Like he was a completely egotistical asshat who didn't deserve her time? That he was what was wrong with so much of the world? Greed, tunnel vision, and a lack of caring for other people.

Her phone buzzed again. Picking it up, she ignored Kaia's message. She needed to update her on the meeting, to tell her to approach C. J.'s "friend." She opened her laptop again, set her phone beside her. They'd see just how friendly the two were when Isabelle put money on the line. She'd bet, double or nothing, that his "buddy" would sell him out for the right amount. And even if Isabelle didn't want to be part of the young women's business initiative, she'd hold the deed, making it so no one could take the space away from them.

Opening Google, intending to look up the program, her fingers hovered over the screen. What *did* people say about her? She'd never needed to know before, but then again, she'd never been so severely unsettled from a meeting that she wanted to buy a building out from someone even if it sat empty for the rest of her life. Normally she didn't run on retribution. Didn't hang onto the past because she was too busy looking forward.

But nothing about the past couple of days was normal.

Her left hand cramped around her phone, making her realize she was holding it too tight. It wasn't like she didn't *hear* things. She knew she was called names by some, respected by others, both by still more.

She would just look. Type in her name and just see if she was as bad as she worried she might be. According to other people. It's what she'd planned to do the other night before everything fell apart. She'd lived thirty-three years without googling her own damn name, and one hour with Elaina shot that to hell.

"Jesus Christ, you don't care about this." If she'd cared about what every person thought of her, she'd have riddled herself with anxiety long ago.

Shake it off. Move forward.

Elaina's voice trespassed again, like it knew how to bypass the barriers: *Trust me, this argument is over. And so is this trip.*

The trip *was* over. It was safe to look now.

Isabelle's fingers shook when she typed in her name.

Accolades. Success. Progress. Women in Business. That's what you'll find. Forbes, Vogue, Vanity Fair, The Economist. *An icon. An innovator.*

She'd never typed so slowly.

I-s-a-b-e-l-l-e C-a-r-o-l-y-n D-u-p-r-e-e-s

Her thumb hovered over Enter.

Mad at herself for the drama, even if no one was there to witness it, she slammed the pad of her thumb down.

Several images of her, but not her, came up first. She scrolled down.

> **<u>Ashland Progress</u>**
> April 10th, 2022—Ashland's Isabelle Duprees has created the go-to spot for all your event needs . . .

Another link read:

> Isabelle Duprees, Owner of Ashland Acres, brings your event to life . . .

And another:

> Isabelle C. Duprees, Owner of Ashland Acres, TripTips Best Venue Award three years in a row.

Busy Bride Magazine
Small Town Diamonds in the Rough.

She clicked the link, read the opening.

If you're looking for a small-town destination wedding full of sweet charm, check out Ashland Acres, which is quickly becoming Tennessee's hot spot for events of all sizes and sorts.

Isabelle didn't even realize she was shaking her head as she pressed the back arrow before continuing to scroll down.

There was another her. And not just any other her.

"No. *No*," she said, her voice ragged, like she'd forgotten how to use it.

She'd left home just before turning seventeen and had never returned. Not once. Not when her mother entered rehab the first time or the second. Not when her grandmother—her dad's mom—died or when her childhood best friend invited her to her wedding.

She'd had a sentimental lapse at twenty-one, when she graduated from MIT. The accomplishment, along with being on her own, with no family and very few friends, softened her thinking and, in a weak moment, she'd reached out to invite Elaina and her mom to the ceremony. The first two invitations she'd sent home went unanswered. It'd hurt more than she'd ever admit to anyone, including herself. Pride and, maybe the tiniest kernel of hope, made her phone, just to be sure they couldn't come.

Elaina had answered the phone, informing her that they wouldn't attend. Her sister had reminded Isabelle that she'd made her choice and walked away, informed her that they were better off without her and hung up. Isabelle hadn't let herself grieve that moment. Instead, she'd promised herself she'd never look back. Never let her past define her future. Never return to the town that took the thing that mattered most: her dad.

"It's over," she whispered, tears tracking down her cheeks. It was *supposed* to be over. But clearly, it wasn't.

Life was full of moments that forced a person to decide who they were going to be at the end of the day. Did she face this head-on? Go back to New York, her *home*, find Jonathan, and slam the door to her past shut? Go home, break it off with him, and never open herself up again so she wouldn't feel so goddamn vulnerable? Face the inevitable truth that she didn't want to leave things with Elaina like this? Admit that she was terrified to go back to the place where she'd been born—where, as Elaina had said, part of her had died? Sun Tzu's words flashed in her mind: *Even the finest sword plunged into salt water will eventually rust.*

It was stupid of her, stupid and shortsighted not to have realized this was where it was all leading. There was no outrunning the past. No burying it deep enough that it never surfaced. Beauty faded, silver tarnished, boxes—even figurative ones—disintegrated over time. Some things were, quite simply, inescapable.

Isabelle needed to go home. She needed to see her mother.

And goddamn it, I need Elaina to do it.

TWENTY-FOUR

On the rare occasions Isabelle had allowed herself to think about her sister, she'd always felt a small sliver of gratitude for the distance between them. There were some people that made you feel like you were surrounded by funhouse mirrors. Looking at them skewed your reflection, altered your image, and made you see yourself in a way that was beyond disturbing. A way that haunted a person in the middle of the night or the early hours of the morning when sleep wouldn't come. Regardless, now that she *wanted* Elaina, her sister was nowhere to be found. Because of course.

Isabelle waited at the reception desk, nails tapping against the counter, her breathing coming in short bursts. She couldn't be certain, but she was nearly positive the clerk on the phone was trying to avoid dealing with her.

The bellman from a few hours earlier came out of a swinging door behind the reception desk.

"Ahh, Ms. Duprees. I hope your meeting went well. Can I help you with something?"

The front desk clerk flashed the guy a grateful smile, confirming Isabelle's suspicions and letting her know she wasn't keeping her feelings locked down as well as she usually did. And that just pissed her off all over again.

"Have you seen my sister? Elaina Duprees. She's not answering the phone and she's cleared out of our room."

His lips twisted in an odd way, his gaze avoiding hers for a moment. "Yes. A car picked her up over an hour ago."

"A *car*? What car? We have a rental."

He splayed a hand on the desk, his eyes going soft. "She asked to go to the airport, Ms. Duprees. I arranged a pickup and drop off for her."

Isabelle reared back like he'd slapped her. She *left?* "She doesn't have a flight." They were driving. Together. It was Elaina's idea!

He shrugged. "I booked it for her. She was kind of upset."

Isabelle pulled in a deep breath, let it out slowly. "Please write down the information for me."

Once he'd done this, she checked out officially, loaded her things in the rental, and headed to the airport, cursing her sister under her breath.

Her phone buzzed constantly as she parked but none of the callers were Elaina. After paying for parking and fighting with crowds, Isabelle realized she couldn't get through security without purchasing a ticket.

She didn't even realize she was rushing, adrenaline coursing through her like a bad virus, until she saw Elaina sitting in one of the connected rows of chairs, staring out the window. The overhead speakers announced departures and listed names of people who were needed at their gates.

A baby with one little ponytail of hair sticking straight up reached out a chubby, cracker-filled hand across from Elaina, offering it to her. Isabelle watched Elaina shake her head, fake a smile, and turn her gaze back out the window.

Isabelle had bought a ticket to Tennessee, which worked

in both of their favors since she was going with her sister now. She'd thought, hoped, to come get her, get her back in the car, but this was easier. Quicker. It would be over sooner.

Rolling her suitcase behind her, she slid into the seat next to Elaina. It was petty of her but the look of surprise in her sister's gaze when she saw Isabelle felt like a small victory.

"What are you doing here?" Elaina glared at her, her jaw tightening.

"Why did you *leave*?" She hadn't meant to ask. She sure as hell hadn't meant to infuse her voice with so much emotion.

"I could ask you the same thing. The answer is probably similar. I left because there was no reason to stay. It's funny . . . you told me that years ago and it hurt. Now, I get it. You were right. No reason to stay. Just because we're sisters doesn't mean we need to be in each other's lives."

The words made Isabelle's heart want to crumple like a thin strip of paper. "I get that you're mad but you don't just take off and not tell someone."

Elaina looked at her, arched her brow.

Isabelle clenched her jaw, forced herself to calm down so she wouldn't make a scene. The baby across the aisle was curling into her mom and Isabelle felt a strange pang she couldn't identify and didn't want to think about.

"I went to university. That's hardly the same thing as taking off on me when we're on a trip together."

Elaina shrugged. "It was a stupid trip. A waste of time. And now it's over. I'm going home."

"I'm going with you."

Elaina sucked in a breath sharp enough to startle the baby. The mom rubbed circles on her back as Elaina turned her body, angled it toward Isabelle.

"What the hell are you doing? You wanted me gone, I'm gone.

Mission accomplished, *Isabelle.* I'm out of your life. Stay out of mine. You have no reason to come home. It's not even your home."

Hanging onto the straps of her purse like a lifeline, Isabelle did her best not to react to words she herself had said so many times. Words that sounded different coming from Elaina.

"The trip isn't over. I'm not getting out of your life. There's one more stop on this road trip from hell, and even after it's finished, after *we* see it through *together*, I won't disappear again. And I won't let you."

Elaina's smile was slow and mean. "You forget, Izzy-belle. You might rule your world but you don't rule mine. If I want you gone, you're gone. Even if you're sitting right next to me. I'll just pretend you don't exist. I've had plenty of practice."

Isabelle could feel other people's eyes on them, knew that they weren't being quiet enough to keep their shit private.

Elaina leaned back in the chair, stared straight ahead.

Isabelle considered her options. She never wanted to overplay her hand. But now wasn't the time for bluffing.

"There's one more stop and I'm scared to do it alone. I need you with me, Elaina. I need you to finish this with me."

It was only because she'd forced herself to look at Elaina while saying this that she saw the way her sister flinched, like her body couldn't absorb the words without a reaction.

Isabelle was nearly positive Elaina was going to hold true to the promise of pretending she didn't exist.

She didn't even turn her head when she asked, "How do you know it's the last stop?"

Gripping the strap tighter to stop the trembling in her hand, Isabelle leaned in. "This latest version of me lives in Ashland, Tennessee."

Elaina's eyes closed, her chin dropping to her chest. Isabelle's hand nearly reached out to touch her sister—to comfort her.

Elaina lifted her head, turned to Isabelle. "And what do you do in this other life?"

Shifting her feet, Isabelle's cheeks warmed. "I own a place called Ashland Acres. It's an event site, from what I gathered. Weddings, parties, whatever. It's weird." She went to parties. When she had to. She didn't typically plan them. Especially for other people.

Elaina's bark of laughter turned several heads their way and drew an annoyed glare from the young mom when the baby started to cry.

"Oh my goodness. That is fantastic. The woman who wouldn't even invite other children to her birthday parties is now playing hostess. That is some seriously poetic justice happening there."

Isabelle tried to shush her but her sister continued. "That doesn't even address the irony of the fact that Ms. You Can't Get Close to Me is planning people's happily-ever-afters."

The mom stood up, sent them both a dirty look and proceeded to pace with the discontent baby.

"I think I just provide the space. I doubt I'm orchestrating the big day," Isabelle snapped.

Elaina's posture relaxed. "I wonder if you walk around in your sky-high heels and power suits yelling out orders." Elaina shrugged. "Guess that wouldn't be all that different than the 'real' you."

The words shouldn't have hurt. Elaina had no idea what Isabelle actually did in her life—this one or any other version. So, why did it hurt like a razor nick to her heart for her sister to be so dismissive of everything about her?

"I'm really glad this is amusing you so much. It's fantastic that you think so little of me. I'm glad you can find the comedy in our acid trip from hell but try and remember, it's not real."

"But it is. Nothing makes sense, but it's as real as it gets. Don't you see? It doesn't matter what you do in any of these versions or the life you go back to. You won't forgive us. Not really. I bet things aren't okay between us in Ashland either. That they never will be. I have to laugh because I don't want to cry. We're never going to be okay."

The nonstop drone of the PA system grew louder as they started calling more gate numbers. Isabelle felt like her heart was hovering on the edge of a steep cliff. It pulsed hard and fast—too fast.

Without thinking, she let go of her purse, loosened her fingers, and reached out for Elaina's hand. She wrapped her own around it, put her head on her sister's shoulder and whispered the words she'd needed all those years ago and the ones she needed more than ever right this very minute. She just hoped they'd be enough. And that they'd be true.

"We're okay. We'll be okay."

IZ

TWENTY-FIVE

The flight was short but between the turbulence and Isabelle's swirling emotions, she felt like she was on the inside of a tornado. Of course, they weren't sitting together, so she had time to think and rethink and second guess and wonder what the hell she was doing with her time and her life. Maybe she'd wake up in her penthouse apartment and realize this was all a bad dream—a little trip down a rabbit hole she had never wanted to explore in the first place.

"Can I get you a drink?" The flight attendant's tag said Alex.

She hadn't even heard or seen her approach. She nodded, following up with, "God, yes."

Alex with the short hair, happy smile, and knowing gaze reached for a napkin. "That kind of day already?"

"You have no idea," Isabelle said, her fingers wrapped around the arm rests. "I'll have a vodka tonic with a lime, please."

The older woman next to her, who was watching a movie with a lead male actor whose name Isabelle couldn't remember but was pretty certain had asked her out at a party a year earlier, leaned over Isabelle's lap.

"Make it two but I'll take Seven up instead of tonic," she said, winking at Isabelle.

For a second, she got caught up staring at the woman whose quick smile and tightly coiled gray hair reminded her of her grandmother—her dad's mom.

"Okay, but if you two ladies start getting rowdy . . ." Alex said, reaching into one of the cart drawers before saying in a lower voice, "I'm going to have to sneak back here and join you."

The looks-can-be-deceiving-grandmotherly woman chuckled. "This flight isn't long enough for me to get rowdy."

Alex *tsked*, passing over their drinks. "Something tells me that's a shame."

When they pushed on, Isabelle held her drink, stared straight ahead at the screen she hadn't bothered touching. There was nothing that could take her mind off all this, so why try?

"The way you're sitting in that seat, honey, you need more than vodka. Fancy girl like you, you look like you need a massage, a week's vacation, and maybe an entire day in bed with someone special." She shrugged, tipped her glass back. "Or yourself. Whatever makes you smile and takes some of the starch out of your spine."

Isabelle found herself amused rather than irritated. "It's been a long . . . few days."

"Always found it strange how time could fly so fast while some days drag so slow. Hell, I feel like I went to bed at twenty-five, woke up fifty, blinked, and turned seventy-five."

Turning her head, Isabelle sipped her own vodka. "If you're seventy-five, I'd like your skin-care secrets please."

The woman laughed, shook her head. "You a real estate agent, politician, or a lawyer?"

Isabelle laughed. "None of the above, why?"

"They're usually the ones with the smooth lines. My name is Maggie. What's yours?"

"Isabelle. It's nice to meet you, Maggie. And it's not a line if it's true."

"Well, thank you, darlin'. No secrets, really. I keep myself hydrated, play nine holes of golf nearly every day, and never go to sleep with my makeup on."

The drink turned Isabelle's stomach and she wished she'd gone for ginger ale. "Golf every day?"

Downing the rest of her drink, Maggie withdrew her earbuds, tucking them into the top of her shirt. "All my friends go on about yoga this and yoga that. No thank you. I want to move and stretch without standing in the same spot. People underestimate how much stretching and range of motion are involved with this sport." She leaned closer, a little twinkle lighting her gaze. "Trust me, keeps me plenty flexible enough."

If she'd been midsip, Isabelle likely would have choked. Apparently, she had the type of face that encouraged her sister and older women to share way too much.

"I'll have to consider it." She leaned her head back against the seat, trying to remember the last time she'd flown coach. She actually didn't travel a whole lot. Too busy. Too eager to prove herself every minute of every day. Too driven. Or so she'd told herself. But maybe she was just keeping her schedule packed so tight in an effort to avoid facing her feelings about anything. Or anyone.

"Whatever's giving you those forehead creases will find a way to work itself out. No sense stewing on it. Best thing about getting old, other than naps, is you stop worrying so much about whether or not everything will be okay."

Isabelle turned her head without lifting it. "My grandmother used to say something similar." She hadn't thought about that, about her grandma, in years. She'd been a bright spot when Isabelle felt shrouded in darkness. "She'd tell me the only thing worrying changes is your heart rate."

Maggie laughed, a deep, rolling chuckle that warmed the air around Isabelle. "She wasn't wrong. When you're young, you're so focused on what's ahead or running from what's behind, you forget to stand still and say, 'Who the hell am I right this minute?'"

"Sometimes you do that and you realize you don't like who you are," Isabelle said quietly, unsure why she was disclosing undigested feelings to this stranger.

"If that's the truth, you change it. You've got success written all over you, from your perfect posture to your fancy pants. Something tells me if you want to change something, you'll do it."

Isabelle nodded, grateful for this quiet moment with someone who could look at her and not want more than she could give. Someone who didn't see all her flaws and mistakes. Someone she hadn't disappointed.

Maggie popped her earbuds back in and went back to her show, but Isabelle forced herself to settle into her own thoughts. Even if she wasn't willing to believe the universe was twisting her into knots in an effort to make her reevaluate things, something inside of her had slowed in the last few days, switched gears. And it made her question her direction. Worse, it made her question herself.

Elaina didn't slow down or wait for Isabelle, who moved through all the tedium of deboarding and finding her suitcase—Elaina hadn't had to check any luggage—without so much as a cursory glance from her sister. It wasn't until they were outside the small airport that Isabelle caught up.

"I have a car coming. It's four minutes out," she said, the thick heat making her stomach roll.

"My car is parked in long-term," Elaina snipped.

Isabelle grabbed her sister's arm, turning her so they faced each other. "Can we set aside the attitude until we figure things out?"

Elaina pulled her arm free. "What's to figure out?"

People pushed and milled, greeted and said goodbyes, hurried around them, the movement making Isabelle feel very exposed.

"You can't take your car. You can't go home to your house. Kaia booked us a hotel and scheduled an appointment tomorrow for us to meet with Isabelle . . . me . . . she goes by Iz. Iz Duprees."

Elaina's brows pushed together. "Cute. That's tomorrow's problem. I want to sleep in my own bed, and honestly, I need a break from this."

"Well, that's really fantastic, but you started this with me and until we figure out what the hell is going on, you can't traipse around town possibly running into yourself. Or me. Or the other me. Jesus." The breath and energy whooshed out of her in one hard exhale. "I hate this."

Elaina's lips pursed, twisted. "Wait. You think there's a different version of me here?"

"I don't know. But until we do, we should . . . I have no idea." How could she have no idea? Sorting through and solving problems were her specialities. *In business.* Her chest tightened uncomfortably. "I never should have started this, but I can't go back. We're here and we need to do this. But . . . yeah, in this version there has to be another you. It complicates something that already makes no sense." People were looking at them and she realized her voice, her pitch, had risen to alarming levels.

Elaina took her sister's arm as a large black SUV pulled up to the curb. "Okay. Breathe. Calm down. Take a breath. Jesus

Christ." Her nails dug into the sensitive skin of her biceps. "Breathe, Isabelle. This looks like Kaia's preferred mode of transportation, so I'm guessing this is for us."

A large man dressed in a black suit who looked more like a secret service agent than a driver came around the front.

"Isabelle Duprees?"

"That's me." *One version of me.* For the first time since she was seventeen years old, sitting alone on a bus to Boston from this very town, she was unsure of who she was. Or who she wanted to be.

They rode in silence to Ashland's version of a hotel. One story, no view to speak of, but the rooms were clean and the fitness center was decent.

Most importantly, they were close enough to Nashville that she could drown herself in hot chicken. She might not miss much about the south but her mouth watered at the thought of eating her weight in the fried food no other state managed to get just right. She and her grandmother had often made it together. They'd spent a lot of time in each other's company with her mom holding odd jobs that never lasted long. When her mom and grandmother had a falling out, Elaina had, of course, sided with Catalina. Since their mom didn't check on Isabelle's whereabouts much, she continued to spend time with her dad's mom when she could.

"Not sure how long you're staying," the driver said as he parked the SUV, "But you're in time for the Ashland Mural Festival. It starts tomorrow. Local artists are showing their work on the sides of businesses. Most of the shops will take part, so you'll get some great deals on food and drinks if you decide to walk through town."

"I can only imagine. Art on the side of Coupon Clippers. Can't wait," Isabelle muttered under her breath as she released her seatbelt, hooked her purse over her shoulder.

Elaina snapped her seatbelt open, let it fly back into its holder with no care or ease. "Listening to you complain about where we come from and what makes our home special will no doubt be the best part of this experience."

The driver didn't say anything else and Isabelle couldn't blame him. She and her sister didn't make casual conversation comfortable. They needed to get back on the same page. Or in the same book at least.

It was probably her imagination, but she felt like Elaina was sizing up the desk clerk. The name, Shayna, wasn't familiar to Isabelle but she hadn't lived here in years. Not that she expected much to have changed but she probably wouldn't recognize too many people. It wasn't like she'd been the popular one, the one who charmed a crowd and made people laugh. No, she'd always been seen as the moody, reserved, stick-up-her-ass sister who couldn't cut loose and let things go. She didn't spend time on social media, so she had no idea what anyone she used to know might be up to these days.

It doesn't matter, she reminded herself. *This isn't actually your life.*

She felt like she was losing her mind and her grip on reality.

Elaina nudged her, bringing her back in a way only her sister could. "Snap out of it. Pull yourself together."

When they got into the room, Elaina looked around. "You could spring for two rooms, you know."

Without even checking the bed, the quality of the linens, the cleanliness of the pillow, Isabelle threw her purse, her overnight bag, and her laptop on the comforter. She sank down, then looked up at Elaina, who stood beside the other double bed.

"Why are you so mad at me?" Isabelle stared at her older sister, her emotions toppling around like a drunk, making her heart ache and her head hurt. "Stop being so goddamn mad at me."

Elaina sat down across from her, the space between them so small that their knees nearly touched. "I could say the same to you."

"I'm not," she said quickly, watching her sister's brows arch. "I'm trying. I've spent years trying to bury my feelings, and in the last four days, I've had to confront them all. It's a lot. And I want this finished. I don't know what will happen after this, but I want this part of it finished so there can be just one version of me." She pressed the heels of her hands into her eyes, not caring about her carefully applied make up. "I can't deal with more than one of me."

"You and me both," Elaina said with amusement in her tone.

With her eyes still covered, Isabelle felt her sister's hand on her knee. She dropped her arms and looked at Elaina, facing her past, her future, and this moment here and now.

Quietly, Isabelle said, "I don't know what we'll find here or why this is happening, but I know there's no one else I could do this with."

Elaina blinked a suspicious sheen out of her gaze. "There's no one else I'd do it for. What do you think happened with this other you? Did you stay or come back?"

Isabelle shook her head. "I don't know. I really don't."

"In good news, Shayna is a friend of mine. A good friend. She didn't recognize me or seem weirded out."

"Okay. That's something." She looked around the room, trying to keep her breathing steady, her heart rate inside a normal range. Over the desk, a large canvas print pulled her gaze. Swirls of color, dark and light, created movement and energy, so much so that it almost pulsed with life, and definitely stood out in an otherwise drab and nondescript room.

"Are you all right?"

She turned her head back, saw Elaina's gaze flit to the picture then back to her. Smoothing the blanket under her fingers, she sorted through the things she'd learned.

Isabelle nodded. "Considering the circumstances, yes. Our meeting at Ashland Acres is for eleven a.m."

"Are we looking for a wedding venue? What's our cover story?"

She hadn't thought that far ahead. "We could do that. Are you getting married any time soon?"

Elaina only laughed. "How about a fortieth birthday party?"

Isabelle smirked. "Sure. We'll say we're planning ahead for you."

When Elaina actually stuck her tongue out at Isabelle, it made her laugh and that eased some of the tension that was making her bones feel brittle.

"It'll be interesting to see a different version of what our town could have been."

She caught herself wondering what the "real" version was like now. She almost asked. But she'd already shown enough weaknesses for one day.

"I'm starving."

Elaina grinned. "Hot chicken?"

"You read my mind."

"Or maybe I know you better than you think."

They cleaned up, got ready, together. They didn't talk more than they had to—which included Elaina insisting Isabelle borrow a pair of jeans and a tank top so she didn't stand out like a 'queen on a haybale'—but they didn't fight. The tension didn't evaporate but it was no longer oppressive. A few more days. She'd be home, preferably in Jonathan's arms after finalizing the details on the Hell's Kitchen property, in just a few days.

She was Isabelle Duprees. She forged her own path, left a trail for others to follow. Surely, she could handle a couple days in her hometown.

TWENTY-SIX

About a fifteen-minute walk from the hotel was a diner that Elaina claimed made the best hot chicken outside of Hattie B's in Nashville. Since she didn't feel like getting back in the car, Isabelle was happy to hoof it and see if her sister was right. She hadn't expected the walk to trigger memories since they'd lived on the other side of Ashland, so she was surprised when long-buried thoughts infiltrated.

Sitting across from each other on fairly uncomfortable pleather seats, Isabelle couldn't help but see the full circle of it all—the first diner and now this one. She glanced around, pleased to see no other version of herself would be serving them.

"Hey, there. What can I get y'all?" a blond, curly-haired waitress asked. She looked like she belonged on the beaches of California rather than small-town Ashland.

"Hey, Carrie," Elaina said, glancing down at the menu. "I'll get a large cola."

Isabelle had watched the way the waitress's blue eyes widened at the use of her name and waited for Elaina to realize her misstep.

When Elaina looked up, her smile faltered, then flattened. "Uh, do you have Pepsi or Coke?"

Carrie nodded. "It's Pepsi. The real stuff, not the knock off cola. How'd you know my name?"

Elaina's smile came back without hesitation. "The other waitress." She jutted her chin subtly to an older waitress delivering food a couple of booths over. She'd sat them at this table. "She said to take a seat and Carrie would be right with us."

Isabelle wrapped her fingers around the menu, let her breath out slowly as the waitress laughed, put a hand on her chest.

"Oh, gosh. That makes sense. Thought you were one of them psychics or something. We've got all sorts coming in for the festival. Last year, a man tried to tell me he was my long-lost grandfather."

"Was he?" Elaina asked, genuine curiosity in her tone.

"Nah. My grandpa's never been lost a day in his life. Sorry about that. Now, one Pepsi for you and how about you?"

Isabelle's stomach wasn't entirely settled yet, so she opted for water and they both ordered the hot chicken platter special with fries and tater tots. She'd need to spend a solid week in her gym after this trip.

When the waitress left them with their drinks, Isabelle leaned forward. "How do you really know her?"

Elaina was looking at something on her phone, a little line forming between her brows. "Oh, our . . ." She stopped, looked up. "Just, we're both locals. That's all. I need to make a call. I'll be back in a minute."

Watching her sister step outside the restaurant, Isabelle tried not to think about how easily Elaina could cover her tracks and how she hadn't done that a moment earlier while looking at her phone. She'd smoothed over her faux pas with Carrie like a pro.

But something was up, either with the call she was making or how she really knew the waitress.

Deciding she had enough to worry about without whatever her sister clearly didn't want to talk about, Isabelle pulled out her own phone, saw a new text from Kaia.

> I've arranged a flight for you from Nashville for the day after tomorrow. Is that enough time for you to do whatever you need to do?

Isabelle hadn't expected any of this to take this much time.

> It'll have to be because I can't stay here longer than that. I'm more than ready to be home.

Kaia responded quickly.

> I could come to you. Help with whatever you're doing.

Isabelle hated that a big part of her would feel comforted by that.

> I'm fine. I need you there. How's the paperwork on the Hell's Kitchen building?

Isabelle knew she was brushing her assistant off with her response and it wouldn't go unnoticed. Kaia's reply made it clear that her 'leave it alone' message was understood.

You were right. He didn't even try to negotiate when I told him you'd give a fifty grand over the asking price. He just wants to liquidate. CJ Rowland has left several unpleasant messages for you.

Isabelle smiled.

I'm good with that. Keep deleting them.

Isabelle waited, listening to the murmuring and chatting around her as the three dots appeared, disappeared, and appeared again. Kaia wasn't the only one who could read people.

Spit it out.

The text that came through surprised Isabelle.

Will you see your mother? I could do some digging. Make sure you don't get blindsided by anything.

Her heart squeezed. She paid Kaia well, but she paid Jasper well too. He didn't make her feel like it would matter to him if things went sideways, if something in any version of her life hurt her. Had she overlooked, or put aside, how much she mattered to Kaia? Because it seemed like the younger woman really cared. She wanted to ignore the idea because if she was wrong, if she let herself care for Kaia as a friend, as a *close* friend, as well as an employee, she ran the risk of being let down. Of being rejected.

You make multimillion dollar deals, negotiate with some of the richest people in the world, and admitting you need her friendship is what scares you?

It's okay. I'm okay. Stop worrying.

She'd spent so long behind self-imposed shields, it was both a relief and concern to learn people actually cared about her well-being.

Who says I'm worried?

Isabelle smiled.

I'VE GOT THIS

Kaia's response was, like the woman herself, quick and to the point.

I had no doubt. Talk soon.

She tucked her phone away. So far she'd dealt with two other versions of herself, choices she'd never considered making, her sister, and coming to grips with a volume of feelings for the people in her life that she'd been shoving down. At this point, nothing could blindside her.

"Here you go," a familiar voice she couldn't place said as delicious-smelling food slid onto the table.

Her gaze moved slowly, along tan forearms covered in swirls of black ink, up over a navy shirt stretched tight by a muscular chest that had clearly filled out over the years, up to a man's slightly bearded face, to a smile she hadn't seen in a forever, eyes she'd trusted and fallen into a lifetime ago.

"Can I get you anything else?" His dark hair was pushed back like he'd run his hands through it. She knew, from memory, he did this out of frustration because he got busy and forgot to cut it. Because he was always on the move, doing something, and inevitably that lush hair would get in his way.

His brown eyes held her captive, jolting her with the reminder that she'd been capable of love once. Of being loved. And wanting it.

"Sorry about that," Elaina said as she came toward the booth.

Isabelle watched her eyes widen, her breath catch.

"Oh," Elaina breathed.

They locked gazes, both sisters recognizing this man despite the years.

Or maybe it hasn't been years for Elaina.

"Yes, *oh*," Isabelle said quietly.

"This looks amazing," Elaina said, once again covering with ease.

Max looked at Elaina but his gaze came back to Isabelle's swiftly. Held.

"I promise you it is."

And when he made a promise, he didn't break it.

"I'm sorry," he said, stepping back. "I don't mean to stare. You . . . your eyes. You remind me of someone."

The girl who broke your heart? The one who left you behind when she ran off to Boston? The one who said she loved you back after you said you'd figure out a way to be together. The one who never followed through. The one who broke her promises.

"She gets that a lot," Elaina said quietly. She sank into the booth across from Isabelle.

Max walked back to the kitchen, but not before turning to look at Isabelle one more time.

"Wow. I haven't seen Max in . . . I don't even know. He went away around the same time as you, came back when he finished college. Then he disappeared again."

Isabelle tried to focus on the food, not the sensation swamping her, one she didn't often feel—regret.

"Then why is he here now?" She shook her head. She wasn't here to follow up on her high school sweetheart. She wasn't here to get sucked into the past. She was here to put it all behind her so she could focus on her future. "It doesn't matter. Who did you call?"

"MYOB." Elaina pulled her plate closer, dug in.

Isabelle nearly snorted out a laugh. "Jesus, you're still twelve. Mind your own business?"

Around a mouthful of chicken, Elaina grinned. "That's right. Glad you remember."

Isabelle dug into her meal. She hadn't realized just how hungry she was with everything going on. Every now and then, she felt like someone was watching her, but when she glanced over to the pass where they put up the food orders, Max wasn't looking her way. He'd been a piece of her past, so she'd had to cut him loose. But she couldn't escape the truth of it all—she'd never let another man in after him. Until Jonathan.

So much for not being blindsided. What was the purpose of him being in this version? She'd figured out by now that she needed to learn from her mistakes. That was the point, right? God, what if there was absolutely no point?

"You know," Elaina said, unfolding her napkin, "When you think too hard, your features become so still it's like you're not even real. It's like you're a cement statue of yourself. Stop overthinking."

"Easy for you to say. Did you just run into your ex?"

"No." Elaina picked up a tater tot and a fry, dragged them through ketchup, and ate them together.

"Do you have a significant other?"

"Do you care?"

Isabelle opened her own napkin and wiped her fingers while she steadied her nerves. When she felt like she was back in control, she met her sister's waiting gaze. "I do. Are you happy? Are you in a relationship? What do you do? How come you never left Ashland?"

Picking up a fry, hoping she appeared nonchalant about the answers, Isabelle let the questions lie between them.

Elaina picked up a fry too. "I'm happy. Really happy. I have a boyfriend. He's a good guy. We're good together. I'm an artist. A successful one. I don't know if my shop—it's kind of a shop slash gallery for local artisans—will be here in this version of your life, but if you ever come back of your own volition, you can visit it. I know you have a good eye for art. We both got that from Mom, and I was impressed by the pieces in your penthouse. You'll like the gallery. I never left because I didn't feel like I could. You weren't the only person that life threw circumstances and curveballs at. But honestly? There was nowhere else I wanted to be. You send enough money—or should I say Kaia sends enough money—that I can visit anywhere I want to. But this is my home."

An artist. Isabelle didn't even realize she was smiling as images ran through her brain of Elaina's style and unique flair. The memory of their mother pulling out paints, glue, recyclables, and godforsaken glitter that got in every damn place, letting them create to their heart's content. Isabelle was never great at it, but her sister had left her speechless more than once with the beauty she could dream up and bring to life.

"I'd forgotten how much you loved to paint. Oh my God," Isabelle said, remembering the picture in the hotel. It'd sucked her in, and she wasn't entirely sure why. Until now. "The painting in the hotel is yours."

Elaina ducked her gaze, focused on her food. "It is. An old one. It's strange because I haven't sold any to the hotels around here."

Immediately, Isabelle pictured her sister's art hanging on the walls of her boutique hotel. Of Jonathan's hotels.

"So whatever version of you we could meet, you're still an artist," Isabelle said.

"I guess so."

There was something about her sister's tone Isabelle couldn't decipher.

It was on the tip of her tongue to ask about their mother. To ask about the last twelve years. To fill in some of the gaps.

As Elaina requested the check, Isabelle felt like a coward for staying silent. It was good, comforting, to know her sister had found success and happiness. Isabelle expected nothing less. But she didn't particularly want a lot of details about how good everyone's life had gone without her in it.

No. She was better off only knowing what she needed to. Just enough to get back to herself. The version of herself that felt most true. The one she'd shed this town to create.

In other words, a coward, a voice in the back of her mind whispered.

TWENTY-SEVEN

When Elaina finished getting ready, they headed out for the day. She'd once again convinced Isabelle that jeans and a light sweater were a better look than her "uptight city girl" attire.

Isabelle had tossed and turned all night, dreaming of Jonathan, remembering Max, falling into memories of her parents and her grandmother. At one point, it had all jumbled together in her brain and everyone she'd left behind or hurt stood in one room, like a lineup of suspects, asking her, "Why?"

She was tired of hiding, of pushing down her feelings in an effort to have control. The truth was, ignoring something didn't make her *not* feel it. It just let her not dwell on it. But when she closed her eyes, pictured Jonathan's face, the way his eyes crinkled when he laughed, the way he looked in an Armani suit or nothing at all, her heart felt so full, it threatened to burst. When she wanted something, professionally, she went all in. She didn't hesitate longer than it took to make sure she had all the pins set up for a strike. Was there a chance she could do the same in her personal life?

Stop being a coward.

Despite demanding it in her mind, her fingers shook as she typed the message.

There's a charity event to promote and fundraise for the Young Women in Business initiative I mentioned.

Just when she'd convinced herself that he wasn't going to respond, Jonathan sent back a single word.

Okay

She hated this. Okay, *what?* Was she supposed to decipher that one word? *Give him more to go on.*

IT'S NEXT MONTH

Another one-word response.

And

Telling herself that he'd put in the work up to this point and it was her turn now, she added the rest.

And I'm attending. I agreed to speak

To distract herself from everything going on, she'd kept a dialogue open with Jenaya Davis, who was more than a reporter. She was spearheading the campaign and looking for powerful women in the New York area to help her launch the idea, make it a success.

After a moment, another message from Jonathan appeared.

You don't like to speak in public

It made her feel exposed, and a little happy, that he knew that about her.

It feels important

Everything about this moment was important. Including his response.

Definitely. And valuable. You have a hell of a lot to offer

"Your turn," she whispered to herself as she typed the message.

Will you come with me?

She exhaled sharply. There. She'd done it. Somehow asking him felt a lot like asking Max if he wanted to go to the spring dance when they were sixteen. Every bit as frightening, and a little exciting.

As your driver?

She laughed out loud, didn't even cut the sound off when Elaina came out dressed and ready for the day.

No

He wasn't finished being a smartass.

Coat holder?

She smiled, bit down on her lip.

Try again

A near giggle left her mouth at his reply. Who the hell was she?

MUSCLE?

Another laugh.

Elaina sat on the bed, slipped on a pair of black flats to complement her skinny jeans. "Whoever that is, keep them forever. I don't think I've ever seen you laugh and smile like that."

She sent her sister a glare with absolutely no heat in it.

As my . . .

Shit. Her what? Boyfriend? That made it sound like she *was* sixteen again.

As the man who gets to escort you to these things from now on regardless of what's printed on Page Six?

She didn't let herself overthink or hesitate.

Yes

She could kiss him for knowing her so well and liking—loving—her anyway. His next response confirmed how well he knew her.

I think you like me 😉

Her heart jumped around in her chest, and she sent him a final message.

I just might.

"We should go," Elaina said. "We'll grab some coffee and then head to Second Street." She stood, trying to peek at her sister's phone.

Isabelle sighed. All of these feelings were making her a sap. But as Elaina tapped her foot exaggeratedly, Isabelle's body begged for caffeine and a smile hovered on her lips—she didn't have it in her to fight the emotions roiling around her entire body.

They walked to Second Street, the heart of downtown Ashland. The closer they walked to places that were so familiar to a distant part of her, the more she felt like she had never left. Streets she'd walked with her dad, her mom, and Elaina. Shops she'd visited. Even if the store wasn't the same as it had once been, the brick buildings and false fronts remained. Time could pass, things could change, but the foundation stayed the same.

She looked over at Elaina as she stopped in front of a coffee shop, her lips turned down. "This is where my shop is. Was?" She looked at Isabelle for confirmation.

"I'm barely keeping all of this straight as it is. If you left a shop behind, then I think *is.* Either you don't have a shop in this life or it's somewhere else. But at least you know it's there, in the life you get to go back to."

A strange look passed over her older sister's features. Isabelle had been so scared about her own shows of weakness, she hadn't realized how hard Elaina was fighting to hide her own.

"What?" She reached out tentatively at first, then with more confidence, put a hand on Elaina's shoulder. "What is it, E?"

"I bought the shop using some of the money you sent. I

never said thank you. I've never said it, but it's set us up. For the rest of our lives, really." She pulled in a breath. "Thank you."

Tears prickled under her lids as Isabelle firmed her lips, giving a short nod. "You don't need to thank me," she said when her emotions settled.

A tall, long-haired man used his back to push the door in front of them open. They backed up, letting the guy, whose hands were full with a tray of coffees, out so they could go in. He smiled at them, told them to have a nice day.

The shop was cute, a bit of a Starbucks knockoff with the shorter version of a farmhouse-style table running up the center, chalkboard signs, and cozy chairs set up to facilitate conversations. It was busy, most of the seats full, a line up at the till, baristas making drinks and grabbing pastries as music hummed through the speakers.

"Looks popular. Maybe I should open a coffee shop," Elaina said, looking around. "It could be tourists. We get more every year."

"Is the mural festival annual?"

Elaina shook her head. "No. I can't wait to see them all. It's a great idea. I'm curious whose it was. I'm guessing between the art and the local businesses joining in, it'll be a lot of socializing and hanging out." She leaned closer to Isabelle. "It's going to be weird to see people I know who don't know me."

Isabelle arched her brows. "Weird seems to be the theme of this road trip."

They moved up in the line as people exited or found seats, and names were called out to pick up their orders at the end of the counter. Little tables lined the left side, near windows that allowed customers to look out onto the street. It was already busy with tourists and locals wandering in packs.

Two things happened simultaneously. As Isabelle's gaze moved around the inside of the coffee shop and landed on an older, elegant, and shockingly familiar-looking woman sitting with a dark-haired, bright-eyed girl of about eight or nine, Elaina sucked in a wheezing breath beside her, abruptly gripping Isabelle's arm.

The older woman turned toward Isabelle, and for the first time in twelve years, she looked into her mother's eyes. Her heart felt like it filled with cement and dropped all the way to her stomach. She thought that was the reason for Elaina's jaws-of-life grip on her arm but when she looked over, she noticed that her sister was staring at herself. Another version of herself.

If anyone knew how surreal this moment could be, it was Isabelle. It'd been a long time since she and her sister had had anything in common. This other Elaina somehow looked older, maybe a little more tired. That didn't keep the smile from her face as she passed a paper bag to a waiting customer across the counter, said hello to another. Makeup-free, with her hair pulled back from her face, she looked a bit thinner but much the same.

Isabelle was caught looking back and forth between her mother and the other Elaina.

When the woman, Catalina, *her mom*, spoke to the little girl, Isabelle started. The little girl's eyes were much like her own. Like Elaina's. Like their mother's.

The other Elaina came around the counter, greeting customers and excusing herself to pass between them. She carried a white to-go cup and a brown paper bag. When she stopped in front of Isabelle and Elaina, they both held their breath.

"Good morning, ladies. Excuse me, please."

She didn't recognize them. She didn't *see* them. Not really.

Elaina still held her arm, and it hurt, but Isabelle let the pressure of her fingertips tether her to the moment.

"Here you go, sweetie." Barista Elaina gave the bag to the girl before leaning over to press a kiss to the top of her head.

A full body tremor racked Isabelle's body. Inside and out. Her skin felt cold.

"You listen to Grandma, okay? I'll meet up with you in a few hours when I'm off."

"You work too hard," Catalina said to her.

"Don't start, Mom. When bills pay themselves, I'll quit," she said, winking at the little girl.

"The murals paid good money," Catalina said in a tone Isabelle could never stay away long enough not to recognize. It was her *I've-said-this-too-many-times* tone.

"Mom. Enough. It's busy. I need to take some stuff out of the oven."

"We're starting with ice cream," the little girl said, hopping up from her spot.

Catalina rose a little more stiffly. She'd aged well but there was no denying the years had been hard on her. "You're not supposed to tell her that, cutie."

Barista Elaina tapped the little girl on the nose. "I know all of Charlie's secrets, Mom. Besides, it was my idea. Fill up on the best stuff first."

Isabelle felt her heartbeat in a third-person sort of way. It beat heavily over her skin, along her spine, at the base of her head, but she wasn't sure she was breathing.

Charlie. Their dad's name.

"Let's go," Catalina said, drink in one hand, taking the little girl's with the other.

Shuffling closer, her gaze once again met Isabelle's, held, and a flicker of something in the older woman's eyes made Isabelle feel like she'd been punched in the stomach. It snapped the breath into her lungs.

Catalina smiled, moved past them. Barista Elaina rounded the counter from the other side and went back to helping customers.

Isabelle felt like she was pulling herself down from the sky, a wayward balloon that had drifted too far, as she sifted through the strangeness, desperate for a glimmer of reality.

"You have a kid in this version," Isabelle whispered, finally looking at her sister.

Elaina dropped her hand, folded her arms in front of her like she was trying to take up less space.

Isabelle studied her sister's profile, saw the hard set of her jaw. She looked unsettled, a bit upset.

They moved forward again until there was only one more customer in front of them.

"Aren't you going to say anything?" Isabelle hadn't meant to hiss out the words like an accusation, but thoughts were tumbling in her own brain. Surely, Elaina was freaking out a bit.

"What do you want me to say?"

Elaina moved to the counter, smiled at . . . herself, who took their order . . . and then moved to the end of the counter to wait. Isabelle could do nothing more than follow.

Her sister didn't meet her gaze while they waited. She didn't look behind when they grabbed their drinks and she led the way out onto the street.

She didn't say a word as they stood in the middle of the road, which had been closed off for foot traffic.

Isabelle watched her the way she might a cobra ready to strike. And then it clicked.

"You're not surprised."

Elaina looked at her. "What?"

"You're not surprised you have a kid."

Elaina sipped her drink.

"I couldn't wrap my head around Belle being pregnant," Isabelle said, her voice unsteady.

"So?"

"So you barely blinked when you saw the little girl. It shocked you to see yourself. But it didn't surprise you to see Charlie."

It felt strange to say the name. Sweet and painful.

"You knew. You knew because . . ." Isabelle started but stopped because it couldn't be true. It couldn't be real. There was no way.

Elaina's face was unreadable as she looked at Isabelle. "You're wrong. I didn't know I had a kid in this version."

Isabelle waited, tense like she was about to zipline across a canyon on a fraying rope.

"I didn't know Charlotte would be in this version."

"Charlotte?"

"Yes. My daughter. Charlie. I have a daughter. Apparently in more than one version of my life. But the only one I knew about was the one I stepped outside to call last night. The one I've been messaging and calling and chatting with the entire time we've been on this bizzarro quest."

Isabelle would have stumbled, possibly fallen, if her body wasn't glued to the spot, if every cell in her body from the neck down wasn't frozen.

"You have a daughter."

Elaina nodded. "I do. And she's everything to me."

Isabelle couldn't breathe but still, she pushed the words out. "I have a niece."

Elaina's jaw twitched. "You do."

TWENTY-EIGHT

Isabelle couldn't pull in a full breath. There was something obstructing her airway. Words? Regrets? Things she absolutely could not undo.

"Izzy-belle," Elaina whispered, crowding her like she was corralling a spooked horse.

"I just . . ." She stopped, didn't know what to say. She just needed to breathe. Which seemed impossible.

"I have to go to the appointment." She turned, nearly rammed right into someone, mumbled an apology, and started walking.

"Isabelle, please."

"I have to go to the appointment." The appointment. To meet herself. One thing at a time.

Elaina hurried alongside her, but she didn't slow down, didn't talk.

They walked a couple of blocks, ignoring hellos from shop owners setting up and getting ready to take advantage of the extra foot traffic the festival would bring.

"I'm going with you," Elaina said, nearly pitching forward when Isabelle stopped without warning.

"No. I need to do this by myself. Please."

The anguish in Elaina's eyes was palpable. Isabelle felt it in her bones. Her sister leaned closer. "Don't you use this as an excuse to disappear on me. Do not take off on me without a word."

Elaina had every right to demand that because they both knew Isabelle had done it before.

"I won't. I'll find you when I'm finished. I won't leave. I promise."

Like she was measuring the truth behind those last two words, Elaina stared at her, lips trembling, nearly undoing the tangled knots tightening themselves in Isabelle's stomach.

"I'll see you soon," her sister said.

Giving a curt nod, Isabelle placed her coffee in a nearby garbage can. She couldn't put anything in her stomach right now. Walking through the crowd, weaving through strangers, Isabelle got lost in her own head, not seeing the faces she passed.

A niece. Her big sister had a kid. And she'd missed all of it.

There was anger simmering, but other feelings burned brighter. Sadness at having missed everything. Regret over deleting messages, not picking up calls. Confusion at how she could know so much and yet not know something of such importance. Despair from knowing that even if she changed the course she was on, there was so much she could never undo.

One side of her brain screamed that Elaina should have told her, but the other side reminded her that she'd closed and locked all the doors, chained them, built a wall so strong and so high, nothing could get through. But this did. *This* seeped through the cracks that had settled in over time, widening them, weakening the wall, and possibly unlocking the door. But before she could even consider walking through it, she needed to finish this.

Ashland Acres was a half dozen blocks up from Second Street. One would think that would make it Eighth Street but other than Second, none of Ashland's streets had numbers. They were all folksy, woodsy names like Dandelion Lane, Foxglove Road, or the street where the three-story home stood like a proud sentinel, Lilac Avenue. No rhyme, no reason. No order. If you didn't know where something was, someone would give you landmarks as a guide rather than streets.

Like any other town, small or large, there were pockets of upscale with dashes of low income. This part of Ashland was older and what Isabelle would call *old money*. The trees that lined the streets, adding pops of color with their blossoms, had been planted long before her time.

Nestled in a multiacre corner lot of a residential neighborhood, the Ashland House, as it'd once been called, had also existed longer than Isabelle. As she stared at the grandeur of the three-story home with its wraparound porch and turrets—a mini castle in the middle of nowhere—she was struck by the realization that, like her, this place had been many versions of itself.

As a child, it'd been a fairy-tale home. Her mother would take them on walks and they'd make up stories about who lived inside. As teens, they called it the Ghost House because at that time, it'd been abandoned for years. Its appearance, owners, and purpose had changed multiple times throughout the years but it still stood, strong and steady, a symbol of endurance and time passing.

It wasn't lost on her that now, as an adult who'd left and come back, it appeared smaller. Less imposing and intimidating. Maybe it was experience or time away that changed her perspective. Or maybe she remembered it all wrong.

She stood at the end of the long, narrow, U-shaped drive, taking in the fresh white paint and dark-blue shutters. The carefully landscaped grounds with cascades of flowers and trees could be the inspiration for watercolor paintings. It was easy to imagine celebratory events here: weddings, anniversaries, birthdays, graduations. A place where families could gather and build memories.

In the distance, a little bridge arched over a small river. They had played there when she was young. When the house had been empty and somewhat run-down, people strolled the grounds like they owned them. Children played in the masses of trees while teenagers made out in pockets of privacy. Families, including her own, had picnics on sunny days.

"Is this your favorite house, Mommy?"

Seven-year-old Isabelle gripped her mom's hand while her father swung Elaina in circles. Her sister squealed with laughter. They'd been looking for dandelions to make a chain but her mother stopped in front of the porch and just stared. Isabelle had stayed quiet at first, trying to figure out what she saw.

"It's beautiful," her mom said, squeezing Isabelle's tiny fingers. "I wonder what it's like inside. I bet they have dance parties in the ballroom and fancy dinners at a table so long it wouldn't even fit in our kitchen."

"I like our kitchen," Isabelle said, not recognizing the subtle hint of envy in her mother's tone.

"Me too, sweetie."

They stood there letting the breeze wash over them. The air smelled like flowers and the sun warmed her skin. Isabelle liked the feel of her mom's hand over hers.

"Do you wish we lived there?" Isabelle looked up at her mom.

Her mother smiled, one of the ones that reached her eyes. When she smiled like that, Isabelle's heart felt like an overfilled balloon. "Are you kidding? Who wants to clean that place?"

"Not me," Isabelle said, looking back at the enormous home.

"Besides, problems exist everywhere, Izzy-belle. No matter

where you live or who you are, life is never perfect and it's rarely easy. Just because a box is wrapped in sparkling paper doesn't mean there's something wonderful inside."

Isabelle stood there, not entirely sure what her mom meant but content to stand and stare, to take it all in while her mother kept her close.

"When I grow up, I'm going to buy you that house," Isabelle whispered just before pulling her hand free and running toward her father. It was her turn to spin in circles. It was her turn to fly.

Isabelle didn't let the tears fall as she stared at the space where they'd once pretended they were flying. She never let herself think about growing up, the time before or after losing her father. Because it hurt and it was easier to blame. To be mad.

But memories could be skewed too, she realized, forcing herself to take a step toward the house. Now that she was here, she admitted to herself, it hadn't been all bad.

The wraparound porch looked like the kind they used for wedding portraits. The sign on the door said Come In, so she did. What had likely once been the entryway was set up as a reception area with a waist-high counter. On the wall behind it hung gorgeous photographs of the grounds and the house at sunset and dusk, with the stars lighting the way and the moon casting shadows. To the right was a gorgeous, wide-stepped, curved staircase and to the left were closed, heavy, wooden-panel doors with ornate carvings. Behind the counter was an open doorway. She barely stepped up to the counter, didn't even reach her finger toward the tiny gold bell, when someone stepped out from the back.

Not someone. *Her.* Like each other time before this, her pulse hammered wildly, and she felt as if her reflection had come to life. Shorter hair, cut in an angled bob, longer in the front, accentuated her jawline. Her smile came easily, like it was always waiting to show itself. Dressed much as she currently was in a plaid shirt and a pair of jeans, the other her came around the counter.

"Hi. You're Isabelle Fairbanks, correct?" She held out a hand and when Isabelle took it, she covered it with both of hers. "My name is actually Isabelle as well, but everyone calls me Iz."

Isabelle swallowed past the lump in her throat. "Iz Duprees." She wasn't asking, just testing how the name sounded rolling off her tongue.

"That's me. You made the appointment through our online booking system, but it looks like you didn't fill out what type of event you were looking to host."

Iz pulled her phone out of her pocket, checked it, and shoved it back. "Let's go to the sitting room. Can I get you some coffee? Tea? Water?" She moved with purpose and efficiency as she walked, sliding open one of the panel doors.

"I'm fine, actually." Isabelle was no stranger to opulence, to the trappings of money. But still, the sitting room surprised her. High-back chairs sat regally next to a stone fireplace that went all the way up one wall. Long, wide windows looked out onto a covered patio. The art was exquisite and if she wasn't mistaken, some of it was Elaina's. A sage-green couch stretched under one of the windows with rounded armrests, gold buttons adding a just-shy-of-too-much splash. "This is beautiful."

Iz gestured to one of the chairs before sitting in the other. "Thank you. It needed a lot of work when I bought it four years ago, but it's definitely been worth it. We're starting to get international bookings, which boosts the tourist industry here."

She sounded so *proud.* So happy and content. "You said 'we.' Do you have partners?" Dropping the strap of her purse so it sat next to her, she did her best to appear nonchalant. There were almost too many things she wanted to say and ask.

"I'm the owner and operator. My best friend takes care of most of the reservations and liaises with contractors for the various events. My sister works here part-time handling event dressings and staging. My mother putters around and actually takes care of most of the flower beds. And my ex-husband helps us with the catering." Grinning, she rested her hands on her thighs. "It's definitely a family affair."

Isabelle wanted to say something but how was she supposed to respond to so many different things that she couldn't imagine being part of her life. A best friend, a relationship with her family.

The last one felt like it was ripped from her throat when she asked, "Ex-husband?"

Iz nodded, her gaze direct. "I know, you shouldn't work with your spouse or ex-spouse, but it works. For us. Better than marriage did. Speaking of which, what kind of event are you interested in?" Leaning to the side, she pulled her phone out of her pocket again, slid it open. "I'll jot down the details and be able to get back to you with a quote within forty-eight hours."

Gripping the armrests, Isabelle had to actively work at keeping herself calm. She'd been married. And divorced. And was clearly happy.

"Are you okay? You're sure I can't get you something?" Iz leaned closer, genuine concern in her identical eyes.

Isabelle needed as much information as possible so she could leave and put this behind her.

You can do this. You need information. Just a conversation.

"I'm fine," she said, pasting on a smile she wondered if her other self would recognize as fake. "I was thinking how much I admire the fact that you've not only created this beautiful place, but you've surrounded yourself with friends and family. I'm constantly at odds with my sister, haven't talked to my mother in years, and I work too much to have close friends."

Or any friends.

Something passed over Iz's features, and Isabelle worried that the woman would shut down, close herself off.

Because that's what you'd do.

"It's not easy, if you want to know the truth. But there are turning points in your life where you ask yourself—is it worth it? Is what I'm hanging onto worth what I'm giving up? It might sound strange, but I was actually in a similar position—not close to my mother and sister. But about ten years ago, my grandmother died and my sister had a baby. Those two things both knocked my feet out from under me and I had to decide what I wanted. Anger is a lousy companion."

The words sank in. *This* Isabelle hadn't missed a thing.

But you're happy with the choices you've made. Look at your life. You don't want to run Ashland Acres and wear plaid to work every day.

Maybe not, but she also wondered how she'd feel, how the last several years would have felt, it she had let go of the anger and resentment. If she'd grasped onto something else instead.

"I'm sorry. I don't usually just spill all of my business like that," Iz said with a laugh. "You've got one of those faces. Maybe it's the eyes. Pulled me in and opened me up."

Isabelle forced a laugh. "No problem. Trust me, I understand." After all, who better to understand that she usually only trusted herself with her feelings than . . . well . . . her?

"Okay, down to business. What sort of event are we hosting?"

For the next hour, Isabelle planned a fake wedding with Iz while trying to figure out how she was supposed to go back to her life in New York when she no longer knew exactly who she was.

TWENTY-NINE

Isabelle joined the crowd on Second Street, listening to the laughter and conversations as people enjoyed the murals, artists spoke, and vendors offered delicious-smelling food. She stopped in a little alcove to admire a gorgeous painting on a cement wall. One woman stood in silhouette, staring out into the great unknown where several paths crisscrossed over one another. Far in the distance, the paths all led to the same place, and if she was interpreting it correctly, it was back to the woman.

Part of Isabelle felt like she ought to be on a shrink's couch, sorting this shit out, but how would she even start? The other versions of herself had elements of who she was now: determination, a formidable presence, drive, and a certainty that she . . . they . . . were where they were supposed to be. Wondering how one of the other hers would react to the version of her that was true, that was real, was pointless, but she couldn't stop herself.

It was a true existential crisis moment—wondering if she was the real deal or if one of them was. She wasn't a fan of things that couldn't be proved on paper and followed up with hard facts. But there was no making sense of anything currently happening to her. She should be in a meeting, heading to a gala of some sort, pretending she didn't notice the way Jonathan's gaze always zeroed in on her in a crowded room.

Instead, she stood alone in a town she knew like the back of her hand, as an invisible stranger. To everyone around her, and to herself.

She was torn between telling the universe, "Okay, message received," or simply telling it to "Fuck off." God, she was tired.

Her phone buzzed with a message from Kaia.

> Am I good to schedule in-person meetings for the end of this week?

Isabelle stared at the text and realized that never, in the eight years Kaia had been organizing her life, had her assistant been forced to ask such a question. Isabelle wanted, badly, to go home to her life and comforts, to her routine and, yes, to Jonathan. But she felt like the energy had been sucked from her soul and replaced with something unidentifiable that she didn't know what to do with. She didn't know how to reboot, restart, and use what she'd learned to redirect.

How could she go back to her regularly scheduled programming with what she'd seen and experienced without letting it impact her? The damage—or maybe, the healing—was already in progress.

She texted back.

> Let's keep things on Zoom for another week and don't make any firm commitments. I need some time.

Kaia responded like she'd already had the message ready to go.

You're scaring me.

She almost laughed. But it wasn't funny.

I'm scaring myself. We'll talk when I get home.

How much more of this could she endure without breaking? She stared at Kaia's response.

Isabelle . . . I feel like it's important to tell you, in this minute, that you matter to me. I'm not sure what's going on with you but you're needed. Exactly as you are. Just know that.

Isabelle sucked in a breath, then covered her mouth with her hand so a sob didn't escape. Leaning back against the unpainted wall, she closed her eyes and breathed in the scents of BBQ and sugary donuts, and listened to the jovial murmurings out on the street.

"Hey." Her sister's quiet voice broke through the noise.

Opening her eyes, she saw Elaina standing in front of her. She'd pulled her hair up into a messy ponytail and carried multiple reusable bags on her shoulder.

"How the hell did you find me?" She was in an alley for God's sake.

One side of her lips tipped up. "Friend Finder."

Isabelle laughed. "No invasion of privacy there."

"They didn't have sister finder, so I went with the next best thing." Elaina leaned against the wall, didn't push further, and if anything, that made the situation harder.

The words Iz shared as they'd planned a fake wedding reception swirled in Isabelle's head. One phone call had changed the woman's path. Isabelle couldn't even remember if there *was* that phone call in her own version. But she had to know.

"Why didn't you come to my MIT grad?"

"Hmm?"

Deflecting. Isabelle turned, faced Elaina with a shoulder against the wall. She didn't have quite enough strength to stand up on her own yet. "Why?"

Elaina looked down at the pebbled alleyway. "It didn't work, timing-wise. You didn't need us there."

"Look at me, Elaina."

Elaina lifted her chin, stared into Isabelle's eyes. "I couldn't. I had some trouble with my pregnancy. I was on bed rest. Even with that, there were a lot of dicey moments."

"You almost died." Even with her sister standing right in front of her, alive and well, the words gutted her.

"We both almost died. There were complications. Mom wouldn't leave me. I told her to go. We had the money. But she wouldn't leave me. She said you'd understand, wanted to tell you."

Isabelle's jaw clenched. "Why didn't *you* tell me?"

Elaina's gaze watered. "You worked from the time you were eight years old to get out of this town, to become something that separated you from your past. I wasn't risking you coming back and getting derailed by me. By this town. I didn't want you drowning in the past when you had so much to look forward to."

Isabelle couldn't form words. They were stuck somewhere between her heart and her throat. All the *what ifs* stabbed at her skin like newly sharpened knives.

Stepping forward, she wrapped her arms around her sister,

pulled her close, and hung on tightly. Elaina's arms fastened around her waist as she murmured assurances that she was okay, that everything was okay.

When she was certain she wouldn't cry, Isabelle pulled back and glared at her sister. "If you had died, it would have seriously pissed me off."

Elaina's laugh was a touch watery, her eyes shiny. "Duly noted. But I didn't. And Charlie didn't. And when we get out of this weird version of the universe we're stuck in, you'll meet her. She knows about you."

Isabelle dropped her arms. "Oh yeah? What does she know? That she has an aunt with a heart made of ice who has more money than kindness? More common sense than capacity to show love?"

Elaina gripped her arm. "No. Stop that. She knows that you and I, that you and Mom, had a falling out. She knows that you're amazing and powerful and someone to look up to. She knows that one day, she'll get to meet you and learn all about how to kick some serious ass in whatever way she wants to. She knows people are flawed, including her mother and grandmother."

"We let him down," Isabelle whispered, grateful the alleyway didn't seem to be on people's radars.

"Dad?" Elaina asked, and then shrugged. "He wouldn't have wanted the last dozen years for us, no. But he always said it wasn't the mistakes we make but what we do after that matters. This is our chance at the *after*, Isabelle."

Isabelle's shoulders dropped, like some of the weight had slipped away. "I want to go home."

Grinning, Elaina looped an arm through hers, pulled her toward the street. "Tomorrow is soon enough. Let's enjoy the festival, go say things we've always wanted to say to people who don't recognize us, and then we'll go get ready for tonight."

Isabelle pulled up short. "What's tonight?"

Her sister gave a little shimmy. "We're going to the club."

Isabelle's groan was drowned out by the people around them.

THIRTY

Unsurprisingly, it was more *country dive bar* than *nightclub*.

Despite the No Smoking signs, a hazy fog settled like low clouds inside. People danced to a band singing an old Springsteen classic. A group of girls waited at the bar for a long-haired, bearded bartender to pour shots. Waitresses moved through the crowd, their full trays lifted over their heads as if they weighed nothing at all. Isabelle had thought lifting her twenty-pound weights was an accomplishment. No way she could lift those trays full of drinks without toppling sideways.

Elaina's hand yanked her through the crowd and Isabelle tried not to think about what body parts she was sliding up against or squeezing through. A gala was one thing but this . . . ? Too much.

"Let's get a drink," Elaina shouted over the music.

Waiting in the short line, her sister bounced along to the beat, clearly energized and happy. Isabelle got caught up in looking around, not hearing what Elaina ordered until she had a pint of beer shoved into her hand.

"Drink up."

Someone bumped her from behind, making some of the

amber liquid slosh over the side of the glass. Firming her grip on her drink, she followed her sister. Eventually, they found a high-top table next to the dance floor—but no chairs.

Sipping her beer, Isabelle raised her brows at Elaina. "Not bad."

Elaina laughed. "See? When you're not snubbing things, you find something you like."

Maybe it was the mass of people or the volume of the music creating an illusion of safety, but Isabelle leaned in, telling Elaina, "I don't really have a stick up my ass. I worry about drinking because I don't want to be . . . you know."

Elaina leaned back, compassion and understanding in her gaze. "You aren't. But I get it. I don't drink in front of Mom, and there's no liquor in her house. But it's okay to cut loose, Izzy-belle. We can switch to Shirley Temples if you want."

It was Isabelle's turn to laugh. They had both felt like princesses when their dad let them order those at restaurants.

The band transitioned into another classic hit. Isabelle was standing so close to Elaina, she felt her sister's hips move in time to the music.

"Barista Elaina works part-time at the coffee house. I went back after you left. She also works with her sister at Ashland Acres and raises her kid."

By some sort of unspoken agreement, they hadn't talked about what either of them had learned while they were apart, except for in the alleyway.

"Iz said her whole family and her ex works with her. I guess she's better at forgiveness than me."

Elaina shrugged, took a sip of her beer, tapped her fingers on the sticky-looking tabletop that Isabelle wouldn't touch for money.

"Maybe. But it's hard to say. You're getting to see the result of a choice, a different fork in the road. Doesn't mean you know how rocky or smooth the path to getting there was."

Since when was her sister so smart? She didn't want to question why it felt so good to have Elaina's validation on the other version of herself.

"Holy shit," Elaina said, her grin stretching.

Isabelle started to ask but saw what had snagged her sister's attention. Max walked toward their table, a beer in hand.

"Hey. How's your visit going? Do you remember me? I brought you your food the other night."

"Of course. That food was unforgettable." Elaina's smile was warm, genuine, and just a little flirty. Of all the things Isabelle could envy her sister for, being able to slip and slide into multiple conversations and moods was high on the list.

"Yes, it was very good. You know what you're doing," Isabelle said, hearing the stiffness in her tone. Purposely relaxing her shoulders, she tried to offer a friendly smile like Elaina.

"Practice," Max said, sipping his drink.

"Were you married to Iz Duprees?" The music dipped just as Isabelle shouted the question across the table.

Elaina lowered her chin, shaking her head as she looked down. "Smooth."

Others cast glances their way, but Max just observed her, measured her with those dark eyes that she'd fallen in love with so long ago.

The music softened, the singer easing into a ballad.

His brows arched, clearly curious. "I was."

"I had a meeting at Ashland Acres today. She mentioned you." A slight fib but Isabelle could add two and two.

Max nodded in understanding. "Right. Yeah. We were married for a while. You want to dance?"

Elaina nudged her before she could respond. "She does."

Isabelle shot her a glare but accepted Max's hand. He pulled her onto the dance floor, the music and scent of sweat, beer, and cologne surrounding them. It was familiar, like curling into an old favorite sweater. Comforting and soothing but it no longer fit quite right.

She looked up at him, saw him watching her. "Sorry if I overstepped."

He stared a moment longer before shaking his head ever so slightly. "No worries. You've got great eyes. They remind me of someone."

Isabelle laughed, lowered her gaze. "You remind me of someone too," she whispered.

"Ever been married?" Max's breath washed over her ear, sending a small shiver down her spine. Not unpleasant. *Just not Jonathan.*

What could she say? Maybe in this life? "No." And because she might never get the chance again, and because if she let herself think about it, she'd always regretted hurting him, she pushed forward. "I'm sorry about your marriage. I can't imagine taking that step and having it not work out."

Max had lived a whole life since they parted ways, and she hadn't thought about him in years. She wondered where he was now, in her reality. *I'm sorry that I hurt you, Max. You mattered to me.* So did Elaina and her mother, she realized. She hadn't wanted to think about them, talk to them, or see them. But they'd mattered.

"I don't know that it didn't work out," he said.

Isabelle lifted her chin, gave him a questioning look.

"The marriage piece didn't. But Iz is one of my best friends. We dated in high school, then went our separate ways. I came back for a visit, we hooked up and thought we could build a life from old feelings. We couldn't. But we built something different."

"That's a very enlightened way to look at a failed marriage," Isabelle said, not realizing how rude that sounded until the words left her mouth. "I'm sorry. I just . . . I guess I can't understand how someone puts aside old hurts and walks away with such an accepting viewpoint."

Max gave her a smile that, back in the day, would have turned her stomach upside down like a rollercoaster. "Divorce isn't easy. Hell, *dating* isn't easy. I figure if you don't make the most of wherever you land, you're only punishing yourself. Anger is about the heaviest thing you can lug around."

She remembered the moment, earlier today in the alley, when she'd felt lighter from letting some of the anger go; from accepting that regardless of what she'd done in the past, Elaina would be part of her future. As she danced closely with Max, she wondered if there was a version of her that didn't hurt him? That didn't walk away so callously?

"How long are you in town?" He'd lowered his head to her ear again, spoke into it softly.

"Just tonight," Isabelle said, pulling back as the song ended.

His grin was sexy as hell, the look in his eyes transmitting clearly. "We could make it an exceptionally good night."

Isabelle held his gaze, let a kaleidoscope of feelings wash through and over her. In her mind, she saw him waving goodbye the last time they saw each other. The fact that there was a version of her life where he didn't hate her for how she'd ghosted him gave her a sense of peace hadn't known she needed.

"I'm flattered," she said, stepping out of his arms. "But I'm with someone and it's serious."

Admitting that to anyone had always terrified her. She didn't want to be judged by who she was dating or spending time with. It wasn't until right this second that she realized the only thing she *should* feel with Jonathan at her side was a sense of satisfaction. Happiness.

Max smiled. "He's a lucky man."

She was the lucky one. She just hadn't realized it until now.

"Goodbye, Max."

He lifted his hand as he moved backward through the crowd, fading out of view. Elaina pushed through the crowd, joining her on the floor with two shot glasses of amber liquid in her hands. "Hey. There you are. Where's Max?"

Isabelle looked at her sister like she was seeing her for the first time. "He left. He asked me to spend the night with him."

Elaina snort-laughed and shook her head. "He was always crazy about you."

Other dancers bumped them but Isabelle held her ground. "Even when I didn't deserve it." She'd gotten lucky that way more than once. "I don't want to keep running from things that scare me." She was done running. From her past. From her feelings. From Jonathan. From her family. From all the versions of herself that existed that she never let herself acknowledge.

She wasn't even sure Elaina heard her until she handed her the shot, lifted her own to her lips, winked at Isabelle and said, "Tequila scares you."

Isabelle laughed, even as she swallowed down the liquid, not enjoying the burn of cheap alcohol. She coughed, shaking her head at her sister.

Elaina grinned, took their glasses, set them on a table and grabbed Isabelle by both wrists. "No more running away, Izzy-belle. We're right here, right now, and we've never had this."

"Had what?" Isabelle felt like she was shouting as Elaina pulled them deeper into the crowd.

"We've never gone to a bar and danced our asses off. We've never let everything go and just gotten lost in the moment.

No past. No future. Just right now. Get ready to shake it, Izzy-belle."

Isabelle's tongue felt thick. "That shot was disgusting." She didn't fight her sister's attempts at making her dance.

Elaina tipped her head back and laughed then lowered her chin. "Yep. Totally disgusting."

More people pushed in, buoyed by the music and energy of others until it felt like they were all dancing together. Lost in a sea of strangers, Isabelle locked down her thoughts of who she really was, where she was headed, and what she'd left behind in different versions of her life.

No matter what happened, whether she rebuilt all of her burned bridges or walked away, Elaina was right; they'd never have this again. This night of anonymity, a chance to live out a moment neither of them had expected. She closed her eyes, anchored by the feel of her sister's hand holding hers and pushed aside all the questions and the worries. Whatever happened tomorrow or the next day or the next, whatever version of herself she faced, she wanted this memory.

THIRTY-ONE

Something was different but with her foggy brain, Isabelle didn't know what. She turned her head to the side, the movement amplifying the steady pounding in her head and at the base of her neck. Elaina was on her stomach, still dressed. One bejeweled arm hung off the edge of the bed, her skirt scrunched, one of her heels askew on her foot, the other one nowhere to be seen.

If Isabelle were checking off a list of things sisters do together, drinking way too much at the local watering hole had been crossed off *hard*.

Easing up from the uncomfortable motel bed, she went to the bathroom and made an attempt to clean herself up. Her flight was scheduled for late that day. She didn't know what Elaina's plan was, whether she'd stay here or come back to New York. She also didn't know what *their* next step was. They'd buried a lot of the animosity and accusations. They weren't besties or likely to talk on the phone every day, but they were no longer estranged.

When she came out of the bathroom freshly showered and dressed in a pair of capri pants, a tank top, and a light sweater, Elaina was still sleeping. Isabelle left her a note, saying she was going for coffee and would be back. Then she did something she couldn't remember ever doing. She tucked some bills in her pocket and left the room without her phone.

It wasn't entirely intentional, but maybe, in the back of her mind, she had no choice but to end up exactly where she did.

The Ashland Cemetery was tucked into a residential neighborhood just past the main part of town. Next to a park which, at the far end, connected to a community center, it sat quietly, shrouded in trees that arched inward like their purpose was to hold in the grief and memories.

A soft breeze blew the scent of flowers and dust. The sound of vehicles purred a few streets over along with a couple of lawn mowers. Isabelle had never imagined herself back here. It had been the second worst day of her life, burying her father.

The first being when she found out he was dead.

He'd pulled several overtime shifts and agreed to more. Catalina had talked him into a family vacation in California. Charlie's whole life was about making his girls smile. It was undetermined whether it was user error or machine failure, but he'd died immediately in the heavy-duty manufacturing plant where he was a foreman. One of the machines short circuited, and from what little details they'd been given, her father had suffered a severe shock with far too many volts to survive.

And like that, he was gone.

A few people walked the well-kept paths. Benches with dedications were set up under trees and in quiet corners. Isabelle turned left at the oak tree that, even at eight, had reminded her of her father when they'd taken this route as a mourning family. Her grandmother had gripped her small hand so tight, she'd left indentations.

Elaina had walked with their mother.

At the end of the path, just around a bend of flowered

hedges, Isabelle readied herself for the ache that would surely come from seeing her father's headstone.

But when she moved closer, she couldn't see it. Not through the person kneeling in front of it, tossing tiny clumps of weeds to the left and right.

"You always were a nuisance to clean up after," Catalina said, her tone light and teasing.

Dressed in jeans and a sleeveless shirt, her hair piled on her head, she leaned back on her feet.

"I miss you, Charlie. Even now. They say time heals all wounds, but I think that's a lie. Maybe if I hadn't messed things up so badly after, maybe it wouldn't still hurt so much."

Listening to her mother talk to her father broke something inside of Isabelle. The regret in her tone, the love that couldn't be unheard, was a heavy-handed reminder that she wasn't the only one who'd lost something. For all her faults and mistakes, Catalina Duprees had loved her husband desperately.

"I wanted to tell you I won't be visiting as much anymore. I'll still come by to update you on Charlie. You'd adore her. She's artistic like Elaina and her smile reminds me of Isabelle's. Isn't it strange how a person can carry pieces of someone else even if they've never met? She's the best of all of us." Catalina laughed. "Not that there was ever much good in me, right? Isn't that what my father used to say? But you, Charlie? You were all that was right in the world and I'm sorry every day that you're gone."

While tears streamed down Isabelle's cheeks, Catalina stood, dusted off her pants, pressed her hand to the tombstone.

"I'm getting married soon. That's why I won't be here, Charlie. I think it's time, probably past time, to let myself move forward. But it won't change how much I love you. You'll always own a piece of my heart."

Isabelle sucked in a breath so sharp it caught, making her

cough. Catalina turned and Isabelle expected her mother to be irritated by having a stranger impose on her privacy.

"Isabelle. *Mi corazón.*" Three words tore down years of barriers, not erasing the hurt but pushing it to the side. *My heart.* She hadn't heard those two words in her mother's fading Spanish accent in what felt like a lifetime.

Frozen in her spot, unsure if Catalina actually recognized her, recognized this version of her, she could only stare.

"Mom?"

Catalina rushed her, nearly knocking her over with the energy behind her hug. She stroked Isabelle's hair, murmuring words and squeezing her tightly. She couldn't make out everything her mom said, but "I'm sorry" came through over and over again until Isabelle didn't know which of them were saying it.

They stood there, rocking back and forth just beside her father's grave, and Isabelle wept like the little girl she'd once been. A piece of her had stayed frozen in time, eight years old and absolutely heartbroken. That little girl cried inside of her, all but collapsing into her mother's embrace.

They couldn't erase the past. But maybe they could move forward.

Catalina pulled back, framed Isabelle's face with her hands and stared so hard, Isabelle wondered if she could see into her soul.

"You recognize me?" Bringing her hands to her mother's wrists, she searched her gaze.

"What? Of course. You're my daughter. I would recognize you anywhere. You're a piece of me." She laughed, the music of it floating through the trees. "What are you doing here?"

Here. She was here, back in her own reality. Or had the worlds meshed together somehow, and this was still an old version of Catalina?

She had to be sure. "I needed to see you. I'm only here until the end of the day. Then I need to go home. To New York."

If this was the real-time version of her mother, New York would make sense to her.

"Just today? That's all I get? It's not enough time to mend fences, to make you understand how sorry I am for everything. To tell you that I'm not the same person. That I'm better than I was."

Fingers still wrapped around her mom's wrists, Isabelle took in the creases around her eyes, the wrinkles that weathered her still-beautiful skin. The hint of gray hair.

"You just told me."

"Elaina went to see you," she said.

"Yes. You're getting married. She told me." Isabelle dropped her hands, stepped out of her mother's grasp. "And I heard you tell daddy."

Catalina lowered her gaze. "I've said no for years. Your father knew him, actually. They were friends. He's a good man." She looked toward the grave marker. "Henry loves me. He's patient with me. He's seen the very worst of me and loves me anyway. I think Charlie would be happy."

Isabelle heard the shame in her mom's tone. She clearly felt guilty for moving on. Stepping next to her, Isabelle took her mom's hand. "Sometimes I forget that his whole life's goal was our happiness. When he died, none of us knew how to find our happy without him. I hope you've found it now. He'd want that. So much."

Her mom's shoulders shook as she turned into Isabelle again, rested her head on her chest like she was the child. Isabelle stroked her back, sorry that she'd let all this time go by, but grateful there was still time left.

The thick branches shaded them from the warming sun

while they stood arm in arm, chatting about nothing because it was easier than facing the past. Isabelle wondered how much they had to sort through and wondered if all those old boxes needed to be opened. Or maybe it was time to put them away for good.

When Isabelle checked her watch, she saw her mom's sudden panic. "You're leaving?"

Firming her lips, she made a split-second decision. "I'll stay a couple more days, but I need to get back to the hotel, make a few phone calls."

The joy in Catalina's face brought back a barrage of memories, reminders of family movies, picnics, walks through the woods. Christmas mornings, birthdays, and her parents dancing in the kitchen. Those moments had often felt so few and far between that Isabelle had shuffled them aside. Maybe if she had focused on those instead, at least a little, if she'd given them a chance to shine bright enough to overshadow the others, things would have been different.

"You'll come for dinner. You need to meet Charlie. Elaina told you about her?"

Isabelle nodded.

Catalina grasped her hands. "Will you come? Let's have a family dinner. I know it doesn't erase what I've put you through, how we've hurt each other, but can we let it go, just for one night, so I can have my three girls under my roof?"

She nodded. It was exactly what her dad would have wanted.

"Will I get to meet Henry?"

Her mom's smile turned shy. "Do you want to?"

Isabelle nodded. "Yes, I do. I might bring someone. I'll have Elaina text you."

"Don't disappear on me, Izzy-belle. I don't think I can stand to lose you again. Not before I have a chance to make it up to you."

Isabelle hugged her mom, a brief squeeze. "Let's put that away, Mom. Tonight, we'll get to know each other again. Let's focus on the future."

"That sounds good to me. I'll see you tonight."

Isabelle nodded, watched her mom walk away, glance back repeatedly, and finally offer a little wave.

Isabelle didn't have her phone and Elaina would likely be worried. She needed to get back to the hotel. As she made her way through town, she detoured past Ashland Acres. Dark shutters hung unevenly, long grass overpowered any presence of flowers, and the porch steps listed to the right while the paint looked gloomy and gray.

Iz was gone. That version of her had faded somewhere into the ether, and Isabelle stood there staring at the crumbling foundation of what she knew could be a thing of beauty and wondered if the point of all of this was to bring her back to the beginning.

Back to where it'd all gone wrong. It might be the only place she'd ever truly be able to set it right.

THIRTY-TWO

They drove in silence toward their mother's house.

Charlie was already there, and Isabelle was more nervous to meet her niece than she'd been on her first date as a teen. It was silly and immature to worry about whether or not the kid would like her. She wasn't even sure how much of a role, if any, she'd play in her family's life after this.

Elaina looked over. "What's wrong?"

"*What's wrong?*" Isabelle gripped her purse against her stomach. "Hmm, let me think. I'm about to have dinner with my mother, who I haven't seen in years other than this morning at my father's grave. I'm probably going meet the man she's about to marry. You have a child who is halfway grown that I've never met, and I invited Jonathan to join me and he said yes and I don't know what the hell I'm doing or how I let everything spiral out of control like this."

Elaina pulled over to the side of the road and turned in the driver's seat. "None of this means there aren't still things to work through. For all of us. It doesn't mean the past is erased or it'll be easy. I'm so happy you're willing to try, that we get tonight with all the people we love. I just want to make the most of it.

I've learned not to squander the beauty life offers you. It can be fleeting, and we think we have control, but we don't. Not over the good or the bad. I know there are still scars. For both of us. But I want tonight."

Elaina's words, the tone of her voice, and the way the emotion pulsed in her eyes, smoothed the rough edges of Isabelle's anxiety.

"I do too." It was true, she realized. Truer than she ever could have imagined it being. "How are you so at peace with everything?" The question had been nagging at the back of her brain for days. Elaina might have been their mother's go-to, but that was hard on a kid—the neediness of the adult in her life, the loss of her father, the discord between her and Isabelle.

Elaina looked out the window, watched a bird swoop down into a treetop. Looking back at Isabelle, she gave a deep sigh. "I faced it. This isn't a judgment so don't get all pissy at me, but you put it all away and moved on. You never really dealt with it. I did that for a while too but then it got to the point where I couldn't keep it tucked away anymore. I was so angry and hurt. I didn't want that for Charlie. I had it out with Mom. God, we fought. It was awful. We didn't talk for weeks. But once I acknowledged what I was feeling, it sort of lessened the intensity."

Isabelle nodded, thinking how that might have been a healthier path. But she couldn't go back, clearly couldn't change the past, and there were a lot of things she *wouldn't* want to be different.

Giving one more brief nod, she smiled. "Let's go. I'm hungry."

"I look forward to getting to know James Bond," Elaina said as she pulled back onto the road.

"His name is Jonathan," Isabelle admonished.

"Jonathan Hottie Pants."

Isabelle snorted out a laugh. "Jesus. If you call him that, I swear to God I'll tell Charlie about the time you tried to get Chad Roland to kiss you by putting on cherry red lipstick and showing up at his house dressed in high heels that were way too big for you, so you taped them to your feet."

Elaina gasped. "Don't you dare. I still have a scar on the top of my foot from where the tape took off skin."

"Some lessons are learned the hard way. Bet you never put duct tape on your feet again."

"Never wore cherry red lipstick again either."

Isabelle wasn't sure what to expect when Elaina pulled into the long driveway of her childhood home. The small ranch with a pitched roof and window boxes she remembered had been transformed, extended, and added onto. They had a decent-sized yard that had always been a little overgrown. Now, it was tended to nicely, the grass short, raised flower beds and fruit trees creating an oasis of tranquility.

"Wow. What happened?"

"Mom never wanted to move but we needed more space. There are things we haven't talked about," Elaina said, pulling up next to a newer Jeep Cherokee.

If she hadn't remembered her childhood home so vividly, she wouldn't have been able to see it in this new version of itself. Whoever had done the work had created the illusion that the house had been designed just this way. It was seamless.

In some ways, it resembled Ashland House, with one story instead of three. It had a strong presence and a happy vibe with the whitewashed siding, the wide porch, and the windchimes dancing in the breeze.

To the right of the house, a smaller structure stood, a pergola joining the main house and the building. A gold metal sign read: *Heart House*. Beneath that was a small line of text Isabelle couldn't read from the car. She got out, walked over to it, ran her fingers along the words.

The first step is the most important one.

She looked back at her sister. "What is this?"

Elaina joined her in front of the sign. "One of the things we haven't talked about yet. Mom got her master's degree in counseling. She helps women get back on their feet. Not just recovering alcoholics but women who've had a tough time, ended marriages, dealt with abuse, made some wrong turns, and just need a helping hand. I do art therapy with several of her clients and some of them sell their work through my gallery."

Isabelle turned to face her sister. She'd been right next to her for days but felt like she was seeing her for the first time. "I had no idea."

"She's made a lot of mistakes. She knows it, lives with it, and tries every day to make up for it. All the good she's done since she finally got sober when Charlie was born, and she still hasn't forgiven herself for letting you down. You coming here tonight might finally help her find closure." Elaina turned to her. "So, no matter how this turns out, thank you for trying. For coming. For being here."

Isabelle swallowed down the lump in her throat. Nothing in her life was what she thought it was. No one was who she'd thought they were. She'd seen things from only one narrow viewpoint, used it to fuel her into a life few could imagine, one she thought was the pinnacle of success, of accomplishment. One that, until recently, she hadn't realized was isolated, lonely, and in many ways, empty.

She'd been happy, living life high up in her beautiful penthouse, thriving professionally and physically. It felt like an illusion now—or just another version of who she could have been.

As they walked into the house, her heart galloping like a wild stallion, she wondered if, when this was all over, she'd know who she wanted to be.

A soft squeak announced the front door opening. Catalina looked at the car, then scanned the yard, finding them by the other building. She clasped her hands, pulled them against her chest like the sight was almost too much for her.

"You're here. You're both here," she said, her voice laced with emotion and disbelief.

Elaina nudged Isabelle with her elbow, grinned at their mother. "I'm always here, so don't pretend all that happiness is for me."

Catalina laughed, opening her arms as she came toward them. Isabelle had let herself feel more in a few days than she had in the last ten years. She was going to need a month-long nap when this was all over.

Both girls were folded into their mother's arms, Catalina kissing each of their cheeks, murmuring endearments in Spanish.

Elaina sniffled and pulled back, which gave Isabelle permission to do the same, minus the sniffling. She was determined not to cry anymore on this trip.

"Where's Charlie?"

"She's got ten more minutes on the Xbox."

Isabelle glanced back at Heart House. "Tell me all about this."

Pulling keys from her pocket, Catalina walked to the bright yellow door with the cute portico awning. "I'll show you."

From the front, it resembled a garage because all the windows were along the back wall. The space was open and airy with a high ceiling, comfortable seating areas, and a small kitchenette in one corner. A couple of doors ran along one wall. Catalina pointed.

"There's an office there and a bathroom." The windows offered a generous view of a little pond complete with beautiful rock edging and a waterfall.

Isabelle walked to the left wall, gazed at the multiple canvases showcasing paintings, sketches, and pencil drawings. From one side to the other, it was nearly a ceiling-to-floor mural of other people's feelings captured and displayed in a variety of frame sizes. She could stare at it for days and not truly absorb the myriad of emotions. It was stunning.

"How long have you been doing this?" She turned to see her sister and mother standing close together. She got that familiar pang right below her heart, a sharp tug. They were and always had been a unit.

Catalina glanced at Elaina. "I finished my master's degree about four years ago. We had two women at first. It went from being a counseling session to group sessions, then sort of morphed into a support group. I do individual counseling, but we have a few different groups with similar backgrounds who meet a couple times a week."

"We do an evening art session for the community," Elaina added. "Anyone can join. Once they're here, those who don't know about what we do can learn, take part. We organize events in town sometimes, have gallery showings."

One person couldn't be a unit. That was an island. And even though Isabelle believed one person could invoke a hell of a lot of change, the power of *more* had an appeal she'd never considered. Because she'd never had someone to lean on. Some of the anger pushed up to the surface because she'd been *eight* when she'd been left stranded, but she choked it back down because she didn't want to focus on it.

"You've done so much," she said, ignoring the twinges of guilt. She'd earned money, paved her own path, bought hotels out from fighting, adulterous couples. She held men at arms' lengths and left parties early to be alone.

"We," Catalina said.

Isabelle blinked. "What?"

"*We've* done so much." She stepped forward, took Isabelle's hands. "You made this possible. You've sent so much money. Because of that, because of your hard work, we found a way to repay what you've given us. I've found a way to heal pieces of myself I never thought I would and I couldn't have done it without you and your generosity. Something I didn't necessarily deserve."

Elaina stepped closer, standing right beside them. "Same. And you know it's true—I wouldn't be doing what I do without you. Not in this capacity. Not with so much ease and peace. I can raise my daughter, send her to school, be part of a community I love and live my passion, help others do the same. Because of you."

It was like writing checks to charities that Kaia chose. Isabelle was removed from the cause or purpose, handing over the money and moving on. It mattered. On a rational level, she knew that. It mattered.

But what her mom and Elaina had built here was about more than money. It was time, passion, energy, and grit. Determination. It was a spark that flickered and grew into an inferno. It started with one small kernel of an idea, a whisper of possibility. Like the Young Women in Business project. Passion plus money could often equate true change.

"I'm hoping you have an accountant? A good lawyer? To make sure you're getting proper tax breaks?" Isabelle asked as her phone buzzed in her pocket.

Elaina cracked first but as soon as she laughed, Catalina joined in. Isabelle's shoulders stiffened. They laughed harder.

"I'm not sure why that's so funny," she said, using the tone she pulled out for meetings that went off the rails.

"Oh honey. For your seventh birthday, you asked if I could get you a 401K," Catalina said.

Elaina snorted with laughter, covered her mouth, folded in half. Isabelle's lips twitched. "I did not."

"Oh, yes you did." She hooked a thumb at Elaina. "Your sister drew you one. I gave you fifty dollars and you asked to invest it." There was more than humor in her mom's tone. It sounded a lot like pride and affection.

A small chuckle escaped Isabelle's mouth. Once it did, the laughter came as they exchanged a round of *remember whens*. Little things that happen in any family, daily occurrences, things said across the dinner table, that were often lost moments after they happened. But they were all there, woven into the history and fabric of who they'd been.

Once some of the laughter subsided, Isabelle straightened her posture again, sent them a mockingly haughty look. "Just because we laughed about it doesn't mean it wasn't a serious question."

Elaina slung her arm around Isabelle's shoulder. "We know. We're good. Kaia helps us with all the details. Whatever you pay that woman, you should triple it."

Isabelle wasn't sure about that, but they'd definitely be having a conversation or two about all the ways Kaia had infiltrated the pockets of her life.

Locking up behind them, Catalina gestured to the house. "Let's go in. Dinner will be in about an hour. We could . . ."

Catalina broke off when a sleek Lincoln Navigator pulled into the driveway. "Uh-oh. Maybe Kaia steered us wrong. I think the FBI is here."

The car came to a stop and Jonathan emerged from the rear.

A grin took over Elaina's face. "Nope. That's Isabelle's hot-as-fuck boyfriend."

Catalina and Isabelle spoke over each other, her mother snapping, "Language," while Isabelle went with "Shut *up*."

Jonathan pushed his aviator glasses to his head then buttoned his suit jacket as he walked closer. Isabelle felt like her heart was literally twirling in her chest. Nothing else could explain the erratic thumping and movement as he closed the distance.

"I see why you like New York," Catalina muttered.

"*Mom*," Isabelle snapped as Elaina laughed again.

"Isabelle," Jonathan said, his tone a bit hesitant but warm all the same.

She'd had days of leading with her feelings, as chaotic as they'd been, so she didn't even think it through before she stepped into him, going up on tiptoes to wrap her arms around his neck.

His strong arms closed around her, pulling her close as he straightened, lifting her right up off the ground.

He buried his face in her neck. "God, I've missed you." His words were muffled but she heard them clearly. More importantly, she *felt* them.

Jonathan set her down but stayed close. "Elaina, right?" He reached out a hand to shake her hand.

It didn't surprise Isabelle when Elaina ignored his hand and went in for a hug. "Right. Nice to formally meet you, Jonathan."

To his credit, he rolled with it, hugging her back while arching his eyebrows at Isabelle.

When Elaina stepped back, Isabelle gestured to her mom. "This is my mom, Catalina."

Her mother didn't hug him but took his hands in her own. "Jonathan. It's a pleasure to meet you."

"You as well, ma'am. I was more than a little surprised to get the invite to dinner," he said. "Pleasantly surprised."

"There's been a few surprises this week," Isabelle added.

Catalina stepped back, clapped her hands together. "Let's go inside. You'll meet Charlie, and Henry will be here soon." She looped her arm through Elaina's.

"Actually, Mom . . ." Isabelle started, then stopped when her mother's eyes widened, a sudden sadness appearing on her face.

"Don't go."

Isabelle shook her head quickly. "No. Not entirely. It's just . . . Jonathan and I need to speak, and I'd like to do that before we all have dinner. I promise we'll be right back."

Jonathan tucked his hands in his pockets while Catalina looked at Elaina, then back at Isabelle. "Where will you go?"

"Not far. I want to show him something. We'll be back really soon."

Catalina nodded. "Okay. Of course. We'll be here."

Because she wasn't entirely sure if her mother believed her, she stepped into her, put a hand on her cheek. "Mom, I'll be back. I need to meet Charlie, make sure my niece knows me. And I haven't had your *leche frita* in over a decade. I won't be long."

Turning to Jonathan, Isabelle took his hand, something she'd never done in front of other people before. "It's basically deep-fried pudding and it's absolutely incredible."

His gaze washed over her, his eyes drinking her in as if he couldn't believe she was right in front of him. "I can't wait to taste it." He looked at Catalina and Elaina. "I'm well-known for my punctuality. I promise we'll be back shortly."

He led her to the SUV, gave her a moment to tell the driver where to go, then closed the privacy screen.

As soon as it hit the ceiling, his hands cupped her face and he pulled her close. "I have more questions than you can imagine, but this first."

He placed his lips on hers and Isabelle knew no matter what might have or could have been, no matter who she was in another version of her life or what she did, there was absolutely no other her she'd want to be than the one right here, in this moment, having the breath kissed right out of her.

THIRTY-THREE

Only the necessity of pulling oxygen into their lungs separated them, but the SUV stopped at that same moment.

A low, needy growl left Jonathan's chest, making Isabelle wish she could curl up on his lap and push the rest of the world away.

"Seriously? That was the whole drive?"

Isabelle smiled, brushed her hand through his hair, so soft against her fingers. When she knocked the sunglasses, he pulled them off, tossed them on the seat beside them.

"Small town."

"I'll say."

When she lowered her hand, he grabbed it, turned it over to kiss her palm with a gentleness, an openness, that boosted her confidence, settled her nerves.

"I want to show you something," she whispered.

Desire darkened his gaze, igniting a matching blaze inside of her but she only grinned, pulled her hand from his. "Come on."

Jonathan lowered the privacy screen and in seconds, the driver opened his door so he could go first, letting him take Isabelle's hand again to help her out.

"I'll wait in the vehicle," the driver said.

"We won't be long, Morgan. Thank you," Jonathan said, keeping Isabelle tucked close to him, his arm around her shoulder. As they walked toward Ashland House and he took it all in, he stopped short. "Wait. Have you brought me here to kill me? Is this where you're going to hide my body?"

Arm wrapped around his waist, reveling in the feel of him against her side in a way she'd never allowed herself to fully enjoy, Isabelle's laughter felt lighter than it ever had before.

"No. And it's not that bad."

They walked up the uneven drive where weeds grew in odd patches, stopping at the porch steps. Close up, she saw the weathered, worn, and aged wood, the damage time and nature had inflicted. She also saw the potential.

"Let's sit," she said, pointing to the top step.

Jonathan eyed her warily, giving the stairs an uneasy glance. "The first time I asked you out, you said to bring something to your place, and if it wasn't Michelin-star worthy, it would be our last date. Now you want to sit on plywood I'm not entirely sure will hold us?"

Isabelle released his hand, took the four steps up and sat down on the top one. "It's been a hell of a week. I have to tell you some things and I want to do it here. There are things you need to know before we go back and I let my family start to care about you." Before she admitted how much *she* cared for him already.

He nodded slowly, hesitantly, a hint of worry in his expression, but sat beside her. She clasped her hands on her knees, not sure she could express all the things she needed to if she looked at him. He'd always been so honest and genuine. So upfront whether it was about his desire for her, his affection, or his irritation. She, on the other hand, had hidden from everyone. Including herself.

"Are you okay?" he asked quietly.

She turned her head. "I am. Physically, I'm fine. I want to tell you about some of the things I've kept tucked away in those boxes. Once I do, you can decide if the things you said, the things you think you want with me, still hold true."

"Feelings don't switch off, Isabelle. Nothing you tell me will change anything I feel. Even if it somehow pushes us apart, I'll always lo—"

She grabbed his knee, stopping his words. "Don't say it. Don't say it again, yet. Let me get this out and if you still mean it, still feel it, then . . . then when you say it, maybe I can say it back."

He gripped her hand, kept it on his knee. His nostrils flared on an inhale, but he stayed quiet, nodded.

Isabelle did her best to keep the story, *her* story, brief.

How she lost her dad and a lot of herself, isolated, estranged, determined, left home at seventeen and didn't look back except for one moment of weakness when she reached out. Rejection she hadn't understood made her sure that whatever path she took, she'd walk it alone.

Because she really did see a future with him, and *wanted* it, she left out the other versions of herself because she wasn't entirely sure exactly what had happened, or how. If she didn't understand it, she couldn't expect him to. No, that would always be something that just she and Elaina shared. Something that, no matter what the outcome, would always connect them.

When she finished and no more words came, she realized she'd fallen into a sort of trance, telling her past and what led her to this moment in a removed sort of way. A narrator more than a participant. But there was nothing removed or distant about the way her heart pounded in the quiet between them. Would Jonathan love the broken, scarred woman who still had a lot to learn? She knew there was more anger to acknowledge and put away, additional healing to do that might bring more hurt. Could he love a woman who could close a multimillion-dollar deal without breaking a sweat but nearly hyperventilated when he'd told her he loved her? One who was more comfortable with the type of vulnerability that existed in boardrooms over ballrooms or bedrooms. One who would stumble trying to figure out how to blend the pieces of who she was and who she wanted to be into one complicated version of herself.

Jonathan turned his body, his grip loosening slightly, like he'd realized how tightly he'd been holding on. "That's a lot."

She nodded, squeezing his fingers. "It is."

"One hell of a week."

"It was."

"You grew up here."

"I did. When I left it behind, I swore I'd never come back. I missed out on a lot because of the choices I made. I have a niece. Charlie. Named after my dad. She's ten."

"I'm sorry you missed watching her grow up . . . but she's got a lot of growing left to do and you get to be part of that."

"I'm not entirely sure I can fully forgive my mother, even though I want to."

Jonathan lifted one hand, stroked it over her cheek, tucked a flyaway hair behind her ear. "Forgiveness is hard. After my falling out with my brother, I didn't know how to put things right."

"You guys seem okay now."

"We are. Mostly. But it's different. When something breaks, you can put it back together, if you're lucky, but it'll never be the same. Sometimes, the cracks show, sometimes it just isn't strong enough to hold, and sometimes, it's so seamless, you have to be looking for it to find the spot where it broke. If you press too hard on that point, it could fall apart again."

Isabelle took a deep breath, feeling like her lungs had expanded fully for the first time in days. "Yes. Moving forward doesn't mean there wasn't damage done."

"It changes you. And that's okay. We're supposed to change. Everyone makes choices they wish they hadn't. You could drive yourself crazy regretting that, or take the first step and go in a new direction. And you don't have to do that by yourself, Isabelle."

The first step. *The first step is the most important one.*

Isabelle stood, moved down to pace along a dusty patch of grass right in front of the porch. Words swirled in her head and her heart like tumbleweeds refusing to settle.

She couldn't wait for the moment to be perfect. Nothing was perfect. *Just because a box is wrapped in sparkling paper doesn't mean there's something wonderful inside.* If that was true, then so was the opposite. Just because they were sitting in front of a run-down house, dust settling on their overpriced shoes, didn't make what she was about to say, about to share, mean any less.

Coming to a stop in front of him, she met his gaze full on. His shoulders straightened, his eyes holding hers like an invisible tether bound both of them together.

"I said 'I love you' once to a boy in high school. I meant it at the time, but I still broke his heart. Even though I was the one to end it, I hated that I hurt him. You realize, as you get older, that you have to go through these things to become stronger. To do better the next time. Except I wouldn't let myself entertain a next time. Until you. You know as well as I do that I've fought my feelings for you every step of the way. You slipped through my defenses, saw the best version of me even when I didn't show it. I'm not the same person I was at seventeen. I'm not even sure I'm the same version of myself that I was yesterday or the one I'll be a year from now. But in this moment, right this second, I love you with everything that I am. It's entirely possible that I've loved you all along and was just too stubborn and scared to admit it. I'm not perfect. I'm going to mess up. Relationships of any kind are not my forte. But you make me feel stronger. I'm a better version of myself than I was before, and I'll do my very best to make sure you don't regret your decision to love me. If you still think you do."

It took all her strength not to crumble onto the steps. Those words and feelings had been building and growing and now that she'd shared them, she felt boneless. Weightless. Free.

Jonathan stood up slowly. Intentionally. Taking the few steps down to her, his gaze hooded, his jawline fierce, he stood right in front of her, so she needed to tip her head back to hold his gaze. One of his hands curled around her waist, the other gently took hold of the nape of her neck.

"My turn?" His voice was husky and deep like he was speaking around his own knot of tangled feelings.

Isabelle nodded.

"I'm not sure it was a decision I consciously made or one my heart made for me but you, Isabelle Caroline Duprees, the *you* right in front of me, the you I met a year and a half ago, the one you are right this second and any other version of *you* that comes along, are all I want. All I'll ever want. I don't take saying it or hearing it lightly. I don't know what journey you took this week but maybe we both needed it. I love you. All of you. Every part of you. Even the parts I haven't discovered yet. I'm not asking for perfect. I'm okay with messy. As long as we're in it together."

After a kiss that held the promise of all the things they'd share, the life they'd build together, he leaned back, stroked her hair off her face.

"What's with the house?"

She grinned. "I want to buy it. With you. Ashland is growing. It's close to Nashville, and there's lots to do around here, even though I wouldn't have admitted that as a kid for any amount of money. I think it would make a great boutique hotel."

He pulled her a little closer. "Oh yeah?"

Focusing on the conversation when he was touching her like this wasn't easy. "Yeah."

"Then, when we visit your family, once we renovate it, we can stay here. Because I love you, but the hotels I passed on the way here scared me."

Isabelle looped her arms around his neck, her laugh echoing in the open space. "Deal."

His fingers tangled in her hair, and he used them to tug her head back just a little, just enough to kiss her.

Letting her fingers trail along his neck, she whispered, "I wish we had more time together now, but I really want to meet Charlie."

"Then let's go. I want to hang out with your family. I want to hear embarrassing stories about you as a kid. We have all the time in the world for you and me."

She knew that wasn't always true, that nothing was guaranteed. Which made it all the more important to take everything she could from each moment.

"Just remember, when we get back to New York, I'm going to ask your brother for the same thing, and he has college stories about you."

THIRTY-FOUR

One of the wheels on the second-hand suitcase was broken, which meant she got a great deal on it, but she wasn't sure if that was enough to offset the annoyance of it.

Even at seventeen, almost an adult, Isabelle knew better than to swear loud enough for her mother to hear. Muttering to herself, she yanked the clunky thing forward, heading from her bedroom to the kitchen.

Her mom sat at the table playing solitaire. She didn't look up when her younger daughter entered the room. With her heart racing and her stomach bouncing, Isabelle braced herself for goodbye. Wanting to go and actually leaving were two entirely different things. There was a tiny piece of her that wanted her mother to stand up and shout, "Don't go! I need you! I love you and I want you here!"

Isabelle sucked in a deep breath, taking a minute to look around the kitchen, to memorize the print of the wallpaper, inhale the scent of the jasmine candle which had nearly burned all the way down. You can always come back, *she told herself. She'd received four scholarship offers—Nashville, California, and two in Boston. She'd known for over two years that she wanted to go to MIT, so it hadn't been a hard choice.*

"Don't run home crying when the world isn't what you want it to be," her mother said, still not looking up. She lifted the stemless wine glass, swallowed back the rest of the red in it.

"If I get a job, I might be able to come back for Christmas," Isabelle said.

"Seems like a waste of money, flying or driving all over the godforsaken country to spend a couple days sleeping in a bed that won't feel like yours anymore."

Isabelle's grip on the handle tightened. "I'm hoping to get a summer internship, so I don't know if I'll even be able to come back then."

Get up, *she thought.* Get up, get up, get up. Hug me. Cry. Leave the room and tell me it's too hard to say goodbye.

When Catalina stood, Isabelle's heart surged. Until she realized her mom was heading to the box of wine on the counter. She poured it, the liquid sloshing up the sides of the glass.

She turned and lifted the glass, her eyes glassy, her smile a ghost of what it once was. "Good luck to you. One day you'll realize running away won't make your problems disappear."

"I'm going to school, Mom. Like thousands and thousands of other kids my age do."

"Plenty of schools right here."

"I'm not doing this again."

"Nothing keeping you here. Go if you're going."

Isabelle waited a bit to see if that was really it. When she realized it was, she turned, blinked the wetness out of her eyes, and left. She was halfway down the driveway, could see the taxi waiting, when Elaina appeared, walking slow like she had all the time in the world.

She stopped short when she saw Isabelle struggling with the suitcase.

"You're really going?"

Letting out an exasperated sigh, Isabelle yanked the case. "Yes. Yes, I'm really going to college. In some households, this is celebrated or seen as an accomplishment."

Elaina walked closer. "Plenty of colleges right here."

"Jesus Christ."

Elaina smirked. "Plenty of churches too."

"Mom doesn't see the point in me coming home for Christmas."

Elaina shrugged. Oddly, it was a better response than defending their mother would have been.

"I gotta go." She stared at her big sister, remembering forts and fights, wondered when and how the chasm between them had grown so wide.

"Guess it's all on me now," Elaina said, tucking her hands into the pockets of her cut-off shorts.

Isabelle scoffed. Like it has been for me for years now? Bills, groceries, yard work, housework, part-time jobs, school, dinners, studying.

Instead, she said: "You could have gone to school."

Elaina snorted out a laugh. "Right. Even if we had the money or I had the grades to get scholarships, one of us has to stay."

She said it like she was doing them both a grand favor when the truth of it was, Elaina didn't want to go anywhere. Isabelle couldn't imagine feeling that way. The thought of staying made her feel like she was trapped in a closed box, the lid immovable, the air dwindling.

She thought of her mom getting up only for wine. "You guys don't need me."

Shaking her head, Elaina pulled her hands from her pockets. "For someone so smart, you sure are stupid sometimes."

The taxi honked.

Isabelle stiffened her spine. "As great as this is, I need to get going."

"Take care of yourself, baby sister." Elaina walked past her, leaving Isabelle standing at the end of their driveway.

"Doesn't look like I have much choice. No one else is going to do it."

"Are you okay?" Jonathan's hand slid onto her thigh as he leaned in, said the words quietly next to her ear.

It would take her some time to get used to the casual affection, to the spark of awareness it struck every time. "Just thinking about the last time I was here."

"I hope you'll tell me about it," he said as other people in the room chatted loudly.

She turned her head. Isabelle might be unsure of how to navigate all of these new waters, but she wanted to—especially this part. "I'll tell you anything."

Satisfaction shimmered in his eyes.

"Are you going to get married, Aunt Isabelle?"

Aunt Isabelle. She'd earned more names and accolades than she could list, but those two words gave her a jolt, a sense of happiness, that she couldn't explain or understand. Jonathan's fingers squeezed her thigh. Whether in reflex or to remind her to answer.

"Do you think I should?" she responded, mostly teasing, still unsure how to interact with a small, adorable human who reminded her, in equal measure, of her dad, Elaina, their mom, and even herself.

Charlie sat down on the floor in front of her, leaning back so she was resting on her elbows. The ease with which her niece had taken to her and Jonathan was astounding. It was as if Isabelle was always meant to be there, at least in the little girl's eyes.

"Grandma is, which is cool. I'm in the wedding. But Mom and Blake always say they will when I do. Which is dumb because I'm not getting married to some gross boy."

Blake, Elaina's handsome and charming boyfriend, who'd welcomed Isabelle with a hug and Jonathan with a hearty handshake and clap on the back, laughed.

"I'm happy for you to keep thinking that, but something tells me you won't always feel that way," Blake said.

He was sitting with Elaina in an oversized chair. Her sister's legs were thrown over his lap, his hand resting familiarly and affectionately on her thigh. There was an ease to them. The little bits of conversation had revealed they'd been together for five years. Charlie alternated between calling him Blake and Dad. He responded with obvious love to either. Isabelle had asked about Charlie's biological father but was told "the only thing about him that wasn't a mistake was Charlie," which quickly ended the conversation.

"You could marry a girl if you think boys are yucky," Henry said.

He and Catalina sat on the other chair a little more primly than Elaina and Blake, but it was clear that they also had an affectionate and loving relationship. Was Isabelle the only one of them who didn't naturally offer or accept physical touch? She hadn't even realized that she had denied herself so many things. Placing a hand over Jonathan's, not missing the surprise in his gaze, she told herself that would change.

"I'm keeping my options open," Charlie said, bringing Isabelle's thoughts back to the conversation.

The adults all laughed and just like that, a new topic landed, and then another veered off that—back and forth like they'd been doing this every Sunday for eons. Like Isabelle hadn't left it all behind without a heavy sense of loss, held onto anger like a security blanket for years, or just experienced the most bizarre week of her entire life.

"It's time for dessert," Catalina said.

Her mother and Elaina had kept their word, making tonight about moving forward rather than digging up the past. It didn't erase it. Just delayed facing it a little. Like walking for a couple minutes in between running sprints. Sometimes you could go farther that way.

Jonathan was one of the smartest men she'd ever met, which was perhaps why she'd been doomed to fall for him right from the start. The combination of looks, humor, patience, and intelligence was too much for anyone to ignore. It shouldn't have caught her off guard that he gave her a look, a barely there head tilt, a suggestion she go help her mom. He knew they were estranged but not why. She'd always told him enough to encourage him not to ask anything more. Isabelle didn't think that would be the case any longer, and strangely enough, it made the weight of it all seem lighter.

Then the boxes have to go.

Isabelle stood up. "I can help."

Those three simple words changed her mother's face, softened and brightened it at the same time.

"That would be wonderful."

Isabelle's stomach danced more following her mom into the kitchen than it ever had marching into even the most hostile boardroom.

They were quiet at first, Catalina pulling an already beautiful platter out of the fridge with the dessert artfully arranged around berries.

"Plates are above the dishwasher," Catalina said softly, tentatively.

"That looks delicious, Mom." Pulling pretty dessert plates from the cupboard, she set them on the counter.

"This will keep a minute. Come with me," Catalina said, reaching out her hand.

Isabelle pulled oxygen into her lungs in a practiced and measured way meant to slow her pulse, to ease her nerves. Extending her hand, she took her mother's. Catalina squeezed and smiled before leading her beyond the kitchen. When she and Jonathan returned to the house, there'd been no time for a tour. They'd settled down to eat and talk and eat some more. Isabelle had forgotten how much food could be consumed when a person was distracted with stories.

The original layout still existed with the entryway leading down a short hallway to a kitchen straight ahead, or the bedrooms if you took the hallway to the right. Just like it had been the last day she was here, the door to her room was on the left, Catalina's a little farther down, a bathroom door, and Elaina's former bedroom door on the right.

"You're showing me my old room?"

Catalina released Isabelle's hand. "I wrote you a letter. More than one, actually. But after you left that day, I wrote all the things I was too stubborn and stupid to say. I've often thought of sending it to you, but I always hoped I'd be able to give it to you in person. I don't blame you for leaving or not coming back, and I know a great night doesn't make up for everything, but I hope . . ." Catalina paused, her breath hitching.

Isabelle put a hand on her mom's arm. "That this is the first step?"

Biting her lower lip, her gaze filling with tears, Catalina nodded, then turned the doorknob.

Her mom walked to the right, straight to a desk by the window where Isabelle's bed had once been, likely to get the letter. But Isabelle stood in the doorway, shocked. It was an office by the looks of it. Beside the desk, next to the window was a huge calendar. It had names and sessions listed, events and phone numbers. The left side of the room had two high-back chairs, a side table between them with an orchid adding a vivid splash of purple color.

But it was what filled the wall straight ahead that had Isabelle's jaw dropping, a little "oh" sound escaping from her throat.

On the wall in front of her were pictures set up much like the display of client artwork. Only this wasn't artwork. It was her family. All of them. It was a collage of the past, memories and moments, the present, and all the things in between. There were framed pictures of Isabelle at the Met Gala, receiving awards, framed magazine photos. They were all interspersed, no real rhyme or reason. A picture of Elaina pushing her in a doll stroller next to a photo of Charlie in a tutu and tiara dancing next to her mom in front of this house. There were photos of Elaina, Blake, and Charlie dressed for Halloween, Henry fishing off a dock.

Even though Isabelle had refused to return phone calls, had put her family out of her mind and compartmentalized her life, Catalina had followed her younger daughter's life, kept up with it, *celebrated* her accomplishments.

Elaina and Isabelle were the kids and Catalina had let them down. Isabelle felt justified in her anger when she'd left, and over the years since. But she'd made mistakes too. She'd hurt Catalina and Elaina by refusing them, lashing out at them the few times she had seen her sister, ignoring their existence.

Despite that, her mother had a wall dedicated to the things she loved most. The people in her life. Years upon years of moments, a visual map of their family in all its shifting forms. Isabelle walked slowly, taking in each photo, aware of Catalina watching her. She stopped moving when she saw a picture of her and her dad. She was maybe five and he'd lifted her high in the air, his head tipped back to beam up at her, and the look of utter joy on her face had her present self reaching out, touching her fingers to the glass, tracing his smile, then her own.

"I miss him," she whispered, not even meaning to.

"He loved you. He loved you so much, Isabelle. We were his whole heart. His everything."

Isabelle nodded. She'd never doubted his love for her.

"I was so sick with your sister when I got pregnant the first time. The delivery was beyond traumatic. I'll spare you details just in case there's any chance of you giving me more grandbabies," she said softly, a hint of humor making her accent stronger.

Turning her face, Isabelle stared at her mother, wondered where she was going with this.

"I said I'd never do it again. I was too scared. I'd spent so much of my life scared. My father wasn't a good man. He was unkind to say the least. When I met Charlie . . . oh, he stole my heart. But more than that, he taught me to trust it. To *give* it. I was the last of three kids and with each child my parents had, they grew meaner and meaner, so to say I was terrified to have you is an understatement. When I got pregnant the second time, I barely breathed for nine months. Charlie promised it would all be okay. That we'd be okay. But I had terrible postpartum after you. He took over in the way he did. A smile on his face, doing it all. By the time you were two, you were a daddy's girl inside and out, and it seemed . . . easier to parent that way. He knew what made you tick like I did with Elaina. But it was lazy of me. Unfair to all of us. The drinking didn't start until he died. I'm full of excuses but in the end, none of them matter."

Catalina took a step forward, turned to stand directly in front of her daughter. "I love you, *mi hija*. No matter how terrible I was at proving it, I always have. I can never undo the damage I've done but whatever happens in the future, please know that I'm sorry."

Tears had spilled over without permission. Isabelle swiped at them impatiently.

"I don't know what will happen from here either, Mom. I don't want to make promises I can't keep just because I'm overwhelmed with emotion."

Catalina nodded, her own eyes filling.

Isabelle reached out and took her mom's hand, the one not holding the letter. "But I love you and I'm sorry too."

Her mother pulled her into a hug so tight, Isabelle felt like it reached her bones and glued her back together.

When Catalina pulled back, she passed Isabelle the letter. "All the things I should have said." She shook her head softly, her gaze clear, her smile wide. "Enough. Dessert. I want to go eat dessert, laugh with my daughters and granddaughter, and marvel at the wonderful men we've all found. I like your Jonathan. And you didn't really answer Charlie's question."

Isabelle slipped the letter into her pocket. She wasn't sure if she'd read it. But she didn't have to decide tonight.

"Mostly because I don't know the answer. He hasn't asked and honestly, things are still new, even though we've been seeing each other for a while."

Catalina hooked her arm through Isabelle's, leading them back to the kitchen. "I didn't know I could be lucky enough to love with my whole heart twice in a lifetime. It's a gift. One you should seize." Her mom turned her head, stopped. "And one you deserve."

Laughter rang out from the living room. It sounded like Charlie was doing stand-up comedy, which made Isabelle smile. Someone turned on music and it drifted through the house.

She didn't know what was next, not the way she usually needed to, with the steps all mapped out, an itemized list on her phone, and several backup plans ready to go. It turned out life didn't always give a warning when it was going to drastically switch directions or make an unexpected U-turn. The only thing a person could do was try to maintain control of the vehicle, navigate the twists and turns as well as she could manage, and not be afraid to turn around and go back if she got lost.

Isabelle picked up the plates while her mother carried the platter. There'd be time for lists and plans later. For now, she wanted to eat dessert with people she loved, focus on the good rather than the hurt. No matter what other version of her existed out there in the world, she was in charge of this one. She got to choose who she wanted to be.

And this version chooses to be happy, she thought as their entrance was greeted with cheers. It was probably more for the dessert but the contentment in her sister's gaze, the excitement in her niece's, and the love in Jonathan's hinted that it might be more.

ISABELLE CAROLINE
DUPREES FAIRBANKS

EPILOGUE

EIGHTEEN MONTHS LATER

Isabelle looked out at the people milling around Pier 83, some hurrying onto the various boats, some just taking in the view. While she'd always appreciated the sight of Central Park through her penthouse windows, this building, the one that housed the Hell's Kitchen chapter of Young Women in Business, was in her top five of places to be.

Kaia entered the office without knocking because once they'd blurred the lines even a little between employee and friend, her assistant had carved out her own special place in Isabelle's world. It was like having another sibling, both annoying and endearing, often at the same time.

"Did you look at the speech I wrote for you?"

Isabelle turned, unfolded her arms, ignoring the nausea that seemed to be her constant companion these days. "I don't need a speech. I'll say what I say when I get up there."

"We have so much press here. The turnout is incredible," Kaia said, rushing around the office, frantically trying to ensure everything was in order.

Walking over to her friend, she stopped in her path. "Kaia."

Kaia stopped immediately, tipping her head back. She'd grown out her dark hair and had it tucked into an elegant twist.

"I want everything to be perfect."

This project was every bit as much hers as it was Isabelle's. Maybe more in some ways, since she and Jenaya Davis had grown incredibly close, taking on the renovations of the space and the implementation of a wider-reaching program that included grants and scholarships for young women.

"There is no perfect," Isabelle said with a grin.

"Who are you and what have you done with Isabelle?"

"We're ready for this."

Kaia nodded. "You're right. I'm being ridiculous. And the silent auction was a brilliant idea."

When Isabelle only arched a brow as if to say, "Obviously," Kaia laughed and her shoulders relaxed.

"I came to get you. You're really ready?"

Looking toward the door, Isabelle thought about the road that had led her here. It didn't always make sense, but it was where she wanted to be. Sun Tzu said, "He will win who knows when to fight and when not to fight." She'd grown tired of maintaining the fight between her and her family. And in the end, the satisfaction of success and knowing she was in the right was a poor trade-off for the simple pleasures she'd discovered from letting them back in.

"Hey," Kaia said, squeezing her hand.

Isabelle thought of what awaited her in the event room that had been repurposed for the black-tie affair.

"I'm ready." She looked at Kaia. "Thank you for everything you've done. Not just for tonight but in general. I'm not sure where I'd be without you." Acknowledging her gratitude was another trick she'd discovered for enhancing her relationships. Sometimes it seemed like there were more nuances in maintaining even footing than there were addenda in a legal contract.

"You look like you but then you go and say sweet things like that, and I wonder what happened on that trip." Kaia said it all with a sassy grin.

"Never mind." Isabelle opened the door, but Kaia put a hand on it.

"Right back at you, boss."

It was enough.

Leaving the office, Isabelle walked down the hallway, then turned right for the side entrance of the stage.

Like the rest of the room, it was adorned with decorations, lights, and beautiful flowers in gorgeous waist-high vases.

Her heels clicked over the hardwood as she made her way to the podium. No awards tonight. No accolades. And yet she felt happier and more successful than she had in years.

The music faded, the hum in the crowd settled, and all eyes in the room turned her way. The spotlight wasn't blinding her for once, so she could actually look out and *see.*

"Good evening. I want to thank all of you for coming tonight to help celebrate and support not only a wonderful initiative but a group of strong, proud, and successful women. Tonight's proceeds from the silent auction will go toward more program options, small business loans, and other necessities like after-school care and housing for women who are trying to get back on their feet."

The interconnectedness of it all came as a surprise to her. She, herself, hadn't come from money but she'd pushed, fought, clawed her way, and succeeded. But that wasn't true for everyone in this room and so many others. Sometimes all the drive and ambition in the world didn't stop circumstance and chance from punching a person in the gut. What they were providing here was the education but also a safety net. That came in many forms for different people from different backgrounds.

She looked around the room, saw her worlds mingling in their fanciest clothes. Business associates who'd come on board, associates, employees, students, small businesswomen, and her family.

"In *The Art of War*, it says, 'Opportunities multiply as they are seized,' and as a successful businesswoman, I've always put a lot of stock in those words. I took opportunity after opportunity to build an empire, and gave interviews telling people that if you wanted something badly enough, you found a way to make it happen. But the reality, what I've recently come to learn, is that it doesn't always go that way. You can plan for everything but it's impossible to control how it all works out. The only thing you have power over is your own reaction. The Young Women in Business initiative is about offering those opportunities where they may not exist otherwise. Tonight, we invite you to mingle, chat, make new friends and associates. Drink the very expensive champagne, eat the delicious food, and bid on the gorgeous auction items, many of which were handcrafted by the women in our programs."

She started to thank them and back away, but something compelled her to stay, to look around the room one more time, stopping every few seconds before letting the words come.

"We don't always take the opportunities we're presented with. They can be right in front of us, but we may be too scared to reach out or accept them at face value. This transcends the business arena. I would be remiss if I didn't take the opportunity right now to thank some people. All too often, we think about our own sacrifices, our own paths. But we aren't alone, even when we think we are.

"So, I want to thank Jenaya Davis for bringing me on board,

Kaia Huxley for being the human equivalent of glue, holding me together in a variety of ways. I want to thank my husband, Jonathan." She paused, found his eyes locked on her. "For seeing the best in me even when I don't show it. My sister, Elaina, not only for the gorgeous artwork hanging on the walls that she contributed to the event, but for her strength. My sister's husband for accepting me as I am. I also want to say thank you to my mom, Catalina, and her husband, Henry, for showing me how freeing forgiveness is. My in-laws for welcoming me into their family and their business. And Charlie." Her niece was bouncing up and down like she had an internal soundtrack blaring. "Charlie. You inspire me. Your optimism and kindness and your unwaveringly fierce love have given me something no amount of money could—hope for whatever comes next. Now, let's enjoy the night."

Applause broke out and she was pretty sure the shrill whistle that rang out was courtesy of Blake. Jonathan was at the edge of the stage when she made her way there. He lifted his hand and she slipped hers into it, smiling as he pulled her close right there at the base of the stairs on the edge of the dance floor.

"Your family is having a wonderful time. Your mother said she framed the invitation."

Isabelle smiled, leaned her head on his shoulder. "She helped organize half of it, for goodness' sake. The invitation was more tongue in cheek than anything else."

"It mattered to her, sweetheart. It was a gesture. You know it and so did she."

"I'm glad they came." It was the truth, even if it was still hard to say.

It wasn't like she hadn't seen them. She and Jonathan had gone back to Ashland for her mother's wedding. They'd dropped in a few times after that to check the progress of Ashland House, even though Blake and Elaina, who'd accepted the job of overseeing the renovations, sent email updates. And of course, Isabelle had been there for Charlie's eleventh birthday. They didn't all talk every day. There were still rough spots and hiccups. But it was more than she'd ever had with them.

"If I didn't know better, I'd think you almost got emotional up there," Jonathan teased, wrapping his arms around her as the band struck up a soft tune and conversations resumed.

"It's important to be appreciative of the people in your life," she said, her tone stiff even as her body melted into his.

He took her hand, turned her so they were dance-gliding on the actual dance floor rather than the outskirts.

"Uh-huh. That's all it was. Just some scheduled gratitude."

She bit back her laugh. "Kaia put it on the itinerary, not me."

Jonathan's lips grazed her cheek. "Of course. Nothing at all to do with pregnancy hormones or that soft heart you keep so well hidden."

She leaned back, put a hand over his mouth. "Shh." She looked around, nearly squealed when he nipped her fingers.

"No one can hear me." His gaze was like his arms—strong, sure, and loving. "I love you, Isabelle. The tough-as-nails boardroom you, the sleepy-eyed morning you, the overthinking you, the cares-too-much-but-is-afraid-to-show-it you. I love you. More every day."

She swallowed down the lump in her throat. "I'm lucky that you do. And I love you too. More than I ever believed myself capable of."

"Which is strange considering you're the most capable woman I know."

"Remember that when I can't tie my own shoes," she said.

Jonathan laughed, pulling her closer and doing what he

did at all these events now: danced with her until everything else faded away and they got lost in the moment. In each other.

Perhaps one of the most valuable things she'd learned in the last couple of years was that there were many versions of success. Emotional, physical, personal, professional. It didn't diminish one area to let them all overlap. Last year's road trip felt like a fever dream, and she might have thought it hadn't even happened if Elaina didn't quietly refer to it from time to time. One night, shortly after she'd returned home with Jonathan, before he'd given up his apartment and moved into hers and they officially meshed their lives together, she'd wondered why *those* versions of her had been out there in the world.

As he'd pulled her close that night, surrounding her with his strength and love, she'd received a text from Kaia letting her know that another huge deal had gone through. That text was followed by one from Elaina saying she hoped everything was good. Then one from her mom. And then Charlie. And as Jonathan held her, it made a strange sort of sense to her. All those versions, and more she likely hadn't discovered yet, were inside of her. Until that trip with her sister, she had locked all the other versions of herself in a vault, showing only the strongest one, the one who defined herself by such narrow parameters. She had nearly missed out on how much more she could be. On how much greater she and her life could be.

She'd thought she had it all because she'd only let herself exist in one specific area of her life. When the boxes spilled over, it had created chaos but it also created a messy sort of beauty that she now couldn't imagine herself without.

Jonathan pressed a kiss to the top of her head, and she knew she wouldn't have to.

ACKNOWLEDGMENTS

Acknowledgments can be a tricky thing to write because there are so many stages a book goes through from inception to landing on the shelf or your e-reader. In that time, so many people play vital roles, whether it's in bouncing ideas back and forth, providing a shoulder to cry on, feeding you when you forget to eat (joking—I never forget to eat), holding your hand through the hard parts, or making it shine. My worry is always forgetting one of those important people who nudged me along the way, who supported me or helped me. I try really hard to thank the people in my life in the moment when they're being my shoulder, rock, or sounding board but if I forget, in the moment, or right here, know that I appreciate anyone who takes part in this entire process and helps me through it.

A few more specific thank yous: Taylor Swift for the song "Right Where You Left Me," which made me reach out to Brendan to ask about short stories because I was stuck on the imagery the song created in my brain. To Brendan, for then sharing an idea that had been shared with him and trusting me to run with it and build an entire world with complicated, multifaceted characters that I grew to love and hope readers will, too. To Fran, for being my champion always. To my family, for being a constant source of support, love, and acceptance. It means everything to me. To everyone at Blackstone who helped this book get from idea to shelf, thank you. To Alicia, Tracy, Melissa, and Anette for agreeing to read and blurb my words. And, thank you to anyone who reads this book, anyone who believes that we each have more than one version of ourselves inside. Embrace every part of yourself.